Formid

Larry Jeram-Croft

Copyright © 2017 Larry Jeram-Croft
All rights reserved.

Cover image: LA(Phot) Handy; Crown Copyright 2005

Also by Larry Jeram-Croft:

Fiction:

The 'Jon Hunt' series about the modern Royal Navy:

Sea Skimmer
The Caspian Monster
Cocaine
Arapaho
Bog Hammer
Glasnost
Retribution
Formidable
Conspiracy
Swan Song

The 'John Hunt' books about the Royal Navy's Fleet Air Arm in the Second World War:

Better Lucky and Good
and the Pilot can't swim

The Winchester Chronicles:

Book one: The St Cross Mirror

The Caribbean: historical fiction and the 'Jacaranda' Trilogy.

Diamant

Jacaranda

The Guadeloupe Guillotine
Nautilus

Science Fiction:

Siren

Non Fiction:

The Royal Navy Lynx an Operational History
The Royal Navy Wasp an Operational and Retirement History
The Accidental Aviator

Prologue

A grey wall of cold rain flew across the Tyne and battered the workers of the Wallsend ship yard. February was always a cold month in the north of England. The workers ignored it and carried on regardless. Welding arcs flashed in the gloom and there was the constant sound of metal being hammered and machinery growling. It was getting late and most of the men in the yard were contemplating the sound of the yard siren signalling the end to yet another day of hard toil. Not that any of them minded the work. The yard always seemed on the point of closure despite its previous successes like building the Royal Navy's flagship, the Ark Royal, only a few years previously. Then there had been the chaos of losing the bid to build the navy's newest warship HMS Ocean. That had almost led to the closure of the company but a miracle then occurred. Not only did an entrepreneur from Holland buy the yard from the receivers but the government, in yet another about face, decided to place an order for another ship similar to Ocean. The design philosophy was to be the same as that for Ocean. HMS Formidable would, in actuality, be based on the design of a merchant ship. In that way she would cost less than a modern frigate but unlike her sister ship she would not be carrying Royal Marines and helicopters, although she could if needed. She was designed around one aircraft in particular, the navy's combat proven and remarkably effective Sea Harrier.

For brothers John and Mick none of this was of any real interest. All they knew and cared about was that there was work for them for several years more at least. They were both skilled welders which was fine when the yard needed them but there was little else for them to do if ships were not being built. Today was Friday and they had their weekend already planned out. The pub this evening and then football tomorrow followed by several Newcastle night clubs. The rest of the weekend would depend on what girls they manage to pull on Saturday night. John was always the most successful at this activity, being taller and better looking, at least that was what he always said. Mick didn't mind, most Newcastle girls went around in packs and if his brother was successful then he almost always was as well.

The two of them were on a staging high up on the side of the ship. The hull was almost complete, soon they would be moving on to internal fittings. One last plate of steel was being swung towards them by a crane. It wasn't particularly large and wouldn't take long to weld into place. The gust of wind hit the slab of steel just as the rain also started to fall and it started to swing. The brothers stood back waiting for the swing to stop. Unfortunately, the crane driver didn't. Maybe he was just keen to get this last job over. Maybe he just wasn't paying attention. It had been a long day for everyone after all. Suddenly, the boys realised what was happening and threw themselves down to avoid the sheet of steel as it swung near them. It may have been a relatively small one but it was still capable of causing severe harm. They were both wearing safety harnesses and hard hats in accordance with the yard's strict safety policy. Unfortunately, neither of them had actually bothered to clip the harnesses on to anything. The wooden slats of the staging were slick with water and very slippery. John was fine but his brother was standing closer to the edge. The safety rail should have stopped him but as he was now lying prone he simply slid wordlessly under it and over the edge. Neither boy even had time to shout. It was over in seconds. Mick's broken body was sprawled over the concrete forty feet below.

Chapter 1

Captain Jonathon Hunt looked up at his new command. It was raining, it was cold and it was bloody windy. He didn't notice. The ship was tied up alongside in the river Tyne at the Wallsend yard. From the jetty, she towered over him, a massive, slab sided, grey wall. From his vantage point, he couldn't see the flight deck at all, although the bulbous swelling at the bow above his head was clearly visible. This was the ramp that would allow his Harriers to take off with more fuel or weapons or both. There was a background growl from the ships generators and the ever present smell of diesel mixed in with the acrid aroma of the seaweed on the jetty side. Sea gulls were making their ever present squawking over his head. Suddenly, he felt completely at home. This was the moment he had been looking forward to ever since he walked over the brow of HMS Prometheus for the last time all those years ago to a world of sorrow. The intervening years had been terrifying and exciting in good measure but this is what he had joined the navy to do. This ship was what he wanted, even what he needed to be whole again.

A gust of wind and rain reminded him that staying standing on the dock was not a good idea. To one side of the ship was a small office block. He walked towards the door hoping it was warmer inside. He knew the ship would be cold, she was a long way from being occupied. His optimism was rewarded with a blast of warm fuggy air as he opened the door. Inside it was just one large space with several desks and an enormous wall chart on the wall facing him. Looking around for a moment, he couldn't see anyone at all. Then a head appeared from behind the desk to his left. Whoever it was had been leaning down to pick something up.

'Yes, and who are you?' The man asked with a frown.

Jon studied him for a moment. Thin and almost bald, wearing a shirt with no tie, he resembled his photograph but with more worry lines on his face. 'Sorry, I'm guessing that you are Commander Derek Murray the current Commanding Officer of Formidable?'

The man grimaced. 'That's one description and who exactly are you if I may ask?'

Jon was in civilian clothes and there was no reason why he should be recognised. He walked over to the desk and held out his hand. 'I'm sorry I should have warned you I was coming. I'm Captain Hunt and will be taking over from you some time in the near future.'

The effect was electric. He stood up and immediately took Jon's hand giving it a firm shake. 'Sir, thank you for coming. Yes, I am Derek Murray as I expect you know. I was warned you might come up before the official handover.'

'I know I should have forewarned you but I was in the area on family matters and decided to come over. I did try to ring but got no answer.'

'Ah well, I've been out most of the morning, as has the dockyard superintendent who works in here with me. So Sir, when are you actually taking over?'

Jon noted a slight longing in Murray's tone. Clearly, he wanted to pass the responsibility of the ship on to someone else. From what he had heard he wasn't surprised.

'Not for another six weeks I'm afraid. I've got a few courses and briefings to attend as you can imagine but also I've been told to take a month's leave. Wasn't my idea but there we are.' Jon grimaced at the remembered conversation with the First Sea Lord. It was a measure of the man that he knew exactly how much leave Jon had accrued and not taken over the past few years. Despite Jon's protestations, he was told in no uncertain terms to take some time off. Formidable wasn't going anywhere for the moment.

Commander Murray looked disappointed but made an effort to keep the look off his face. 'Would you like the tour Sir?'

'Can you spare the time? I know you're very busy.'

'Of course Sir. Maybe I could offer you a coffee and give you a quick brief first?'

'Sounds good Derek. And just to confirm, you will be staying on as my Weapons Engineer Officer is that right?'

'Yes Sir', he answered as he filled two mugs from a kettle on a shelf behind him. 'Sugar?'

'No thanks. Julie Andrews please.'

'Ah, white, none.' Derek laughed. 'Coming right up Sir.'

The two men took chairs by the large wall chart. 'Can I ask what you know Sir?'

Jon looked thoughtful. 'I've been told the party line, that there have been a few problems and that commissioning has slipped a few months but little else. Hopefully, you can give me the full picture?'

Derek thought for a moment. He had heard about this man. Who in the navy hadn't? He had already formed the opinion that here was someone who would want the whole picture warts and all. With a mental gulp, he decided that trying to sugar the pill was definitely not the right tactic.

'Technically, we are behind the programme but not by much. Yes, there have been teething problems but not much more than one could expect from a new class of ship.'

'But surely she is similar to Ocean? Not exactly a new class?' Jon asked.

'Different enough Sir. Ocean only has diesels. We have two Olympus gas turbines as well as we need the speed for fixed wing launches. Ocean has no serious weapon magazines, we have six. Also, someone in their wisdom decided we needed a more sophisticated Action Information System. The one we have has been nothing but trouble. But none of these are an issue in isolation. The problems really started back in the autumn.'

'Ah, you mean the accident I take it?'

'Yes Sir. A welder was killed when he fell off a stage dodging a sheet of steel swinging from a crane. It was very carefully investigated and as the silly bugger hadn't followed clear Health and Safety instructions to have his safety harness clipped on it was deemed an accident. That said, the crane driver took it very badly and has had to have counselling. But frankly, I wonder what century some of these ship workers are living in. Ever since, there have been, how can I put it 'issues'. You won't get anyone to say it to your face but they all think Formidable is an unlucky ship and you can see it in the care they take. For example, we flashed up the first diesel last week and almost wrote off the engine because some clown didn't fit the sump drain plug properly and most of the oil ended up in the bilges. We investigated of course and found the culprit but he swears he did it up tight. Of course he would say that, he didn't want to lose his job. But then you get the mutterings that there was something more to it. It's not everyone of course but there are enough stupid superstitious men around to make a difference.'

'Shit, that's all we need. I've seen this before you know. It's the same with sailors. Once word gets around it becomes an excuse for sloppy work and then more mistakes happen and then more credence is given to the rumour.' Jon observed tight lipped.

'Glad you understand Sir. My hope is that when our first draft of navy staff arrive in a couple of weeks we can get back on track. Would you like to look over her now?'

'Yes please.' Jon took the proffered hard hat and the two of them went out into the rain.

Two hours later, they were standing in the hangar. The ship was eerily quiet. Temporary lighting was strung everywhere. Jon had been shown as much of the ship as was accessible. Most of the accommodation was finished but the Operations room resembled something out of a horror film. There was clearly an incredible amount of work yet to do.

'So, tell me Derek, will she really be ready in two months? It seems impossible.' Jon asked as he looked around the cluttered mess of the hangar.

'Well, the aircraft lifts are in and the propulsion has been tested as much as we can alongside and as you've seen the accommodation is about complete. We have internal power and all the generators have been set to work. It's not as bad as it looks. You should have seen it only six weeks ago. My view is that as long as there are no more silly delays then yes, we should be ready for our first sea trials by then. There will still be a great deal to complete even after the trials but I think that we should be able to make our commissioning on time.' Derek said with a note of cautious confidence.

Jon wasn't quite so sanguine but there again he had never stood by a ship as it was being built and Derek had been here for over a year and had a much better feel for the project.

'Let me take you up to the bridge Sir, that's finished. It will give you a much better view.' Derek suggested.

The two men went into the ship's island and made their way up several ladders until they could enter the bridge. The consoles were all in place as was an extremely comfortable looking chair for the Captain. Jon went over and jumped in. From his vantage point, he could see the whole forward part of the ship. This was the view he would be seeing for the next two years.

'All we need is a few aircraft Derek but I see what you mean. Let's just hope the rest of the ship can get to this standard in time.' Suddenly the wave of optimism that he had experience when he first saw the ship which had steadily been eroded during his walk around her returned in force. Of course there would be issues with a new ship but there was no such thing as an unlucky one. It was the people who made a ship what she was and they weren't even here yet. He would take his leave and then come back and make this marvellous machine the smartest and most efficient ship in the fleet.

Chapter 2

The sun was getting low on the horizon and making the distant islands glow gold. The sea still retained its deep blue colour but was slowly darkening as the light faded. Jon was feeling mellow as he sat at a table at the hotel veranda bar and the first beer of the day slipped down. The cold liquid was making the outside of the glass become frosted in dew. He was suddenly grateful for having been ordered to take some leave. He hadn't really relaxed like this for years and it felt good.

He looked across at his companion and she smiled back. 'Penny for your thoughts Jon? You were somewhere else then,' Ruth, his girlfriend or partner, he wasn't actually sure which, asked him with a gentle smile on her face.

'Yes, I suddenly realised I was properly relaxing for the first time in ages. Despite or maybe because what happened today, I at last, felt able to let everything go,' he said almost wistfully.

Ruth laughed as she looked at the small, coin sized, rubber ring that was on the table between them. 'A near death experience often does that I'm told. You suddenly realise what you've got.'

Jon looked at the 'O' ring. 'Maybe but I'm not sure what was the biggest scare. That little bloody thing or the even bigger bloody thing with teeth. Mind you, that's something I've always wanted to get up close to, so I shouldn't complain.'

Ruth just looked at him as if he was mad.

That afternoon they had been out diving. Something they had been doing all week from an Egyptian dive boat operating out of Sharm-El-Sheik, the place they had both selected to go on holiday. Despite being early spring, the weather was warm and sunny which made a pleasant change from the almost continuous rain and gales of England. It was one of the reasons they had decided to go there. Both of them had dived before although they were both a little rusty. The dive centre soon brought them back up to speed and they had had a fabulous week exploring the various sites around the area. One morning they had visited the famous wreck of the Thistlegorm which had been discovered by Jacques Cousteau many years previously. She was a Second World War military freighter that had been torpedoed and went down crammed with military equipment. Even now one could swim amongst the remains of motorbikes and tanks on her decks.

Despite the novelty of the wreck, they both preferred the reefs that were so vibrant with life and brilliantly coloured coral. Many divers liked to go deep but both Jon and Ruth preferred the shallower water where the sun brought the colours to life. However, that morning they had been talked into a deep dive, not the least because there had been a chance of seeing a shark. Jon had always wanted to see one in its natural environment. Ruth wasn't so sure but after some persuasion had agreed to go along. At thirty metres, it was quite dark and much of the coral had gone to be replaced by rocks and sand. After twenty five minutes swimming slowly along with the others of the group and with no sharks in sight, Ruth had caught a glimpse of something moving in one of the crevices of the reef wall. She turned to catch a glimpse of a very large octopus. Sensing it was being watched, it immediately changed colour and disappeared. Ruth knew it was there though and swam slowly in looking for it. Jon had seen her turn and went to see what she was hunting while the rest of the divers slowly swam on. Suddenly and with no warning, Jon was out of air. For a second he couldn't work out what the hell was going on. Sucking on his regulator had no effect. Then he heard a massive noise from just behind his head. He turned as fast as he could but all he caught a glimpse of was a silver trail of bubble heading up from above and behind his head. Completely confused, he realised he was starting to panic and it was a long, long way to the surface. Luckily for him, Ruth heard the same roaring sound and turned around to see a massive plume of bubbles streaming from the top of Jon's air bottle. Not quite sure what was happening, she did know that the cut throat signal that Jon was doing meant he was out of air. Abandoning her search for the octopus, she swam towards him as fast as she could while reaching for the spare regulator that was clipped to the front of her jacket. Later, when they could laugh about it, they couldn't decide whether she gave him her regulator or he just grabbed it. Either way, the look of relief on his face as he took his first gasp of air was easily visible through the confines of his mask. Once they had settled for a few seconds Jon grabbed Ruth's air gauge to see how much was left in her tank. It was low, they had been at depth for some time and there was no sign of the other divers now. He gave the surfacing signal by raising his thumb upwards and Ruth nodded. It was going to be a close run thing as they didn't dare ascend too fast and really needed a stop at five metres for three minutes as well.

Holding on to each other, they carefully controlled their ascent. As they reached five metres, Jon indicated to Ruth to stop and he checked their air. They still had fifty bars of pressure. In theory this was what they needed to surface with but now they were so close to the surface it wasn't really an issue and they needed to decompress having been so deep. They had just settled into their stop when Jon saw Ruth's eyes open wide at something behind them. Before he could react, she put her hand to her forehead held vertically in the universal sign for a shark.

Jon spun his head around and saw something out in the blue quite far away. At first, he couldn't really make it out as it was heading directly towards them. Then suddenly, it came into focus. It was definitely a shark and getting closer all the time. The nearer it came the bigger it got. Jon was remembering what the Divemaster had said. Sharks didn't like to get too close to the reef so if in doubt head towards the coral. The only problem was that the coral wall they had been exploring was now quite a distance away from them. There was no way they could swim to it in time.

Jon made another signal to Ruth to stay put and the two of them watched the massive animal swim around them. It was at least three metres long and a deep grey in colour except for a white tip to its dorsal fin. It had a sharp nose and there was the white glimmer of teeth in its apparently smiling mouth. It didn't seem at all put out to see them. It also didn't seem in the slightest interested in them. They must smell of rubber and aluminium to him Jon guessed and they weren't flailing around on the surface looking like a wounded fish or turtle as most swimmers did. He indicated to Ruth to slowly start heading for the surface. It could be the wrong thing to do but they would be running out of air soon and then they really would be in trouble. Suddenly, with a flick of its tail, the massive animal headed straight towards them. There was absolutely nothing they could do. It swam so close they could see its eyes and then, as quickly as it appeared, it was gone, back out into the blue.

They continued their ascent and their heads broke surface. The bright sunlight and dappled surface of the sea was an amazing contrast to the blue world below them. They both spat out their regulators and inflated their jackets, Ruth with her remaining air and Jon by blowing in his oral inflation tube.

'Jesus Ruth, that was an interesting few minutes,' Jon exclaimed in a wave of adrenalin.

Ruth looked rather less impressed. 'Maybe but where the hell is the dive boat?'

They both looked frantically around and then Jon spotted it some distance away around the reef which showed itself as a brown smudge near the surface. 'Over there, I suggest we swim for it with snorkels and our masks on. If our big friend comes back we can keep a look out and also get close to the reef.'

Ten minutes later they were being hauled out at the back of the dive boat. The others had already made it back and were starting to worry about them. Their Divemaster, immediately looked at Jon's tank and diagnosed a blown 'O' ring. It was only a small circle of rubber but acted as a seal against the thousands of pounds of air pressure in the tank. He gave it to Jon as a souvenir and more importantly promised to ensure that all the dive centre's tanks were checked. When they described their encounter with the shark they were met with universal jealousy from the other divers. They were told that it was almost certainly an Oceanic White Tip which was very rare this far north in the Red Sea. It didn't help Ruth's equanimity when it was explained that they were rated as the fourth most dangerous shark in the world and apparently accounted for nearly all the attacks on survivors in the Pacific in the Second World War.

Jon took another deep draught of his beer. 'So I almost died at thirty metres and then we almost got scoffed by an FBF. An interesting day to say the least.'

'Alright, I'll bite. FBF?' Ruth asked not sure she wanted the answer.

'Efffin Big Fish,' Jon explained. 'It's a technical term. I not sure that women would understand.'

The remark got him quite a hard kick under the table. 'Oops sorry,' he apologised. 'Standard naval way of explaining things. FB followed by the letter of whatever you're talking about.'

Ruth smiled. 'So are you looking forward to your FBS then? She's going to have women on board isn't she?'

'Yup. Never had that before. Should be interesting. I suppose as the skipper, I get my choice of the pretty ones.'

Just for a second Ruth thought he was being serious but then realised he was teasing her yet again. 'Just be careful Mister Hunt. I kick hard as you might have noticed. Anyway, if you could be serious for just a moment, are you looking forward to it?'

'Do bears poop on the Pope's balcony? Look Ruth, I joined the navy to fly and then I grew up a bit and learned to command ships. I can honestly say that commanding an aircraft carrier has got to be the pinnacle of my career. I get a new and very large ship to play with and then fill it up with aircraft. What more could I want?'

'But you won't get to fly, you're not a Harrier pilot as well are you?'

'Well no, I'll leave that to the younger lads but there will be at least one helicopter on board for routine delivery work and I've still got Wanda the Wasp to play with back at Yeovilton.'

'You're so lucky,' Ruth said wistfully. 'The things you've done in your career. I wonder what trouble you'll get into now the navy has given you such a big toy to play with.'

A cloud passed over Jon's face. 'I've got to make her work first my dear. When I was there the other day she was a mess but I can understand that, she's still in build after all. What worries me a bit is this reputation she's already got for being unlucky. It's all bollocks of course. A ship is only as good or bad as the people in her but once these things get started they can be very hard to turn around. Anyway, that's enough about her Majesty's bloody Royal Navy, we're on holiday. Let's get some more drinks in, have a bloody good dinner and go to bed. You know the effect a large dose of adrenalin has on the male libido.' He said with a rather lecherous grin.

Ruth looked affronted. 'Typical bloody male. I got quite scared too you know.'

Later that night as they lay in a tangled, sweaty heap in their bed. Jon's mind was in a whirl. Instead of feeling sleepy, he felt alive and awake. It was clear that Ruth was awake as well.

'Come on Casanova,' Ruth said leaning on one arm and looking down at him. 'What's up? You're normally snoring your fat head off by now.'

'Hmmph, thanks for that. I think we need to talk. Let me grab some scotch from the fridge and we can sit on the veranda and look at the moon.'

'Shouldn't we put some clothes on first?'

'Why bother, no one can see us and frankly I rather like the way you look with nothing on.'

Ruth gave a wry smile at his remark but said nothing.

The cool night air was soothing and Jon poured two large measures, added some water and handed one to Ruth.

They sat in silence for a few minutes and then Jon plucked up the courage to speak. 'Ruth, we need to sort something out. We've been seeing each other now for quite some time. Should we make the arrangement more formal?'

Ruth let out a bark of laughter. 'If that was a proposal Jon, it's one of the worst I've ever had.'

'Oh, you've had many have you?' he asked rather huffily.

She realised this was difficult for him and immediately felt guilty. She had wondered if this would ever happen and had already made up her mind. She just hoped he wouldn't be too disappointed.

'Jon, I've had the same thought you know,' she saw he was about to speak. 'No, just let me have my say. You know how my last marriage ended but you probably don't know the main reason. You see, I can't have children. I had to have a hysterectomy when I was young. I'm perfectly fit but a family is out of the question. That was why Mick left me in the end. Now, I don't know if you want a family or not but it won't be with me. On top of that, I'm quite aware that no one will ever replace Helen, even though its years now since she died. You can only have one love like that in your life. After my divorce, I swore I would never marry again but after meeting you I did almost change my mind. In the end though, I've become so independent and happy with my life that I don't want to change it. Let's face it, you're going to be away for most of the next few years anyway. So sorry, the answer is no, if that is what you were going to ask. However, I would love us to carry on as we are. There's no one else in my life and I really like you and being with you. Who knows, maybe in a couple of years things might change but not now.'

Jon didn't say anything and Ruth started to get worried that she had offended him but she had to be honest. Just as she was really starting to get concerned, he gave a little chuckle. 'Thank you Ruth. You've just summarised my own feelings very well. I like you a lot you know. I don't want a family either, that desire left me when Helen went. But I wasn't sure that if I didn't ask then you might take offence if that makes any sense at all. Because I'm very happy with our arrangement if you are.'

'Good, I'm glad we've got that off our collective chests,' she replied.

Jon looked over at Ruth's pert chest. 'You know, adrenalin can have quite a long lasting effect.'

Chapter 3

All too soon their holiday was over and Jon was back to work. Willingly of course and it was with mounting excitement that he peered out of the taxi windows for his next sighting of Formidable. The weather was much improved which helped. At first, when he saw her alongside the wall he was disappointed. She looked very much the same as last time but it didn't take long to start seeing important difference. There were two brows now giving access to the ship. Everything looked tidy and there were far less workmen around her. What was more interesting was that there was clearly a welcoming party waiting for him at the rear brow. No one was in uniform but neither was he. They all seemed smartly turned out in business suits. There was one exception. One of them was female and even from this distance looked quite attractive despite a rather formal looking dress. He realised he was going to have to get used to this from now on

The taxi drew to a halt and Jon handed over some money, telling the driver to keep the change. He couldn't be bothered to ask for a receipt, he was far more interested in getting on with things.

He was about to climb out when one of the men came over and opened the door for him. 'Captain Hunt Sir?' he asked.

'That's me,' Jon replied as he climbed out and held out his hand.

The man shook it with a firm grip. 'Paul Taylor Sir, I'm your Executive Officer.'

Jon quickly studied one of the men he was going to have to rely heavily on over the next few years. He was short, with close cropped sandy hair and could clearly do with losing some weight but Jon could already feel a nervous energy emanating from him. It might be nervousness at meeting his new Captain but Jon suspected it was something more. After all, he had read all his Heads of Departments Service records and knew them on paper at least. Paul Taylor came highly recommended. Surprisingly Jon had not come across any of the team that had been appointed to support him but the navy was still a big club and Jon had been away from the mainstream for some time.

'Let me introduce you to the others Sir.' Paul said. 'You already know Derek Murray the WEO. This is David Johnson your Marine Engineer, Mike Perry the Air Engineer, Jim Prior your Supply Officer and Amelie Smith the ship's navigator.'

Jon shook all their hands putting faces to the reports he had looked carefully at. It wouldn't take long to get to know them all and then there would be a mere five hundred or so more faces in due course. Suddenly, he realised the mountain he was going to have to climb. He stood back and took in their eager expressions. 'Well thanks for getting together to greet me. We'll all get to know each other pretty well and pretty soon I expect. You've probably heard a little about me, I've been in the media a few times.'

A small laugh met this remark. Jon was very well known for some of his past exploits. Luckily not all of them, he mused.

'Whatever you've heard, please forget it. We start afresh today and we have a big job on our hands. What I would like is for Derek and Paul to stay with me and take me through the general programme. Then I'll have an individual face to face with everyone later today.'

Taking the hint all but the named two left. Paul turned to his new Captain. 'Sir, why don't we go to your cabin on board. Derek and I have set it up to give you a full brief.'

Jon was slightly surprised by the suggestion. 'Is it all finished? It was a complete mess last time I was here.'

Derek gave a short laugh. 'I think you'll find we've made excellent progress since then Sir. Come and have a look.'

As they walked through the ship to Jon's main accommodation, he was amazed to see the transformation. Gone were the tangles of temporary wiring. All the wall panels were in place. The whole ship looked and felt like a real warship. He turned to Derek. 'You were right Derek but I'm staggered at what has been achieved in just a few weeks.'

'Told you Sir,' Derek replied. 'The yard really dug out and as I said at the time, all the major work was already complete by then. Most of what you saw was cosmetic. Here we are Sir, this will be you harbour accommodation, you've a much smaller sea cabin one deck below the bridge.'

Jon was ushered into a palatial space. There was a large table, several comfortable looking arm chairs and a desk.

'Your heads and bedroom are through there Sir,' Derek pointed to a door off to one side.

Jon looked around, comfortable it certainly was but it would need some personalisation. The walls were bare, with the exception of an oil painting on one wall. Jon went over and studied it. 'Where on earth did this come from?' he asked.

'I'm guilty of that one Sir,' Paul replied. 'We've got a replica in the wardroom but that is the original. I raided the silver store in Portsmouth last week to get mess silver. There's a fortune stored there from all the ships that have decommissioned over the years. They've also got loads of oil paintings and I spotted this one. It's the last Formidable as I'm sure you recognise. The painting is of her taking part in Operation Torch, the invasion of North Africa in nineteen forty two. I've also asked the yard to make us a battle honours board which their shipwright shop has promised to do. It will be quite large as the ship was in just about every battle of the Second World War.'

'I know,' Jon replied. 'I read up on her some time ago. Let's make sure the new one does just as well. So, grab a seat gentlemen, tell me where we are at.'

Just then the main door opened and a Petty Officer walked in with a tray. 'Petty Officer Steward Jenkins Sir, I'm your steward. I've got coffee and a few biscuits. I can get lunch for you whenever you want it.'

'Hang on a second Jenkins, I know you. Didn't we serve together in Prometheus?' Jon was pretty sure he recognised the face. His steward smiled, clearly flattered at being recognised so fast.

'Yes Sir, I was one of the wardroom staff. I'm amazed you remember me.'

'I never forget anyone from that ship Jenkins. We had some interesting times.'

'Indeed we did Sir. I was in one of the First Aid parties. You kept us all busy on one particular occasion I seem to remember.' Jenkins replied with a grin. 'Let me know about lunch when you've decided Sir.' And he quietly slipped out of the room.

Paul Taylor was impressed by the exchange. 'You've got a good memory for faces Sir. I'm not sure I would remember someone from a ship's company so many years later.'

'Ah, we had some good times in that ship Paul. My task and yours now will be to make sure we know as many of our people as quickly as we can. You know, I'm amazed. In Prometheus we had a complement of two hundred and fifty seven and in this ship, which is over five times the size, we only have three hundred. It just shows how modern technology makes warships easier to operate.'

'Don't forget the Air Group Sir, that will be another two hundred or so when they are on board,' Derek said.

'Good point Derek. Anyway, let's grab a coffee and get down to business.'

The morning passed in a blur for Jon but he summarised after a couple of hours. 'So we have some of the ship's company on board already but the ship is now capable of hosting her full complement. However, we will only get about another hundred before we start initial sea trials in ten day's time. Which is all we need for the first ones anyway. We do manufacturers shake down trials before we move on to full acceptance. Once they're out of the way, we have our commissioning ceremony when we finally get to fly the white ensign. Then it's on to shake down for the whole ship plus first of class flying trials and finally the dreaded Basic Operational Sea Training. All this will take about a year and then we finally get to play with the fleet.'

'That's it Sir,' Paul responded. 'I don't think anyone will get bored.'

'That's an understatement Paul,' Derek said. 'As for her material state, all propulsion has been tested alongside. All electrical generation is up and running. The command systems are now working and believe it or not Sir, the Ops room no longer looks like a hand grenade has exploded in it. The yard believe we will be ready in time and for that matter so do I.'

'Good,' Jon responded. 'What could possibly go wrong?' he added drily.

He pulled stumps at lunchtime but invited his two Commanders to stay although he banned any more talk about the ship while they were eating. Instead he dug around a little further to find out more about the people behind the job titles. It appeared that Derek's main occupation when away from the ship was playing golf. Jon had to admit that he had never played but was happy to take up the offer of a lesson at some time in the future. Paul was also a diver but apparently also had a historic Sports Car he occasionally raced. His offer to take Jon to a race was even more attractive.

Paul looked at his Captain. 'So Sir, what about you? You've said you're a diver but I heard a story about owning a helicopter is that true?'

Jon laughed. 'Absolutely right, it's no secret. When I couldn't fly professionally any more, I found that I just couldn't stay away. We found her at the old Dartmouth Flight hangar. It's a bit of a long story but she's now with the Historic Flight at Yeovilton but I fly her when I can.'

Derek was intrigued. 'What sort of machine Sir?'

'Oh sorry, she's an ex-navy Wasp. A friend's kids named her Wanda and it's stuck.' Jon replied.

'Sir, if you don't mind me asking. There's a story doing the rounds that you were involved in some sort of incident in Scotland recently and that you were flying the Wasp then?' Paul asked warily.

Jon sat back and thought. He knew that there was going to be a trial very soon and he was going to be called to give evidence. There were going to be heavy press restrictions but even so he wouldn't be at all surprised if most of the story got out. After all, chasing a retired Air Marshall up to Scotland and getting him arrested as a Soviet spy as well as the murderer of his wife was pretty sensational. The fact that his XO already knew something was clear evidence that things were already leaking.

'Look chaps, I can't tell you the whole story, not yet at least. But yes, it resulted in someone being arrested. Someone I had a personal interest in seeing caught. Once it has become public I'll give you the full story, alright?' Jon said looking hard at the two of them.

'Of course Sir,' Paul said for both of them.

'And we need to discuss something else along those lines if you don't mind?'

His remark was met with interested looks.

'I already alluded to it when I met everyone this morning. Look, I've been lucky, if that's the right word, to be caught up in the limelight on a few occasions. Probably the most public one was the hijack of the Uganda and my involvement in catching that Russian spy.'

'And when you lamped that journalist at Culdrose,' Paul said without thinking.

Jon frowned. 'Not my finest hour I'm afraid.'

'I'm pretty sure the ship's company don't see it that way Sir,' Paul responded. 'I've already heard a few remarks.'

'And that's the point chaps. It won't be possible to ignore it but I want us to look ahead. I'm fully aware of how the lads will talk but I really don't want to dwell on it. If that makes sense?'

Paul answered. 'I think we all get that Sir but it's going to be very difficult for me because there is one thing I need to thank you for personally.'

'Oh what's that?' Jon asked slightly surprised by the look on his XO's face.

'The Uganda incident Sir. My son was on board.'

Chapter 4

The Jury foreman stood and the courtroom hushed. 'Gentlemen of the Jury on the charge of Treason, how do you find the defendant?'
The foreman didn't hesitate. 'Guilty.'
'On the charge of attempted murder?'
'Guilty.'
'On the charge of manslaughter?'
'Guilty.'
The courtroom exploded in noise. Jon looked at the man who had killed his wife and betrayed his country all his life. The man he had hunted down. Air Marshall Peter Johnson stood stony faced and didn't move. There was no look of surprise or regret on his face. It had amazed Jon that he had bothered to plead not guilty at all, such was the wealth of evidence against him. But now, at last, it was over.

Brian tugged Jon's sleeve. 'Let's get the hell out of here. They won't sentence the bastard for weeks. Hopefully, the rear entrance will be clear.'
Jon nodded and the two men took their leave as the uproar continued. It wasn't often such a senior military officer was arraigned for such crimes. The press were going to have a field day and Jon wanted no part in it. They left the central court of the Old Bailey and Jon took them both down a side corridor which ended in a small lobby. There were double doors that opened on to a small side road at the back of the building. The doors had small glass panes and Jon could see that there was no one there. He took out his mobile phone and sent a prepared text message. Within minutes an old Ford pulled up and he beckoned Brian with him. They ducked out and straight into the car. Before Jon could put his seat belt on, Ruth who was driving, set off quickly and clear of the court building.
'Bloody hell Ruth, slow down a bit,' Jon exclaimed. 'It's only the press we're trying to get away from, not a bank robbery.'
Ruth laughed. 'If you could see the scrum outside the front you wouldn't say that.'
'How the hell did they know,' Brian asked from the rear. 'I thought the whole thing was under a D Notice.'

'You may not like them Brian but they're not idiots,' Ruth replied. 'Slapping a reporting restriction on something only makes them chase the scent even harder. Despite the restrictions, the outside of the court is a public space and they'll have had people watching who comes and goes and you two have been here right from the start. And as you know, today it's been announced that there will be a statement made to them as soon as the trial is formally over, which is why they are out in force today. So I'm sorry but be prepared to be harassed for a while. Oh and Jon, I strongly suggest your previous tactic of knocking one to the ground won't work a second time.'

'It didn't exactly work that well the last time, even if most of my ship's company think differently,' Jon responded.

'Well, I hate to tell you but a certain Mister Simon Gross is now working for a major newspaper. I didn't tell you this before but the notoriety he gained from being thumped by you on national television down at Culdrose after Helen died, was enough to get him on to the staff of one the more disreputable rags. Sorry but he was one of the throng outside.' Ruth said.

'Shit, that's all I need,' Jon muttered.

'Don't worry old son,' Brian replied. 'I'm sure he will have the sense to stay out of the range of your right hook this time.'

'He's a sneaky bastard. He won't try the same tactic again, I'm sure,' Jon said. 'But I don't suppose he has any love left for me. Anyway, it's over as far as I'm concerned. Even if they decided on pressing only those three charges when there so many others they could have used. Johnson won't be leaving prison for the rest of his life. Bugger it, let's forget about today and go and have a drink. Where are we meeting Rupert?'

'Not far now,' Ruth replied. 'I'll park here and the restaurant is just over there at the edge of the square.'

Ten minutes later and the three of them were just sitting, when Ruth's brother and Jon and Brian's old friend, Rupert Thomas arrived, looking very dapper in a business suit.

'Rupert, good to see you,' Jon said standing. 'How's the world of spooks and spies.'

Rupert shrugged. 'Same as always Jon, ninety nine percent boredom and the rest is bloody paperwork. Unless you're around that is, then everything always seems to get interesting. I hear that bugger Johnson is going down?'

'Yes, guilty on all three counts.' Jon replied.

'And thanks to you old chap,' Rupert stated.

'With a little help from you, Brian and Wanda.' Jon replied. 'A team effort I would suggest. Right what can I get you to drink?'

They all took their seats and the waiter came over with menus. They all stopped talking to order. When the waiter had gone, Brian who had been relatively quiet tapped his wine glass to get attention. 'Hey you three, I've a little announcement of my own to make.'

They all turned to look at him. 'I'm leaving Dartmouth and they're giving me a ship. It's one of the new Type 23s, HMS Hampshire. So, you and me both Jon.'

'Bloody well done,' Jon replied. He wasn't surprised. He had been lobbying the Naval Secretary on Brian's behalf ever since he had returned from Serbia but that would have to stay secret. 'She's just out of build as well isn't she?'

'Yes but further on than yours. We commission in a month and then on to trials and BOST. The previously appointed skipper was taken ill last month. So I get to step in at the last moment. They had me down for another 23 but this is by far the better deal. I get the latest ship and a chance to work her up my way.'

Ruth looked at both the men. 'I think I understood about half of that but I do get that its good news for you Brian, congratulations.'

'Thanks Ruth, although I'm not sure that Kathy is all that delighted. I'm going to be away quite a lot but she knew that when she married a naval officer.'

The conversation continued in a light hearted manner for the rest of the meal. But all too soon Jon had to make his apologies. His train wouldn't wait and he was eager to get back to his own new charge.

Half a mile away, Simon Gross was in his editor's office. The editor was looking at some rough copy that Simon had produced. 'Bloody hell, they've convicted one of our senior military as a bloody Russian spy. This is going to run but you're very sparse on details Simon. There must be a lot more to it than just this.'

Simon nodded. 'That's just a digest from the formal statement. It makes no mention of who he is meant to have tried to murder or who he killed by accident. Nor does it say how he was caught and who did it. You know how these things work. We are going to have to ferret around for weeks to find out anything and then they'll probably slap a gagging order on us. Look, I've got a different idea. You know I've been keeping an eye on who has been attending. You might remember a little fracas down in Cornwall a few years ago?'

His editor laughed. 'Too bloody right, you stepped to close to a bereaved husband and asked just about the wrong bloody question possible and got yourself a straight punch to the face. It's why my predecessor hired you and it's why I keep you in the background even now.'

'What would you do if I said that I'm pretty sure that that bereaved husband played an integral part in bringing this spy down and that it might even have something to do with his wife's death?'

'Eh? How do you work that one out?'

'He was a witness at the trial and made a sneaky escape out the back afterwards. He has something to hide.'

'No hang on, he used to work for the Air Marshal in the MOD. He was responsible for getting that other spy arrested. That would be why he was there,' the editor looked sceptical.

'Ah but what you don't know is that they were both in Serbia recently working for the UN. I have my sources and they say something odd happened although no one will say exactly what.' Simon looked pleased with himself.

'Yes, he rescued a French pilot. The French gave him a bloody great medal. Come on Simon, is this part of your personal vendetta because he made you look a fucking idiot on prime time TV?'

'Boss, I won't argue with you over that,' Simon replied. 'But this Captain Hunt has now taken over command of the navy's latest aircraft carrier. All I'm asking is that you let me keep this story live while I see what I can dig up and maybe keep a close brief on what he does now.'

'Fair enough but keep me in the loop. We will need hard facts or the ministry will come down on us like a ton of bricks.'

After Simon had left, the editor sat back. Despite what he had said, he liked his staff when they had a personal axe to grind and Simon definitely did. It kept them on their toes and made them dig just that little harder. Also he agreed with the man. There was more to this story if it could be ferreted out, much more.

Chapter 5

Jon woke to the alarm clock in his main cabin with the dappled light of the sea and morning sun reflecting on the ceiling above his head. For a few moments he luxuriated in the feeling that he was home at last before suddenly remembering what day it was. He quickly jumped out of bed and headed for his shower. As he was washing away the sleep he heard a door open and the cheerful voice of Petty Officer Jenkins announce that his breakfast would be ready when he got out of the shower. He quickly dried and dressed himself in his working rig of dark blue pullover and black trousers. On his feet, he put on his 'steaming bats' the standard black naval shoes with reinforced toe caps worn by all sailors at sea. Because today that is where they were going. Formidable was sailing for the first time today.

Breakfast over, he checked his watch and headed for the bridge. Normally this sort of briefing would be held in the main briefing room that was used by the squadron but it was one of the spaces in the ship that was yet to be finished. As he entered the large space he could see out of the armoured glass windows that the weather was set fair. It was as forecast, with a light wind and a mainly blue sky. Already gathered and waiting for him were his HODs, the First Lieutenant and Chief Bosun's mate, normally referred to as the 'Buffer', and a sprinkling of other relevant ship's staff. He would soon know all their names but for the moment was glad everyone was wearing name tallies. 'Good morning all,' he called cheerfully. 'Let's get our brief out of the way. The yard superintendent and harbour pilot will be along in half an hour and I want us to be ready in all respects. Commander you have the floor.'

Paul Taylor took a step forward. 'All hands on board and accounted for Sir. We will go to Special Sea Duty men at ten thirty. The First Lieutenant will be in charge forward and Lieutenant Pearson will be on the quarterdeck. As discussed, we will use Procedure Bravo, hands will man the upper deck but in working rig.'

'Excellent,' Jon replied. He already had some working knowledge of his crew but it was early days yet with the fleshpots of Newcastle not far away. He was glad that all of them had managed to make it back on board. 'Engines?'

The MEO took centre stage. Both diesels up and running Sir, all ships systems are checked out particularly steering and generation. We are at eighty per cent fuel. We flashed up the two Spey gas turbines yesterday but don't intend to use them today as you know. However, they will be available at about fifteen minute's notice if we need them for anything.'

'Good, you never know with so many untried systems all having to work properly first time.' Jon said. 'WEO?'

Derek Murray looked down at a clipboard. 'All radars flashed up Sir but the Action Information system is in navigation mode only. We are still waiting for our full software suite but it should be fine for today. The new Global Positioning System is working well and the automatic chart display on the bridge is up and running.'

Jon turned to his navigator. 'How do you want to play that Pilot?'

'As discussed Sir,' Amelie Smith responded. 'I will run a standard visual plot for the whole trip especially the pilotage in and out of the river. Although we will have the harbour pilot in charge, I will give you a standard navigation narrative. My Yeoman will manage the GPS plot and when we are back in we will run a comparison assessment of the system.'

Jon nodded his agreement. The GPS system was relatively new to warships and he had no intention on relying on it until it had proven to be one hundred per cent reliable and even then there would always be a conventional visual plotting system running as back up. 'Thanks Amelie. We will have our first leaving harbour navigation brief after this meeting and then I will want you to make sure the harbour pilot is happy with it as well.'

Jon then stood back and regarded his team. 'Thank you all for the incredible hard work that has gone into getting ready for this day. I will make a broadcast to the ship's company before we leave to thank them as well. However, please remember that the Queen doesn't actually own this ship at the moment. We sail under the red ensign and that technically means she is still owned by the yard. This is a brand new class of ship with many untried systems yet to prove their effectiveness so we take it slowly and carefully. Caution is the key today. Let's have a successful first sailing. Right, off you go. Let's get the Standard Operators Checks completed in good time and I expect to sail on time. Amelie, let's go and look at your navigation plan.'

Everyone left except Jon and his navigator, who led him over to the chart table where she already had several large scale charts ready.

'Amelie, I haven't really had much of a chance for a chat,' Jon said. 'And for that I apologise but it's all been rather hectic for the last few weeks as you know. Before we go into talking about passage plans, tell me a little about yourself.' Jon was still finding it a little odd talking to a girl wearing Lieutenant Commander's stripes in such a situation, which was strange he mused, bearing in mind that he had been married to one of the navy's first female officers. In some ways, Amelie reminded him a little of Helen although physically she was much smaller and had short, wavy, black hair. Actually, she looked more like Ruth. However, there was the same look of determination in her eye that he remembered. The same air of competence.

'Died in the wool Executive branch Sir,' Amelie said looking him in the eye. 'My father was in the navy and I joined the WRNS before applying for a full commission as soon as I could. I was at Dartmouth the term after your wife Sir.'

Jon nodded, noting the hesitation in her voice. 'Don't worry Amelie, I know it's a sensitive subject but it's in the past now and nothing can change that.'

'Yes Sir, well I went on the Warfare training courses but my heart has always been for navigation and seamanship so I specialised in that in the end. I've served in two frigates before this appointment as well as one shore job teaching at HMS Dryad.'

'Yes, you come highly recommended. What about your life away from the navy? I hope you don't mind me saying but I notice a ring on your left hand.'

Amelie blushed slightly. 'Yes Sir, I've only had that a few weeks. He's a Lynx pilot like you used to be. We met some time ago when I was doing a course at Yeovilton. He's an instructor on 702 Squadron at the moment.'

'Well with him there and our likely itinerary over the next year or two I hope you get the time to see some of him.'

'Don't worry Sir, we both know the situation, we're not planning anything more for a year or two. Not until the end of my time in this appointment.'

'That's a sensible attitude. Who knows what the next few years will throw at us. What about hobbies, interests that sort of thing?'

'Sailing Sir. I did my Yachtmaster Offshore last year and my father owns a forty foot Jenneau which he keeps on the Hamble.'

Jon laughed. 'So, even your spare time involves being at sea. Actually, I did my Skippers ticket as well recently when I was at Dartmouth so who am I to talk. Anyway, time is moving on. Take me through your cunning plan to get us out to sea.'

Four hours later and Jon was starting to relax. Leaving the wall had been straightforward. They had the use of two tugs who pulled the massive bulk of the ship clear and then turn her around in the middle of the wide river. Once heading the right way, the ship had gently got underway using her two diesels and headed out to sea. The navigation was relatively simple and once into the North Sea, they started a series of simple shakedown trials. Once Jon was content that his bridge crew were on top managing the ship he went walkabout.

Starting forward, he visited all the major machinery spaces and was gratified to see that all was well. He then stopped off in HQ1 the ships control centre for machinery and damage control. The MEO was in charge there and despite a few minor gripes was happy with the way things were going. The Ops room was a dark quite cave, lit by the lights from the various displays. Because Formidable was built on merchant ship lines and costs had been kept down, she only had four close in weapon systems for self-defence and no sonars. Her weapons would be her Harriers once they were embarked and so she had a good powerful radar for watching the skies. Unfortunately, as the WEO had said earlier, the software system that managed the ship's radars and controlled the aircraft had yet to be set to work so there was little work for the team. However, they were making the best of it and starting to get familiar with the systems as much as they could.

As lunch time was approaching, he made his way to the Junior Rates galley area and managed to speak to as many of his sailors as he could. He had already started to put some names to faces and saw this as one of his major tasks over the next few months. The lads all seemed in good heart. He got the strong impression that despite it being early days he had the making of a good crew. His final stop was the empty flight deck. All the marking were in place but none of the aircraft handling equipment had been delivered so there were none of the four wheel drive tractors or fire fighting equipment he would expect to see in the months to come. It was a windy, lonely place but he couldn't suppress a shiver of anticipation for when it would become a busy, noisy and dangerous place. A place from which his ship would generate her full capability.

But that was for another time. He made his way back to the bridge very happy with all that he had seen. They would be at sea for the rest of the afternoon then return to the yard. Day running like this would be the norm for the next two weeks then they would hopefully sign her off from the yard and set off for Devonport for their official commissioning.

Chapter 6

It had all been going too well. Jon wasn't surprised that they started having the odd failure as they put more stress on the ship and her systems. On the third day, they had tried a full power trial with both diesels and both gas turbines driving the ship. They had managed a respectable twenty eight knots before the port gearbox had started overheating. It quickly cooled as power was reduced but there was clearly a problem not the least because the other gearbox seemed fine. A cautious return to harbour had followed and then they had to stay alongside for an extra day until a blocked oil cooler was found to be the culprit. The next day all was well and the ship managed a sustained twenty nine knots for over an hour. This was a little more than the design specification and Jon was more than happy. There would be many occasions when his ship's capability to generate a strong wind over the deck would be critical to flying operations.

Then the forward aircraft lift jammed. Unlike American carriers that had side lifts, like her sister ship HMS Ocean, Formidable had two aircraft lifts set into the flight deck itself. The rear was only a few feet from the stern, the forward one was actually adjacent to the ship's island. Unfortunately, the access from the island to the flight deck, while not directly next to the lift, was close enough to make it dangerous if the lift was not in the raised position.

Jon and Dave Johnson, the MEO went to inspect the problem.

'Hydraulics have failed Sir,' the MEO said as the two men stared down the dark hole in the deck to the cavernous hangar below. 'The yard staff say they know why. It's a failed pump but it will take a couple of days alongside to fix.'

'Damn, how come the rear lift is working then?' Jon asked, suspecting he already knew the answer.

'Separate systems Sir. Designed that way to ensure one pump failure doesn't bring both lifts to a halt.'

'Hmm, I wonder if it should be the other way around so if one pump fails the systems can be cross connected so the remaining pump can power both lifts. If it's going to take the people who built the ship two whole days to replace the pump it's not likely to be something your people will be able to do at sea, is it?' Jon asked.

'Probably not Sir but I'll look into both those issues and let you know what the yard says. I think we also need some form of automatic barrier here so that when the lift is down, even during normal operations, then there is no risk of people falling down it as they exit the island. It's fine now but on a black shitty night things could be a lot different.'

'Good idea Dave, get on with it and keep me informed. I guess I had better go back to the bridge and turn us around. I don't suppose the lads will mind a couple of extra runs ashore.' Jon said and turned to go back into the island and up to the bridge.

When he arrived, he picked up the microphone for the ship's main broadcast. 'Do you hear there, this is the Captain speaking. I'm afraid we are going to have to return to harbour earlier than planned to fix our forward lift and will be staying in for a couple of days. As it's a Wednesday already I will look to giving everyone an extended weekend's leave.' He could hear a muted cheer from below decks even this far up. 'But don't think I'm going soft. We are going to have to catch up on the other work we are missing and then you can all look forward to BOST. Captain out.'

He put down the microphone and smiled at Amelie who was the current Officer of the Watch.

'I didn't hear a cheer to that second announcement Sir,' she said with a grin.

'I'm not surprised,' Jon said. 'Have you done any Work Ups Amelie?'

'One Sir, in Chester a couple of years back. And I know how much hard work they can be.'

'Hard work but fun if we approach it the right way,' Jon replied. 'Anyway navigator, you can take us home please.'

Two hours later as evening fell, the ship entered the river Tyne once again. The harbour pilot had come on board before they entered but Jon was so familiar with the approach that he rarely said anything now. She slipped past the breakwaters at the entrance to the river and slowed down for the four and a half mile transit to the Wallsend yard. It always amazed Jon how many large ships had sailed from here over the years, not the least the Mauretania in 1903. And then a succession of warships up to the modern day including both the navy's previous carriers the Illustrious and Ark Royal. And here he was in command of the latest one. He often felt like pinching himself to confirm his good luck was real. Not that he would do so with the bridge staff all around him. His two tame tugs were waiting for him a little further on but he was getting so confident in handling the ship now that he was almost tempted to do away with them. Unfortunately, Formidable still technically belonged to Swan Hunter and it was a risk he couldn't take.

As they approached the yard with the two tugs ready to push their charge onto the dock, Jon ordered both engines to stop. With the way the ship still had on, they should be perfectly placed to coast to a halt in the correct place. The tide was ebbing past them and he probably wouldn't even need to go astern.

Suddenly, the loudspeaker above his head woke into life. 'Bridge this is the machinery control room. We have a defect on the port diesel. We have lost throttle control and can't shut it down.'

The effect on the bridge was electric. Jon grabbed his microphone. 'This is the Captain, confirm you can't stop it?'

'That's correct Sir,' Jon recognised the MEO's voice. 'It's not responding to our controls and even though we tried shutting off the fuel supply it's still running. It's possible it's actually burning its own sump oil and I've no idea how long it will run for.'

'Do your best MEO we're not far from the dock. Right, Officer of the Watch I have the ship, pipe hands to Emergency Stations, make the emergency sound signal for not under command and hoist the visual signal.' Jon looked over at the signaller manning the maritime VHF radio. 'Yeoman get on channel 16 and warn all local traffic of our problem and tell the tugs I will need them to help as soon as I sort out what we can do.'

For a second Jon was distracted by the blast of the ships siren and then the main broadcast alarm telling the crew to get to their Emergency Stations. But then he was alerted to the next problem by the quartermaster who was steering the ship. 'Can't hold her, Sir I've got full port wheel on but can't hold ships head.'

Jon realised that port propeller was now forcing the ship into a starboard turn that the rudders were unable to compensate for. He had a choice, he could restart the starboard engine which would give him rudder control but then he would be heading further up river and it got very narrow very quickly, not to mention the bridges he couldn't get under. Even with rudder control re-established they wouldn't have room to turn around. There was only one thing he could do and only a few seconds in which to do it.

He grabbed the main broadcast as it was probably the quickest way of getting his order understood and acted on. 'Fo'csle this is the Captain, emergency release the port anchor.'

It was standard procedure to keep one anchor ready to drop in case of power failure when leaving or entering harbour and they had the port one prepared today. No one had really considered using an anchor for the exact opposite of power failure but it was all Jon could do. He prayed that the First Lieutenant who was in charge up forward understood the problem and acted swiftly.

Jon turned to his left. 'Yeoman, have the tugs responded?'

'Yes Sir. They said they would keep clear until you wanted them.'

'Tell them I am dropping my port anchor and will probably swing violently when it digs in,' Jon didn't add his fear that if the anchor didn't hold they were going to hit the jetty very hard.

He looked out of the bridge window knowing there was just about nothing left to do. He might as well watch the train wreck as it happened.

There was a muted rumbling from forward. 'Anchor has been released Sir,' Amelie called.

Suddenly, there was a jerking shaking motion through Jon's feet. He knew it was the anchor being dragged across the river bed and digging in but then pulling out. The concrete wall of the jetty was getting really close now. Suddenly, the bow of the twenty thousand ton ship dipped sharply and the swing to starboard abruptly stopped. The bridge crew all had to grab something to stop being thrown off their feet. The anchor had dug in at literally the last moment.

Almost immediately, the intercom came alive. 'Bridge, machinery control room, we've managed to shut the bloody thing down.'

Jon offered a prayer to whoever was watching over them. They had managed to get away with it. Then Amelie called to him and pointed out to the shore. By now, it was starting to get dark.

Jon looked to where she was pointing. 'Oh fuck,' he said quietly to himself. All the lights on the shore had just gone out.

Simon Gross had never been to Newcastle and had been pleasantly surprised by how modern the city looked. Wallsend was another matter. It was very much the product of the tail end of an industrial revolution that had long gone. Finding the shipyard had been quite easy as the large cranes dominated the skyline even now. He had come up to the yard for a look at this new ship and was surprised to see her in the process of coming alongside. His plan was to ask around a little and see if there were any chinks in her Captain's armour. One thing he had no intention of doing was to get too close to the bloody man. Unless of course he was on solid ground this time and preferably without live TV cameras on him. He would take his time and have his revenge cold.

As he watched the great grey vessel approach the dock, despite knowing next to nothing about ship handling, he could sense something going wrong. Suddenly, the air was torn apart by blasts from the ship's siren and then he could see something dropping off the ship's bow. He quickly realised it was an anchor and that definitely wasn't normal. Then the ship shuddered to a halt still well clear of the jetty and pointing back out towards the centre of the river. Completely nonplussed, he realised that something had gone seriously wrong just as all the street lights around him went out.

He sat for a few moments trying to understand what had just happened. It didn't take that long to come up with a fair guess and that was all he needed. Grabbing his camera he started shooting. 'Got ya, you bastard,' he muttered and then he reached for his mobile phone.

Chapter 7

Jon woke up the next day already dog tired as he had only managed a few hours sleep. What had started out as a successful emergency procedure then became a further cascade of problems. With the ship stopped, the next problem was getting her alongside the dockyard wall. The tugs quickly positioned themselves alongside the ship ready to push her sideways. The problem was that the anchor was firmly caught on something on the riverbed. Jon had a pretty good idea what that was and didn't want to damage the main electrical power line they had clearly done serious damage to any further. In the end, they had paid out all their anchor chain as the ship was edged closer to the dock. Unfortunately, it wasn't long enough and so they were forced to let the whole lot go and drop to the bottom. It was either that or stay stuck out twenty yards clear of the shore.

Once alongside, Jon had despatched Derek Murry ashore to alert the authorities as to what had happened and start the inevitable round of apologies. In the absence of anyone appointed to be the ships Public Relations Officer Jon agreed with the XO's suggestion that Amelie Smith take on the role. It wasn't long before the telephones began ringing and local reporters started asking what had been going on.

Meanwhile, Jon and the XO had to draft a signal to various authorities to appraise them of the incident. It didn't help that in theory the ship still belonged to the yard and therefore lacked a formal command authority as would be the case once she was commissioned.

Luckily, the local power generation company worked quickly to reroute power to the area. They even had a working contingency plan for losing an underwater feed across the river and the lights were all back on within an hour. Jon breathed a massive sigh of relief when he saw the street lights flicker back into life. Eventually, the situation settled down. There would be much to do over the following days. There would have to be an enquiry and report into what had happened and no doubt they would be asked all sorts of questions. Deciding who would have to pick up the bill to repair the power line was going to be an interesting debate and Jon had no idea how that would be dealt with. They would also need to arrange for a team of specialist divers and equipment to see if the anchor could be recovered or whether a new one would be needed. The only saving grace was that the Swan

Hunter chief engineer came on board and apologised for the problem clearly accepting that the strange behaviour of one of his engines was the root cause of the whole incident.

It was after two in the morning when Jon managed to get to bed and he was up, bleary eyed again at seven.

'Morning Sir, breakfast is on the table and a large pot of coffee to go with it,' PO Jenkins called cheerily. 'Is there anything else?'

'Yes, could you ask the Commander and MEO to join me and rustle up some food for them as well please? A working breakfast is in order I think.' Jon asked.

Fifteen minutes later, the three men were sitting at the table and discussing the events of the previous day.

'So MEO, how the hell can a diesel engine keep running like that?' Paul Taylor asked. 'It seems bloody odd to me.'

'Actually, it's not that uncommon,' Dave Johnson replied. 'A simple failure of the throttle mechanism can do it although shutting off the fuel should then stop it. But have you ever had a car engine run on after you turn off the ignition? It's a similar effect. As long as there is something in the cylinders to ignite under compression the engine will keep running. In this case, we think some of the piston rings failed, probably after the full power run which pressurised the sump and blew oil up into the cylinders which kept it running.'

'How the hell did you stop it then?' Jon asked. 'Did it run out of oil?'

'No Sir,' Paul replied. 'I reckon it could have run on for over half an hour. One of my chiefs took a bloody great spanner and managed to unbolt several of the fuel injectors which lost compression on those cylinders and eventually the whole thing ground to a halt.'

'That sounds a brave move MEO,' Paul said. 'Is he alright?'

'Yes, just a couple of burnt fingers but I would like to consider putting him forward for some form of award. As you say, it was a brave thing to do.' Dave said.

'I agree,' Jon said. 'Write him up Dave and let me see what I can do. However, I assume that the engine is now damaged and will take some time to repair and what guarantee can we have that this won't happen again?

'Actually, the yard think it will be quite easy to fix it as it's designed to have easy access to individual cylinders. There is also a decompression system that is used to start it. They are suggesting an override for it which will allow us to decompress even when it's running. So we will never have the problem again.'

'Good,' Jon said. 'Keep me informed. It could have been a great deal worse as I'm sure you appreciate. Let's face it we were bloody lucky.'

'I think some quick thinking helped Sir,' Paul said. 'Not sure I would have had the presence of mind to drop the anchor that fast. I would probably have had us under both shafts heading towards the Tyne Bridge at ten knots. Now that would have made the headlines.'

Jon was just about to reply when there was a knock at the door and Amelie Smith's head peered around it. She was holding something in her hands.

'Yes Amelie, come on in.' Jon said to her. 'Do you have some news?'

Amelie came in holding a newspaper. 'Yes Sir. As I got a pierhead jump into being the PRO I made sure to get all the national papers this morning. There's nothing about us except for this one.' She handed the paper to Jon who spent several minutes looking at the front page.

The others kept silent while he read then he looked up and passed it to his XO. 'In case you didn't know, the man who wrote that is a Mister Simon Gross, he's the journalist I had that little disagreement with at Culdrose.'

Paul finished reading and passed it over to Dave. 'That's all we bloody need. How the hell did he get all that information and how on earth was he there to photograph it?'

'Captain Calamity and His Unlucky Ship,' Dave said out loud. 'With a photo of us stuck in the middle of the river. And the bastard has managed to dig up the dirt on the poor chap who was killed during the build. Jesus Sir, he's got all your past exploits here but has even managed to put a spin on them making out they were your fault in the first place. What the hell do we do?'

Jon looked grim. 'About this particular article? Absolutely nothing, we ignore it. However, Amelie I want you to prepare a release on what actually happened and contact the PR people in the MOD and see if we can at least get a true account to the papers. Let me see it when you've roughed it out. No more than two pages let's keep it simple. I'm far more worried about the effect on the ship's company. I was hoping to put all this 'unlucky ship' stuff behind us but what with jamming lifts and run away engines and now this crap we seem to be going backwards.'

'So what do you think off all this crap in the papers Taff?' Leading Seaman 'Dinger' Bell, the ship's quartermaster on the ship's gangway asked the Able Seaman at his side. Taff was the Bosun's mate and between them they were responsible for running the ship's routine while alongside.

Anyone looking at Taff would have seen a grizzled middle aged man. On his arm were three red stripes which to the uninitiated would look like the Sergeant's stripes on a soldier. They were, in fac,t good conduct badges awarded to sailors after years of service. To see them on such a lowly rank as Able Seaman said a great deal about the wearer. A 'Three Badge AB' was a rarity in modern times as all seamen were specialists of some sort and actively encouraged to gain promotion as soon as they could. For his length of service, Taff could easily be a Chief Petty Officer had he wanted. However, like a few others in the navy he had decided early on that he was completely happy as an Able rate and had no desire whatsoever to move up the chain. He looked over the side at the scruffy dock wall. 'Dunno, it's all crap in the papers isn't it? I only read the Sun for the tits, don't care about much else.'

'Oh come on Taff,' Dinger responded. 'How many ships have you served on? I reckon the skipper did a bloody good job yesterday and all he gets is a hard time.'

Taff continued to look gloomily over the side. 'Yeah well, you serve in a ship not on it and it's not the first time an engine wouldn't quit. I was on a Ton class minesweeper going into Vernon in Pompey some years back and the same thing happened. Bloody diesel stayed running and we clobbered the dockyard wall good and proper. Suited me as we were in dock for over a month instead of dicking about at sea. Thought the same might have happened yesterday but the skipper did about the only thing he could I reckon.'

'Yeah, I reckon he's a good one,' Dinger said.

'All bloody officers are the same,' Taff said gloomily. 'Even this one. He thinks he's some bloody movie star, he does. All that crap in the papers about that hi-jack and that stuff he did in the Falklands. You mark my words he'll be the same as all the others. Never met a bloody officer yet who gets my respect.'

Formidable

Dinger reflected on Taff's words. He never had anything good to say about officers, the ship or the navy for that matter, yet here he was after years of service clearly quite happy with his lot. Dinger reckoned that much of it was a front but didn't say so. He knew he would get nowhere.

'Good morning Able Seaman Jones.' A voice said from behind them both. They froze and came to attention. Neither man had been on board long but the Captain's voice was easily recognised.

Jon laughed. 'Stand easy chaps, I was only stretching my legs. How's it going Killick Bell?' Jon asked.

'All quiet Sir,' Leading Seaman Bell replied. 'We're expecting another draft of lads later on and there's more stores coming on board but otherwise all routine.'

'Good but don't expect it to stay that way. No doubt you've seen the papers. I wouldn't be surprised if the press start sniffing around soon. I've asked the Officer of the Day to station himself here to keep them at bay. Right, good work both of you and I hope you have a good weekend. Leave will be piped from midday.' Jon turned and walked further aft towards the quarterdeck.

'Well bugger me sideways,' Taff said in amazement. 'Maybe I got the blighter wrong after all.'

'Oh, what did he say to amaze you Taff?' Dinger asked surprised that his taciturn companion could be stirred to such words.

'Well, we've both only be on board a week and we've been bloody busy the whole time.' Taff replied with a note of awe in his voice. 'Yet without even looking, he knew our names. And on a bloody great steamer like this. Fuck me that takes the biscuit.'

Jon chuckled to himself as he walked away towards the stern. His hearing was quite acute and he caught Jones's last remark. Now that almost all the ship's company were on board, he had spent quite some time with the Commander going through the personnel records. The ship's staff were the direct responsibility of the Commander as the Executive Officer but Jon always made a great effort to get to know his people and with barely more crew than his last ship he had already made good inroads. One thing he had specifically done was to identify certain characters as early as he could. No doubt as they all settled down many more would come to the fore but a three badge AB was a rarity in the navy these days. Someone with that experience would be a good sounding board for the whole lower deck and Jon intended to use him for just that purpose. Not that he would be telling him that of course.

Chapter 8

Jon breathed in the heady mix of Somerset fields and unburnt kerosene. It was a smell that took him back to his roots as an aviator. As he got out of his car on the south dispersal he was met by the noise of turbine engines and rotor blades. He looked over the other side of the airfield where he could see several Sea King Mark 4s burning and turning. A Lynx was hover taxying over to its squadron dispersal area. He wondered if he had actually flown any of the aircraft he could see and reckoned the odds were pretty good that he had. Suddenly, his attention was taken by the roar of two Sea Harriers performing a run in and break over his head and then turning hard into the circuit downwind to land. It was all so familiar. It felt like home. In recent years he tended to come here at the weekend when the place was reasonably quiet. Just a few gliders and light aircraft and that was when he would get Wanda out for some fun. Seeing the place like this forcibly reminded him what a busy and important place it really was.

The ship was still alongside the wall and undergoing specialist Harbour Acceptance Trials or HATs as they were generally known. Once complete they would move on to the final sea trials, SATs and then, the ship would be ready to finally commission and fly the white ensign. Jon had left the ship in the charge of his HODs so that he could travel down to the naval air station and meet elements of his future Air Group. He was also about to meet the final member of his command team. Commander (Air), normally known as 'Wings' would be in charge of all aviation when they were at sea. The fact that they had yet to meet was unusual but Tim Malone had been abroad at the Embassy in Washington and had only just been released. Jon was looking forward to the meeting because unlike the rest of his command team they knew each other quite well. They had learned to fly together.

There was only one concern that Jon had over his new Wings. It wasn't strong enough for him to turn down the appointment but Jon clearly remembered his interview with the boss of the training squadron based at RAF Leeming all those years ago. As the senior member of his flying training course and the course leader, Jon was called in for his leaving 'horoscope' first.

'Come in Jon,' Lieutenant Commander Gifford called when Jon knocked on the door. He went in and sat in the proffered seat noting the photographs on the wall. The boss had been a fixed wing aviator of the old school and most of them were of Sea Vixens and Buccaneers although there was one of a group of young officers lined up in front of a small jet.

The boss saw his gaze. 'It's a different world now Jon. For the better some might say. That photo you're looking at was my training course, there were sixteen of us and you might be surprised to know that only three of us are left alive. The early Scimitars and Vixens were not the safest machines to fly. Still, I wouldn't have missed it for the world.'

Jon had been fascinated by the Fleet Air Arm from a young age and knew quite a deal about the early days of jets flying from carriers but to see the results of those machines in such a stark fashion really brought the dangers home. He knew that things were much better now but he also knew that flying from a ship was never the safest activity one could partake in.

'Must have been bloody exciting Sir,' he replied tactfully.

The boss snorted in amusement. 'That's definitely one way of describing it. Anyway, that's not why we're here is it? We need to review your results and decide where you should go next.'

Jon immediately picked up in the sub text of the boss's remark. There were only two options at the end of Elementary Flying Training and those were to go to helicopters or jets. Most weren't given a choice so that must mean he was one of the few that were going to be given one. He had wondered if this would happen and had given it a great deal of thought. He didn't think the boss was going to be too happy.

The boss took Jon's silence as all he needed, so he carried on. 'We debriefed your final handling test last week when we did it, didn't we? And as I said at the time, I felt it went pretty well. In fact, your whole performance has been extremely satisfactory. I shouldn't tell you this now but I know you can keep a confidence. You are the top student on the course and so I am really happy to offer you the chance to fly the Harrier. What do you say?'

Jon looked the boss in the eye. 'I would have been daft not to know that I was doing quite well during training Sir, although I hadn't realised I had done that well. But because of that I've been mulling over this possibility should it arise for a while. I'm sorry Sir but Harriers are not for me. I'd like to fly helicopters if you don't mind.'

Formidable

The boss looked surprised. 'Goodness, I wasn't expecting that young man. Would you care to enlighten me as to why?'

'Can I speak candidly Sir?'

'Of course, the door is closed. Ignore my rank tabs.'

'Sir, several reasons. I'm a General List officer and want to make a full career in the navy. If I go Harrier, I will be out of the loop for several years while I convert to the Jet Provost and then the Hawk. After that, I have to do a Harrier conversion followed by operational training on the Sea Harrier. Once I'm on a squadron, there is only one type of ship to operate from and little chance of flying any other aircraft type. If I go rotary wing, I will be back at sea and operational within a year. I have the choice of various marks of Sea Kings, Wessex, Wasp and the new Lynx to fly. These aircraft operate from almost every type of ship that we have. Also, forgive me for saying this but the scuttlebutt in the crewroom was that anyone selected for fixed wing would be the top performing student. However, several of the instructors have pointed out that landing a helicopter, on the back of a small ship, at night, in rough weather, with no chance of any diversion, probably requires as much skill as any required for flying a jet.'

'Hmm, that's a point for debate young man but as I've never had to do exactly that I don't suppose I'm really qualified to gainsay it. However, I do take your point about variety. Of course there is always the chance of exchange flying with the RAF or other navies so you wouldn't necessarily be stuck with the Harrier.'

'Which would put me out of the loop even more Sir. I'm sorry but I've made my mind up about this. I assume that I am allowed to make this choice?'

'Oh yes, we would never force it on anyone. Well, I've only got one place on offer so young Malone will be given the option instead. I just hope it doesn't make him even more insufferable.'

Jon laughed at the remark. Even though it was probably slightly inappropriate for the boss to make such a comment about a fellow trainee. The problem was that Tim Malone seemed to want to make sure that everyone knew about his previous experience. His father obviously had money because by the time Tim joined the navy he already had several hundred hours flying in light aircraft and even owned his own little Cessna and boy, did he go on about it. Despite several attempts to burst his balloon by various members of the course, nothing seemed to dent his arrogance. It wasn't helped by the fact that he was clearly quite a good pilot, yet another fact that he was prone to boast about. Being selected for fast jets would be like pouring petrol on a fire Jon realised.

'Well, the RAF can manage him for a while Sir,' Jon remarked. 'And life at Culdrose will be much quieter. But please don't tell him I was offered the chance first. He'll take it the wrong way I'm quite sure.'

The boss grunted acknowledgement and wished Jon luck.

He was jerked back into reality as he spotted Tim Malone walking out of the squadron building that Jon had parked by. Clearly someone had been keeping a watch. As they closed the distance between them Jon had a few seconds to study the man. He was surprised how little he had changed. His full head of red hair now had a few streaks of grey at the temples and there were creases around his eyes but he still looked as slim and fit as ever.

Jon offered his hand in welcome. 'Tim, good to see you, it's been too long.'

Tim's handshake was firm and he seemed to be genuinely pleased to see Jon. 'And you Sir and welcome to 888 Squadron.'

'Thanks Tim and how are you? All sorted after coming back from the States?'

'Yes Sir, my wife and I have bought a house down in Plymouth and we've managed to move in already so that will be really handy for the ship when she gets there. Do you like the new squadron's number? I managed to talk the Admiral's staff into it.'

'Oh, that was you was it? Well done. Having the number of the most successful squadron to operate off the last Formidable was a great idea.'

Tim was clearly relieved that his new boss liked the idea. He knew from the past that Jon was a Fleet Air Arm buff and had studied the branch's history extensively. That he already knew about 888 was hardly a surprise. 'And the ship Sir? How is she faring?'

Jon grimaced at the question. 'Teething issues as I'm sure you'll not be surprised to hear. We almost clobbered the dockyard wall the other day as you probably saw in the papers but I'm sure they'll all be sorted and were still on course for commissioning.'

'Great, well come on in Sir. I've got the Squadron CO and his boys ready to meet you and a little treat in store as well.'

Jon was introduced to a bunch of fresh faces, none of which he recognised. Even Pete Moore the CO of the squadron was a stranger but they all seemed genuinely pleased to meet him and hear about the progress of the ship. As a squadron, they had only formed up a few months previously and were still busy working up to operational capability but it seemed that they would be ready when the ship was, which was good news. He sat in the crewroom and spoke with them all for some time over a cup of coffee. The atmosphere of a squadron crewroom was unique. Probably something to do with, the rows of coffee cups on the wall over the sink, the Uckers board set into the central table and the stacks of old flight safety calendars piled up below the flight safety notice board that included the latest 'Tugg' calendar. It had clearly been tidied up for his visit. He knew it would normally be much scruffier unless the Senior Pilot was on a purge. Jon was taken back to his days in places like these and for a moment felt sad that he would never be able to live in them anymore. The best he could expect was to be the occasional guest like today. However, he was very impressed by the morale and keenness of the pilots who all seemed eager to get with the job and join the ship.

'Now Sir,' Pete Moore said. 'I would like to offer a swap if that's alright. I hear you own that Wasp that the historic lot further down the line have hangared? They wheel it out occasionally.'

'Yes but don't worry, she won't be embarking with us if that's what you're concerned about.'

'No Sir,' Pete laughed. 'My first tour was on Wasps before I transferred to the Harrier. I was going to suggest that if I can have a go in her with you, when you next fly her, then you can have a go with me.'

'Eh? What in?'

'If you look out of the window Sir. That black Harrier belongs to us for the moment and she's a two seater. Fancy seeing what a real aircraft can do?'

'Bloody well try to stop me.'

Four hours later, they landed back on at Yeovilton. The flight had only been for an hour but several more were needed to brief Jon on all the procedures necessary to fly in the aircraft. Jon was seriously asking himself whether he had actually made the right decision all those years ago after training. He hadn't had so much fun for ages. They had flown out over the Bristol Channel and tried some general handling at thirty thousand feet. Jon knew the area well from his past experience but at that height and speed everything was different, as was the amount of 'G' they pulled in the turns. On returning to the airfield, he had been given the chance to hover the Harrier and was surprised how easy it was compared to a helicopter, although he hated to think how fast you would have to react if the motor packed up. Finally, he tried a running take off from the dummy ski jump launch ramp that had been built at Yeovilton to practice deck take offs. Jon was keen to experience this as he would soon be watching it as a regular occurrence from the bridge of Formidable.

They climbed out of the machine once the engine wound down. Once on the tarmac, Pete Moore turned to Jon. 'Was that alright Sir? You seemed to be enjoying yourself.'

'Oh yes, fantastic and I didn't barf, which no doubt you are glad about because as a Captain I would have pulled rank and claimed the right not to have to clean it up.'

'Good point Sir,' Pete laughed. 'It does happen quite often as I'm sure you know.'

'So, when do you want a blast in a real aircraft? I'm here for the next few days so we could take the Wasp up tomorrow if that suits. I need to get some hours in to keep my licence up to date.'

'Fine by me Sir.'

'Now, there is one other thing I need to talk to you and Wings about. You both live in the mess don't you?'

'Yes Sir, during the week, as both our wives are in Plymouth.'

'Good, then let's get together over a beer this evening and I'm buying.'

Chapter 9

'Jesus, it really is time they knocked this place down,' Jon said as he looked around the wardroom bar. 'The décor's not that bad but let's face it, it's still a load of tarted up old wartime huts.'

'Apparently, there is a plan to do just that Sir,' Tim Malone said. 'They're going to put up a new building next door and then bulldoze the place. The only problem is that the new site on the playing fields used to be a Roman Army camp and they're going to have to do a full archaeological survey and God knows how long that will take.'

'Or they could do what they did at Culdrose some years back,' Jon suggested. 'They had just finished the new mess but hadn't actually moved in when some clown left a cigarette in the wrong place and it all caught fire. At least that's what I heard.'

'Frankly, it surprises me that this place didn't burn down years ago,' Pete Moore said. 'Your old lot, the Junglies, seem to have a predilection for setting fire to pianos on regular occasions.'

Jon laughed. 'Good God, are they still getting away with that? When I was a Jungly CO we were being read the riot act over it and that was some years ago.'

'I'm afraid it still happens and of course the fixed wing community look on in horror,' Tim observed wryly.

'Yeah right, Tim. I popped in to talk to the air station CO this morning as a courtesy and we had a chat so don't try that one,' Jon said with a grin. 'Now, this is actually what I want to talk to you two about if you don't mind. I'm treading on my Commander's toes a little as this is really his business but as we are here and I have first hand experience of mixing aircrew with ships, I thought it wouldn't do any harm. Also, Paul Taylor has never served in a carrier before so I wanted a word in advance.' He looked hard at the two men.

'Go on Sir,' Tim Malone said. 'I think I know where this is going.'

'I'm sure you do Tim,' Jon replied. 'But I just wanted to make my position clear. I have no issues with aircrew keeping non standard hours compared to the ship's officers and drinking at sea, as long as they're not flying of course and even a modicum of bad behaviour is fine. But I want it under control please and I will be looking to you two in particular to police it. In addition, I would like the whole Air Group to see themselves as part of Formidable's company not just

Formidable

visitors using the flight deck and hangar as a mobile airfield. How you foster that attitude I leave up to you but I'm sure you know what I mean.'

Both men nodded. Pete Moore spoke first. 'Already ahead of you Sir. Wings and I spoke to your Commander the other day and we agreed on a design of ship's Cummerbund which we will use rather than a squadron one. I've also been saying all this to my guys, maintainers and aircrew both. Your Commander is also commissioning various ship's unofficial rig items like those American baseball caps with the ship's name on it and we have an order in for them. I know these are only little things but we have to start somewhere.'

'I've also been talking to the Sea King squadron that's going to be providing two cabs for plane guard and delivery work Sir. It's harder for them as they rotate their Flights but they seem to be on message.' Tim added.

'Bloody hell, you two seem to be well ahead of me. I have to say I'm very pleased. I've seen things go badly wrong before, even in small ships. Let's hope we survive the first mess dinner.' Jon said smiling.

'If you'll excuse me Sir?' Pete said as he stood. 'I have some paper work to catch up on.'

'Of course Pete. Oh and I've asked the Historic Flight to get Wanda out for a ten o'clock launch tomorrow. I assume you still want to be reminded what a real aeroplane is like to fly?'

'Wouldn't miss it for the world Sir. Goodnight.'

Once he had gone Jon turned to Tim. 'He seems to be the real deal Tim. Sorry if I had to make the point about aircrew and ships but if we start out on the wrong foot it will be a nightmare to correct.'

'Understood Sir, I've been there as well.'

'Anyway, how are things with you? We haven't really met up since all those days ago in training.' Jon asked. 'You did well in the Falklands I seem to recall. Two kills wasn't it?'

'Actually only one Sir the other was only a probable. So that puts us on a par.'

Jon laughed. 'Well said Tim. And how do you see your posting to the ship? Was it what you wanted?'

'Well, like you Sir, the navy won't let me fly any more so this is the next best thing. What I would really like at some time is a drive. You've already had Prometheus.'

Did Jon detect a note of bitterness in Tim's reply? He would have to tread carefully. 'Yes, well, maybe that was the bonus of not getting stuck in the fixed wing world but you've had a squadron and an exchange with the US Navy on A7s which sounds like great fun. Not many Fleet Air Arm pilots get to do conventional carrier flying any more.'

'Don't get me wrong. As you say I've had a great career so far but I don't want it to stop here and warship command must be the next important step.'

'Well, all I can say is do well with Formidable and who knows what will come next.'

'Oh, I have every intention of doing just that Sir.' Tim responded with an edge to his voice.

Clearly, his Commander (Air) still had strong ambitions. Jon thought. They had never really got on that well during training but it was good to see that his attitude seemed to have mellowed a great deal since those days. However, Jon made a mental note to try and see how he treated those below him. It wasn't unusual for officers to present one picture to those above them and a completely different one to their subordinates. Leopards rarely completely changed their spots.

'If you'll excuse me now Tim. For some reason I'm quite knackered. It must be after pulling so much G all afternoon. I'll take Pete flying tomorrow morning and then I'll down to Devonport to see friends for the weekend. I'll head back to the ship on Sunday night. When will I see you up there?'

'I've only got a few more loose ends to tie up here Sir, so if I join formally on Monday will that be alright?'

'Absolutely, I look forward to showing you the navy's latest wonder weapon. Do you want me to give you a lift? As I said, I'll be driving up the night before and I assume you'll be at home for the weekend as well?

'Yes please, that would save a train journey.'

'Excellent, let me have your details and I'll pick you up Sunday evening. Good night.'

'Good night Sir.'

Formidable

Jon had arranged to go down to Plymouth for the weekend to meet up with Brian, Kathy and the kids who had taken a married quarter there while he was commanding Hampshire. He had also managed to persuade Ruth to join him so it was the perfect weekend. He had taken Ruth up on to Dartmoor and introduced her to the open moor. It was one of his favourite places to walk. That evening they all went out for a meal with a babysitter to do duty looking after the two girls at home.

'So Brian, you haven't told me how it's going on your new steamer. Are you settling into the heady delights of command yet?'

'You did warn me Jon. It's being cut off from the wardroom I find hard but I've got a good bunch of officers and the ship's company seem sound. We'll find out soon as we start BOST in a fortnight. How about you? How's the ship coming on?'

'Well, as first of a class of one, we seem to be having our fair share of teething troubles. No doubt you saw we made the headlines recently?' Jon asked.

Brian laughed. 'Yes and I saw who wrote that crap, so I suspected it's just a little far from the truth.'

'Actually, it was factually reasonably correct. It was just the spin that bastard put on it.' Jon replied. 'Anyway, it's all fixed and won't happen again, the engineers have done some modifications.'

'What about your people Jon are they shaping up?'

'Actually, I'm not sure at this stage. I've never served with any except Wings. But if the amount of effort they are expending is anything to go by we should be fine.'

'And Wings? Don't forget that I was with you when we all did the initial aircrew training together, survival training and all that.'

'Oh yes, I'd forgotten that you knew him. Anyway, he seems fine. He certainly has the right attitude to integrating the Air Group into the ship. I suspect the years have knocked a lot of corners off him, although he was quite late making his Brass Hat. It might have been because he spent so much time abroad. We'll just have to see. I'm giving him a lift up to the ship on Monday so I'll have a few hours in the car to dig deeper.'

Ruth looked sternly at the two men. 'Can we stop the shop talk now please? Apart from the fact that I only understood about half of it, you two can blather on about it when the ladies aren't present.'

'Seconded,' said Kathy.

Chapter 10

In some ways, the drive up to the ship had been frustrating. Even though it was late on a Sunday, the M5 and M6 were their usual snarl and then once they had cleared the Pennines the A1M was blocked for over an hour, presumably by an accident although by the time the traffic started moving again there was no sign of what it might have been. However, on another level Jon had found it quite illuminating. He had always found that sharing a long car journey with someone generated a sort of intimacy that was almost impossible to manage anywhere else.

The two men had chatted about their respective careers and even a bit about their private lives, although Tim had been very careful to steer away from anything relating to Jon's previous wife. Jon's impression that Tim was feeling frustrated with his career was only reinforced and he just hoped it wouldn't affect his performance.

As they finally neared the ship, Jon decided on a little test. 'Tim, once you've settled in, there are a couple of things I want you to do for me.'

'Yes Sir, what would that be?'

'Well, as you well know we are expected to operate eight Sea Harriers and two Sea Kings. Also, we could possibly take on a Lynx Flight as we will have some magazine space for a limited number of Sea Skua missiles for them. However, I remember how many aircraft Invincible managed to operate during the Falklands and it was far in excess of what she was meant to carry. I would like you to head up a working group and come up with a contingency plan for what sort of overload we could manage. In addition, I want you to consider the ramifications if the extra cabs are not naval aircraft.'

'Eh? Sorry Sir what on earth do you mean?'

Jon laughed. 'Sorry, I should have been clearer. When I was at Flag Officer Naval Aviation a while ago getting briefed, there was talk of RAF GR7s operating from sea. It's an idea that's been floating around for some time. Talk to the AEO and other HODs about the difference in support that we would need and let me know what issues it might raise. Everything from technical support to manpower issues.'

'Over what period Sir? Because that will have a significant effect on the result.' Tim asked.

'Good point, it's not something we could sustain for a long period so let's say three months as a planning time frame.'

'Bloody hell Sir, do you honestly think the Crabs would go for that?' Tim sounded unconvinced.

'Not their decision in the end is it? And anyway, it's only so we have a contingency plan up our sleeves.'

'Yes and it will be a damned good way for me to learn the ship and her people,' Tim replied.

'Exactly.'

They arrived at the ship two hours later than planned. Jon had left instructions that unless he was in uniform and on ship's business then he did not require to be formally greeted at the gangway. However, the Commander had clearly decided to ignore that as both he and the Officer of the Day were waiting for him at the top of the brow. For a moment, Jon was worried that there was some sort of problem but was soon pleased to hear that all was well and in fact, the harbour trials had all been successfully completed. After introducing Wings to Paul Taylor, he took his leave and headed for his cabin. The weekend had been great fun but quite tiring and then he had had the drive back to the ship. A bath, a large scotch and a good sleep were on the agenda although not necessarily in that order.

The next morning Jon was woken by the ship's broadcast.

'FIRE, FIRE, FIRE, Fire in Three Echo Two generator space. Fire and Emergency party muster in Three Echo cross passage.' The broadcast went on to repeat itself. Jon wasn't listening as he threw himself out of bed and grabbed some clothes. He did it with some frustration as in a situation like this he actually didn't have anything to do. The initial reaction would be managed by the Officer of the Day and then with the MEO and Commander on board they would take over if needed. Fires on warships were not uncommon and were very often minor matters, quickly dealt with. All personnel on a warship had to undergo basic fire fighting training before being allowed to serve at sea. Jon had done a refresher only a few weeks previously. He would soon know whether he would be needed but that didn't stop him from getting ready just in case.

Suddenly, his internal telephone rang. He sprinted across the cabin and grabbed the receiver.

'Sir, it's the Commander here, you'd better come down to HQ1. We might be needing you.'

'Give me a summary Paul,' Jon demanded.

'Bad one Sir, not sure quite how bad at this stage but we've at least one casualty.'

'I'm on my way.' Jon shot out of his cabin and made his way to HQ1 the ship's main emergency coordinating centre which wasn't far from his harbour accommodation and one deck down. As he entered, he could see the Commander and MEO standing around the main ship's state board.

He went to join them and the MEO turned to him. 'As you can see Sir, the generator space has been evacuated. We're boundary cooling all around as well as above and below. Unfortunately, we had to pull the firefighters out after there was an explosion. Not sure what it was yet but my best guess is the air bottle used to start the diesel engine cooked off. Two men were injured and one is critical. The doctor is getting them both to the Sick Bay.'

'Is the fire still burning?' Jon asked anxiously.

'Probably not now Sir. All the fuel supplies have been isolated and the whole space is now completely shut off. It's sealed tight so all oxygen supplies are gone.'

'Why the hell didn't they do that first MEO? Why send anyone in at all?' Jon demanded.

The MEO looked embarrassed. 'Sir there's meant to be a Halon drenching system in all the generator spaces. When the Fire Party Chief tried to operate it he found that the operating lever was jammed. He tried everything to get it to move but in the end he felt he had to get people in to shut down the fuel supply if nothing else. They used a water wall and got to the fuel cocks but that was when the explosion happened.'

The conversation was interrupted by a voice over the emergency broadcast. 'HQ1 this is the Officer of the Day. We assess that the fire is out, we'll continue boundary cooling and monitor temperatures until we assess its safe to make a re-entry.'

'Sounds like the Officer of the Day has his head screwed on right.' Jon observed. 'Commander, MEO you keep on it until it's all over. I'm going down to Sick Bay. Give me a full brief once you're happy that the dust has settled.'

Formidable

Without waiting for a reply, Jon headed out of HQ1 but not before he heard a muttered 'bloody ship, what's she going to do next?' From one of the ratings. He decided to ignore it for the moment. His priority was to see after his injured men. But the remark worried him in more ways than one.

Sick Bay was busy. It was clear that more than two of the firefighters had felt the need to be checked out. Jon spotted the Principal Medical Officer. 'PMO, what's the situation?' He asked.

The PMO, a harassed looking Lieutenant Commander, with the red strips between his rank stripes on his shoulders denoting his medical status, looked up. His expression changed when he saw who it was. 'Not good Sir. Most of the men here have minor injuries but I'm terribly sorry but Leading Stoker Mathews died about ten minutes ago. He had internal injuries and there was nothing we could do.'

Jon flinched at the news. 'And someone else was badly injured?'

'Yes Sir that's Able Seaman Jones. Although it's not as bad as we first thought. He was knocked unconscious in the explosion but they managed to drag him out. He's concussed and we need to get him ashore for X rays but I'm pretty sure he'll make a full recovery.'

'Can I see him?' Jon asked.

'I don't see why not. He's behind those screens there.'

Jon parted the curtains and saw Jones lying in bed looking wan. A bandage was wrapped around his head and over one eye but he was awake. 'Morning Able Seaman Jones, I'm glad to see you're alright,' Jon said smiling.

'Take more than a knock on the head to take me out Sir. Good solid Welsh bone that is,' Jones replied. 'Mind you, I've had to tackle some fires in my time and that was a good one. How is Mathews? He was bloody brave. He threw himself in front of me, he did.'

Jon didn't know what to say for a moment. 'Sorry Jones, the doc just told me he didn't make it. But I'll want the full story from you when you're up to it. It sounds like he was very brave.'

'Tell that to his wife and little kid Sir,' Jones replied sourly. 'This bloody ship is trying to kill us all.'

Jon almost said something sharp but reined himself in. He knew it wasn't the ship but once sailors got something into their heads, it was hard to talk them out of it and Jones was in no shape for a lecture.

Jon left Sick Bay a few minutes later. There would be all sorts of things to get settled now. And he needed to get together with the

Commander and sort out priorities. But deep inside he knew what the long term problem was going to be and he was going to have to come up with a way of solving it.

Chapter 11

Everything was put on hold for the next week while a Board of Enquiry was set up. With the ship already cleared for sea trials, there was little most of the ship's company could do although the Commander made great efforts to keep the people occupied with extra training and getting the ship immaculately clean.

By Friday, the enquiry was complete and Jon called a meeting of the HODs to discuss the way ahead.

When all the Commanders plus the First Lieutenant and navigator were present, Jon started. 'First things first everyone. So that you know, the President of the Board of Enquiry has just debriefed me. The findings will now be passed over to the local Coroner but it's unlikely that anyone from the ship will be called to account, in fact, probably the opposite. Leading Stoker Mathews is going to be given some form of posthumous award. Commander, please look into that and make me some recommendations please. I also want to commend AB Jones and the Fire party Chief Petty Officer. Now, I know most of you probably know most of this but I want us all singing from the same hymn sheet please. So, as to why the fire started, it appears that at about five in the morning the shore supply tripped. The generator was running in standby and automatically took some of the load. But as shore power came back on almost immediately, it caused the generator to stay powered up instead of reverting back and with no load now required, it started to over speed and then overheat. WEO can give the full details to anyone who wants to know more. Sometime later, it burst into flames. Luckily, the fire detection system worked and we were alerted in good time. Unluckily, the automatic fire suppression system didn't bloody well work for the same reason that the Chief couldn't operate it manually. Because it uses Halon gas, there's a physical safety lock on the operating valve that has to be removed once the system is installed and the yard forgot to remove it. We've checked all the other generators and machinery spaces that have the same system and none of the locks had been removed. They have now.'

'Bloody hell Sir,' Wings interjected. 'Someone's head is going to roll for that.'

'Yes,' Jon replied grimly. 'It's something the builders should have done as a matter of routine. It's not up to the Board of Enquiry to lay blame but there is every chance that criminal charges, probably of manslaughter, will be made against whoever it was who had the responsibility of safely installing the systems. Now this brings me on to my why I wanted all of you here. This was not the fault of anyone in the ship nor was it the fault of the ship itself and I want all of you to get the message across. You all know what the lower deck are like and what with that welder being killed during build, various mechanical mishaps and now this latest incident, there is bound to be all sorts of buzzes flying around the mess decks. We've all served in ships that have had their problems and ours are no worse than any other. I want you all to do your best to convince your people that this is not unusual and keep morale up.'

There were heads nodding all around. The Commander summed it up for all of them. 'Yes Sir, we've all heard the odd remark and we'll do our best. Getting to sea next week will be a great tonic. This enforced week alongside really hasn't helped.'

'Good,' said Jon. 'Now let's talk detail about the sea trials.'

A week later, the atmosphere on board had improved markedly. The ship had received its first aircraft on board. Firstly a Sea King and then a Lynx had carried out a series of deck landings and then finally a Sea Harrier from the test establishment at Boscombe Down had come on board and conducted a series of take offs and landings. Once the ship was commissioned, the aircraft would all be back for a far more detailed series of tests for First of Class flying trials which would give the ship the operating windows she would need to be effective. However, these first landings proved that the ships facilities were adequate. This was everything from making sure the flight deck paint was grippy enough, to ensuring that the lifts were actually big enough to strike aircraft down into the hangar.

However, the real icing on the cake was that now the trials were over the ship was heading south towards the channel and then would make its way to Devonport for commissioning. Jon was sitting in his chair on the bridge as the Harrier made its last take off and headed into the distance. He turned to Amelie Smith. 'OK Pilot, let's take her to her new home.'

Formidable

The next morning Jon was on the bridge as the ship entered the traffic separation scheme through the narrows between Dover and Calais. It was without doubt the most crowded piece of water in the world and despite the two way system it was still a piece of ocean that any Captain was glad to be clear of. Up ahead of Formidable there was a large ugly container ship that really looked as it should capsize with such an enormous amount of deck cargo.

With such an important passage to make, Amelie Smith was on watch. She was supported by a junior sub lieutenant who had just joined the ship in order to get his bridge watch keeping certificate. Jon knew his Christian name was Bertie but he hadn't had time to get to know him better. There would be plenty of time for that.

'Coffee Sir?' the Bosun's mate asked.

'Oh, yes please,' Jon replied taking the mug gratefully. Although he had spent some time in his sea cabin last night there had been so much traffic which he needed to know about, he had barely two hours sleep and was starting to feel the strain.

'How on earth do they load those container ships like that?' Amelie asked, echoing Jon's earlier thoughts. 'It looks so ridiculously top heavy.'

'I think there's a lot of it underwater as well Amelie,' Jon replied. Suddenly, he was remembering another merchant ship in the Gulf a few years ago. That one was heavily laden but with a far more deadly cargo than the ship ahead of them. 'You would be surprised how stable they really are.'

'You had an encounter with one in the Gulf didn't you Sir?' Amelie asked. There had been stories going around at the time but she was pretty sure the real story had never been public.

Jon considered the question. The fact that the ship had been carrying a modified SCUD missile with a nuclear warhead that was going to be fired at Israel was something that was never going to be made public. He stuck to the agreed party line.

'Yes, you're right, although she was a grain carrier not a container ship. She had been hijacked and an Iranian crew were on board. They had fitted a gun on the bow. The feeling was that they were going on some sort of suicide raid up the Shat al Arab waterway. Prometheus intercepted her but she fired on us. We sank her.' He stated simply.

Amelie seemed taken aback by his matter of fact rendition of what must have been a very dangerous incident. 'But weren't you damaged as well Sir?'

Jon laughed. 'Yes but that was earlier. A little encounter with an Exocet. Mind you, the American cruiser we were with copped a great deal more damage.'

'I would love to hear the full story some time Sir. What with the Falklands, the Uganda incident and your time recently with the UN, you've had an interesting career to say the least.'

'Interesting maybe but sometimes just a little too interesting,' Jon replied thinking that luckily the public weren't aware of a few other 'incidents' in his career.

Both of them were interrupted by an urgent call from the quartermaster who was steering the ship using a small joystick control on the other side of the bridge.

'The ship isn't answering the helm Sir. I've got fifteen degrees of starboard rudder on and the rudder isn't responding,' he reported with a note of panic in his voice.

'Shit, Amelie, make a broadcast to that effect. Bertie is that tanker still right behind us?' Jon asked, his mind whirling.

The ship's head was already starting swing well to starboard. 'Stop port,' Jon called. With the port shaft stopped the ship's heading steadied but she had slowed down significantly.

'The tanker is still there Sir,' Bertie reported, 'And she's closing fast.'

'Right Yeoman, get on the VHF and tell her we have a problem and ask if they can manoeuvre clear. Then put an all ships call out and include Dover control.'

He then turned to Amelie. 'How far to the coast and more importantly how far until the water is too shallow?' Knowing that the tanker behind them was unlikely to be able to take much avoiding action, he realised he had no choice but to try and get out of her way. 'Half ahead port,' he ordered. 'Revolution one five zero. Any steering yet QM?'

'No Sir, the rudder is still jammed.'

With both shafts turning again, Formidable started altering course to starboard again under the action of the jammed rudders.

The broadcast from HQ1 broke into life. 'Captain Sir, MEO here. As we were at Specials, I had two of my guys in the tiller flat. They

Formidable

say the hydraulics have failed. They're about to engage hand steering but it will be very slow.'

'Just get the bloody things straight MEO. I can use the shafts then.'

'Oh fuck,' Bertie was at the port side of the bridge staring at something astern.

Jon ran and joined him. The bow wave of the massive tanker was only about a hundred yards off Formidable's stern. The carrier was now almost ninety degrees off course and heading towards the nearby coast. It seemed that the massive bow wave and cliff like bow above it were going to hit them. 'Pipe hands to emergency stations,' Jon yelled. 'Full ahead both engines.' Full ahead was an emergency order, only used when every ounce of power was needed. Jon prayed it would be enough.

While the broadcast alarm started to blarc out and the call for the ship's company to get to safety was being made, Jon just stared. Unlike the incident in the Tyne, there was little more he could do.

Amelie joined him. 'Plenty of water until we're within half a mile Sir. Oh shit,' she gasped as she saw what was coming at them. Jon felt his ship slowly stop her out of control turn. The stokers in the tiller flat must be centering the rudders at last he realised. Now that she wasn't turning, her course was taking her away from the tanker a little faster. His ears were suddenly hit by blasts of the tankers siren. 'Silly sod,' he said to Amelie. 'As if that's going to do anything except make giving orders harder.'

'It's alright Sir, she's going to miss us. Her bearing is starting to draw ahead.'

Jon immediately realised she was right. If they were going to collide then the bearing between the two ships would remain steady. The tanker was definitely edging ahead and clear. Even so, the massive bow only missed them by feet. A great wall of rusty steel was suddenly rushing past them. As the bridge of the tanker came abreast, a man with what looked like an officer's hat on came out and looked across at them. Their respective bridges were of similar height. He gave an ironic salute and then the danger was over.

'Stop both engines,' Jon called. 'Pipe stand down from emergency stations and for the cable party to close up. Yeoman, tell Dover coastguard we would like to anchor inshore until we fix our steering.'

'Aye aye Sir,' the yeoman answered.

Jon turned to Amelie who still looked shocked. 'Funny how fast things can happen isn't it Pilot?'

'I think you were right about things being able to get too interesting Sir,' she replied.

Chapter 12

'Well that went well,' Jon said to the Commander ironically.

'Could have been better Sir,' Paul responded. 'Once again the builders have covered themselves with glory.'

'And made us look like total dickheads. Having to be towed into Portland was the final straw. The sooner they sort out my ship and bugger off the better. Still, at least they made enough of a repair so that we made it to Devonport in time for commissioning. Being followed by a tug all the way in case we broke down again was hardly impressive though. What's the latest?'

'As you already know Sir, it was hydraulic failure again,' said the MEO who was also present. 'First the forward lift and now the steering gear. The same type of pump is used for both. I can give you the gory details if you want.'

'No, spare me. I'll read the ships enquiry report in good time but if that's the case why wasn't it checked after the ones that power the lifts failed?' Jon asked in an exasperated tone.

'It was Sir and it seemed fine. The aircraft lift pump failed due to an overpressure. They're still not sure exactly why but the steering gear was under virtually no load. However, in both cases it was the same component that failed. The yard guys say they can fit higher rated pumps and that should solve the problem. They weigh a ton and that was why we had to be alongside to get a crane adjacent.'

'Shouldn't have shut the bloody dockyard at Portland then should they? We could have got the job done straight away.' Jon said to no one in particular. 'OK, so when are we going to be operational again?'

'By Friday,' the MEO said. 'So, commissioning on Saturday is still a goer.'

'Good, we'll have a planning meeting to thrash out the final details this afternoon,' Jon said.

Saturday morning broke bright and clear, which was a relief to everyone as the forecast hadn't been good. Jon's steward had spent serious time on his number one uniform. The ceremony was due to start at two in the afternoon and as soon as he had had lunch Jon prepared himself. His shoes shone like mirrors and his medals all gleamed with a high polish. His sword was belted around his waist and his main aim was not to trip over the bloody thing at the wrong moment. He took a final look at himself in the mirror of his harbour cabin and decided he looked the part. He knew his ship did as well. The Commander had been working the ship's company hard all week and she was gleaming. He left his cabin early to have a final look around before heading to the gangway to be ready to meet the great and the good as they arrived for the ceremony. He was also expecting Rupert and Ruth as his personal guests and they would be staying for the evening for a private dinner party along with a few other close friends like the Captain of HMS Hampshire and his wife, Brian and Kathy Pearce. Brian's ship was moored further up the dockyard. But first there was all the pomp and ceremony of a major warship commissioning ceremony to get right. After their embarrassing entry into their home port, Jon was determined the day would go off well.

Well pleased with what he had seen, he made his way to the aft brow. Several Admirals including the First Sea Lord, who would be taking the salute, would be arriving in due course. The Commander and Officer of the Day were already there and saluted smartly.

'Good morning Sir,' the Commander said. 'We're all ready, I'm happy to report.'

'Excellent Paul, I've had a quick look around and she looks wonderful. Please pass on my thanks to the men.' And then turning to the gangway staff he continued. 'And that includes you Able Seaman Jones, good to see you up and about again.'

Although he kept a straight face, Taff was delighted to be singled out in such a way. Not that he would ever admit it to his mess mates, he had a front to keep up after all. 'Thank you Sir, it'll take more than a knock on the head to keep me down.'

'I don't doubt it Jones,' Jon replied with a smile. What Jones didn't know was that during the ceremony, he was going to be called forward for a CinC's commendation for his part fire fighting in the generator space. Jon was quite looking forward to the look on his face when it was announced. There was also going to be the announcement of a medal for Leading Stoker Mathews although that would not be so happy an occasion as it would be a posthumous award.

Jon turned to the Commander. 'I think our idea of using the hangar for the ceremony was a good one Paul. As usual, they got the bloody forecast hopelessly wrong but there is the chance of a shower and we don't want the high and mighty getting wet.'

'Yes Sir but we will still do the march past on the flight deck if we can. There's far more room and you know Jack and his ability to march. The more space we can give him the better. I'll literally do a rain check as the padre is winding up and then we can make a decision.'

'Good thinking.' Jon replied knowing what the Commander was getting at. Sailors were trained to march in basic training and got little chance to practice after that. After the actual commissioning dedication, the only sailors to march would be the especially prepared guard as there was no room for the ship's company as a whole to manoeuvre around. Even with the extra practice they had had over the last week, Jon knew they wouldn't make much of a show on Horse Guards Parade. In fact, he was just praying they managed to stay in step.

'And the dais and prayer lectern are at the forward end of the hangar and not on the aft lift. Also both lifts have been mechanically locked into place,' Paul added with a slight smile.

Jon nodded. He had reminded the Commander of a well known naval novel where the story was that the aft lift had been used for the ceremony of a carrier's commissioning and it had started to raise itself half way through the Chaplain's dedication. It always struck Jon as being a surreally funny story but it was definitely not one he wanted repeated in real life, especially in his ship.

'Right then Commander, let's gird our loins and get this done,' Jon said as he spotted the first car with a significant amount of gold braid in it approaching the brow.

At seven o'clock that evening, Jon flung himself into a comfy chair in his cabin having divested himself of his jacket. 'Coffee please Jenkins,' he called out as he kicked off his shoes.

As if by magic, Jenkins appeared with a tray containing a steaming mug and large pot for refills. 'Your guests Sir, when will they be arriving?'

'Good question, they've been hijacked by the wardroom but have promised to be here by seven thirty. Is everything ready for dinner?'

'Oh yes,' Jenkins answered with a grin. 'The menus have been printed as you requested and the galley have done us proud.'

'Good and did you enjoy the ceremony Jenkins?' Jon asked. 'It all seemed to go well from where I was standing.'

Formidable

'Like a Swiss watch I thought Sir.' Jenkins responded but Jon caught the carefully crafted reply.

'Come on Jenkins, it's just the two of us now. What did you really think?'

'Well Sir, that's the fourth ship's commissioning I've attended and in the old days we just got on with it. It was a ceremony for the ship by the ship. You might see the port Admiral but no more. Nowadays every man and his dog attends from the First Sea Lord downwards. It just didn't seem to have the same family atmosphere, if you see what I mean.'

Jon got the point. A commissioning ceremony was very much meant to be the first real bonding time for a ship's company. Yes, the sailors would all moan about having to get out their best rig and stand to attention for a while. But underneath it all there would hopefully be the first stirrings of pride in their ship. With such a top heavy attendance and the media present as well, it probably seemed more like a circus than anything else. Jon knew why of course. Formidable was a capital ship and had attracted a great deal of media attention, not all of it good. Also, with the navy now so small compared to even a decade ago, the maximum PR value had to be milked from this sort of occasion.

'Well it's done now. We've work up to look forward to. That should keep us busy,' Jon said.

'Done a few of those in my time as well Sir,' Jenkins observed wryly as he tactfully made himself scarce.

Jon downed his coffee and made a quick dash to the shower and then changed into a suit. He knew the other men had brought a change of clothes with them and the ladies were all dressed to the nines anyway. Not that he knew much about it but the girls had all said that they were happy to stay in their glad rags.

It wasn't long and there was a knock on the door and the Commander put his head around. 'Ready for guests Sir?' he asked.

'Yes of course Paul, come on in everyone.'

Rupert, Ruth, Brian and Kathy came in with Paul. Jon could immediately tell that the wardroom had done their best to ensure his guests had been given suitable hospitality. He knew Ruth well enough by now to be able to interpret her expression. She looked happy and at ease. Her normal reserve had vanished as she planted a large kiss on his cheek.

'Lovely day Jon. I'm so glad it all went well. So, this is where you live, it's certainly large enough.'

Jon barked a laugh. 'Unfortunately, I don't get to see it often enough. When we're at sea, I have a little rabbit hutch below the bridge in the island.'

Before anyone else could speak, Jenkins entered with several bottles of champagne and glasses. He pulled the corks and poured them all glasses before retiring quietly.

Jon looked at his friends. He had made strenuous efforts to stay off the booze at the reception after the ceremony but at last he felt he could let his hair down a little. He raised his glass. 'A toast. To Formidable,'

They all repeated the toast and then general conversation broke out. It seemed that everyone had enjoyed the day and soon it was time to sit down for dinner. Jon had thought hard about what he wanted and with several non naval guests had decided on a little naval education. Once seated, the guests were able to pick up the menu cards placed in front of them.

Brian was the first to get the joke and burst out laughing. 'Oh dear Jon, are you trying to put our guests off their meal?'

Jon looked blankly at him, trying hard to keep a straight face as Ruth then read the menu. 'Jon what on earth?'

He looked at her with the same straight face. 'Good naval dishes my dear. I thought it was time you were educated a little more into our ways.'

'Alright, I know what Spotted Dick is but what on earth is 'Shit on a Raft'?'

Before Jon could answer Rupert joined in. 'And Baby's Heads Jon?'

Even Kathy who had been a naval wife for years was slightly puzzled. 'Unlike our poor civilian chums I know what those are Jon but 'Spuds Agratin? That's one even I've not come across.'

'Sorry, you'll all find out and I promise you will enjoy it. Just be grateful I've not included 'Herrings In' I could never stand those.'

He suddenly received a none too gentle kick from under the table. 'Come on, oh great and wonderful Captain what are you poisoning us with.' Ruth demanded.

'Oh alright, they're all dishes that are loved by the lads and the wardroom too for that matter. OK, Shit on a Raft is devilled kidneys on toast. In fact, any food served on toast is 'on a Raft'. Baby's Heads are individual steak and kidney puddings. Traditionally they are made in little round tins and when turned out, resemble the aforementioned toddler's heads. As we're having kidneys to start, they will just be steak pies this time. But, I'm surprised at you Kathy. Surely you know what 'Agratin' is?' He looked around the table and saw Brian and Paul grinning.

It was Rupert who got it first. 'Au Gratin, with cheese.'

Jon laughed. 'Spot on Rupert. Sailors always like to simplify things. And just to finish off the savoury course of Cheesy, Hammy, Eggy is exactly what it says. Very much a naval favourite.'

He was saved any further explanations as Jenkins appeared with perfect timing and served the aforementioned starter of kidneys on toast.

The evening was a great success. The food was enjoyed by all despite the various naval descriptions. Jon had invested in some seriously good wine and the talk flowed more as glasses were refilled. He was glad to hear that Brian's ship had completed her Sea Training and was now formally part of the operational fleet. He was also interested to hear what Rupert was up to. As usual, Rupert was reticent with any detail but he did give some indication of what issues were keeping MI6 busy.

'You may find this odd Jon but at the moment it's the bloody Chinese we have our eyes on,' he said in response to a question.

'Really? I thought they were still bootstrapping their economy. Surely, they're not a threat?' Jon responded.

'No, not in that sense,' Rupert replied. 'Your point about their economy is a good one but it won't be long before that takes off, believe me. And their military is still quite weak. What they are trying to do is increase their influence by generating a presence abroad in developing countries. They're in the Caribbean, in several of the poorer islands and more worryingly making inroads into several African countries. There's not a great deal we can do apart from keep an eye on what they are doing but it's taking much of my time at the moment. Anyway, I shouldn't worry too much. I can't see an aircraft carrier being much use in darkest Africa.'

'Maybe,' Jon replied. 'But don't forget that ninety percent of the world's population lives within a hundred miles of a coast and that includes Africa.'

The conversation drifted on and all too soon the food had been cleared away and the port decanter started its stately tour of the table. By midnight, everyone was feeling the effects of a long day and Jon politely made suggestions to wind the evening up. His last guest to leave was Ruth. The others had already made their farewells, even Rupert and Jon was pretty sure this was all planned. He didn't mind.

Ruth shut the door and turned on him putting her arms around him and kissing him soundly. 'Thank you for a wonderful day and showing me just a little of your new girlfriend. By the way Rupert and I came in separate cars.'

'Hmm, she may be a girlfriend but she can be bloody awkward at times, unlike you my dear. Now look, you know you can't stay the night. It's not allowed for the sailors so how would it look if they saw you leaving my cabin in the morning?'

'Who said anything about the morning and anyway my pink chit to get into the dockyard expires at two. So that gives us plenty of time. How big is the bed in the Captain's cabin anyway?'

Chapter 13

Zhang Li looked over the wide nondescript valley. It was mainly dark brown scrub with a few stunted trees. 'What am I looking at?' he asked the surveyor.

The other man was not Chinese, he was from Wales in England and the two of them couldn't have been more different. Li was small and light framed with dark black hair and a pock marked face, a legacy of childhood smallpox. Despite his lack of stature, he had piercing intelligent eyes and an almost perpetual sneer on his face. He was clearly in charge. Max Llewellyn didn't look Welsh. A shock of receding red hair topped a large muscular frame. He looked more Scottish than Welsh although his accent would immediately give him away. It was a very hot day and there were large sweat stains around both his armpits as well as sweat streaming down his face. In contrast, Li could have been in the Savoy Grill for all the weather seemed to be affecting him.

Max turned to his boss. 'The lake, Mister Zhang. That's what we want you to see.'

Li turned his gaze to the bottom of the valley. He couldn't see a lake. 'What lake? All I see is some white ground.' His tone was sceptical with its usual condescending tone.

'Sorry Mister Zhang. Yes. You're right but it's that large white flat area. It's a salt lake like the Bonneville Flats in the USA but even bigger. If you look at this end you can see where a river sometimes floods it. At the moment it's the dry season so it's all dried up.'

Li had no idea where or what the Bonneville Flats were but was damned if he was going to show his ignorance to this barbarian. 'Alright, but it hardly looks like a source of wealth to me. We have similar things in China.'

'Not like this one Sir. Let's get back into the cars and go down. It's easier to show you than explain.'

The two men climbed back into the Land Cruiser that was in the middle of the convoy. In front and behind them were open topped trucks, each containing a dozen armed soldiers. At the front of each was mounted a large half inch machine gun. It was the bare minimum needed to travel safely in the anarchic lawless part of Africa. Max sat gratefully back into his seat letting the air conditioning cool him

Formidable

immediately. The Chinese politician wrinkled his nose in distaste at the smell of sweat but said nothing. The convoy started off again down a rough road that meandered down the side of the valley. As they neared their destination Max pointed to their left. 'You can see the dried up river bed clearly now. When we first saw this we weren't surprised. This sort of geographical feature is common in this area. We know of at least six others within two hundred miles of here. As you know, we were primarily looking for copper or other useful minerals. It was when one of my team decided to track the river back that we realised there might be more to this. That and one other key feature.'

'What has the river got to do with it?' Zhang asked.

'Normally, these lakes form in the valleys where they are fed by rivers that bring the rain down from the surrounding hills. It only rains once a year and flash floods are common. The water pools in places like this and then they slowly dry up, leaving the chemicals that have been washed down. It takes millennia for any deposits to build up and they are normally very sparse. Not here. The average depth of deposit is over twenty metres thick although you wouldn't know that by looking at the surface. To have been caused in the normal way, this lake would have to have been here for millions of years and the hills aren't that old by an order of magnitude.'

'So what caused it,' Shang asked in an exasperated tone. When was this bloody man going to get to the point?

Max wasn't going to be browbeaten. He needed Zhang to fully understand exactly what they had here. 'Obviously, the water that feeds the lake has to be unusually full of minerals that's why we decided to track the source of the water. But we couldn't find it. It goes half way up the valley and disappears into the side of the hill. My men aren't caving experts but they did manage to get a little way inside and the whole hill there is riddled with caves and channels caused by water erosion. Most of the minerals that were in the hill are now lying on the ground. They've been washed out and are ready to be taken by anyone who wants them.'

'Hmm, except for the fact that there is virtually no government around here and if you're correct and word gets out then this whole area will become a war zone.'

'With respect Mister Zhang, you have the ear of the government in the capital and they do have an army. They've been pretty good at looking after my team so far.'

'Yes but it's one thing to give protection to a small party of geological surveyors and quite another thing to protect a site as large as this could become. There are no real roads and certainly nowhere to land an aircraft. Is this really going to be worth it? The costs will be enormous.'

Just then, they rolled to a stop next to three large tents. Several western people and one Chinese came out to greet them. Max introduced them all and then led Zhang into one of the tents. Inside, there were benches with various scientific instruments and other inexplicable devices. Max led Zhang over to one of them.

'It's actually a very common material. Sea Water is full of it but it's totally uneconomical to extract. There are a few other places in the world that have commercially viable deposits, mainly in South America. However, we've never come across or heard of concentrations at this level. Let me show you.' Max said and he reached over into a jar which clearly contained some of the salt from the lake and put it into a glass jar which he then held over a small flame. The salt started to melt and gave off a white vapour. When all the vapour had stopped, all that was left was a rather disgusting black mess. Max then poured in clear liquid. 'Now, if there is any present it will turn a pale blue. As a rule of thumb, bearing in mind that this is just a crude demonstration, the darker the colour the more concentrated the sample is. He swirled the contents around for a few seconds and it started changing colour. Within seconds it had turned so dark blue that it looked black.

'There you are Mister Zhang, the most concentrated deposit of Petalite in the world. Or more significantly the richest source of Lithium in the world and whoever owns this will revolutionise and control the world market for energy storage.'

A few hours later, after they had been given a meal, Zhang Li left as he had arrived. Although this time, the big Welshman stayed behind with his team with instructions to carry on with the survey work.

However, Zhang had not been straight with his Welsh colleague. He wasn't the commercial envoy from the Chinese Embassy in the capital, although that was his official title and indeed that did take up some of his time. He was, in fact, the local intelligence officer but who coincidentally had a degree in geology. It was one of the reasons he had been posted to the country in the first place.

After the initial report had been received, he had contacted Beijing and his orders had been clear. If the discovery was true, then no one was to find out until measures had been put in place to ensure that China would have control. And the discovery was clearly true. The potential, not only for wealth for his country but more importantly for power over other nations was immense. Lithium was already soaring in price as more and more developments in battery storage technology needed more and more of the precious material. Soon, it would be the new gold standard and whoever controlled this discovery would reap immense rewards. Not only that but the person who managed the discovery was sure to reap his own personal rewards.

He had already left instructions with soldiers at the camp plus a little incentive in the form of more cash than they would ever have seen before. As his little convoy crested the hill they had descended earlier, he suddenly heard the distant popping noise of gunfire. There would be no one to testify about the discovery now. The soldiers conducting the massacre had no idea what had been found and probably wouldn't have understood the significance of it anyway. Everyone who did know was now dead, except for Zhang. He didn't particularly like the thought of what he had had to do. But the stakes were massive both for his country and for himself. Despite his distaste, he couldn't help letting a smile of anticipation cross his face.

Chapter 14

Jon stood on the bridge of Formidable as she made her way past the breakwater at Plymouth. Up ahead of them was a large yellow buoy which they would be tying up to. Once again a breakdown was changing their schedule.

'It's the only sensible option Sir,' Commander Sea Training said to Jon. 'You'll need full power at times, you know what us Sea Riders like to do at no notice.'

'I know Mark,' Jon replied. 'But it's just one thing after another. HMS Ocean isn't having these problems.'

'She's made by a different yard and doesn't have to stretch herself like you do Sir. She can launch helicopters with just about any wind over the deck. The Mark 2 Harrier needs all the wind it can get, especially when the weather's hot.'

Just then Dave Johnson appeared. 'Permission to come on to the bridge,' he asked routinely and then came over to the two men even while Jon was nodding.

'Well MEO, what's the gory truth?' Jon asked.

'The port gas turbine Sir. It looks to me like the compressor ingested something, possibly a nut or bolt. It's academic because the whole engine is trashed.'

'And are there spares to hand?'

'Yes Sir, Rolls Royce have one on the road to us now it will be ready to be fitted tomorrow morning. The whole job will take two days. At least the ship is designed in a way that gives good access.'

'Mmm, that's better than I expected. Well Mark, can you re-jig our programme? We could do the harbour week we were due to do later on instead?'

'I'll nip ashore as soon as we're on the buoy Sir,' Mark replied. 'And talk to the FOST planners but I don't see why not. It should be possible and it will keep us on track. Your Basic Sea Training package needs to be completed in a month or you won't be able to progress to Operation Sea Training on time and there are a great deal of other assets involved in that as you know.'

'Good, make it so. Now, excuse me while I try not to clobber this bloody great mooring buoy.'

In fact, Jon wasn't too despondent. After commissioning, they had spent several incident free weeks at sea conducting first of class flying trials. These involved getting all the aircraft types the ship was required to operate on board and then exploring the limits of what they could do with various wind speed and sea states by day and night. It had all gone extremely well. The aircraft, several types of helicopter and a Sea Harrier, had been flown by test pilots from the test squadrons based at Boscombe Down in Wiltshire. Once complete, the ship was issued with its SHOL or Ship Operating Limits. This meant that once she had finally completed her Basic Sea Training or BOST she would be able to embark her full air wing and proceed to OST, her full Operational Sea Training. The first package was conducted by the dedicated training team in Plymouth and involved testing all the ships capabilities from fire fighting to receiving foreign VIPs. For OST she would come under the scrutiny of FOF3, the Admiral in charge of all large aircraft carrying ships, as well as the navy's amphibious force. Once all this was complete FOF3 would become Formidable's boss and dictate where she went and what exercises and operations she would conduct. Jon couldn't wait. The training package was a hard strain on everyone and he, like the rest of the ship's company, were keen to get on with a real job after endless weeks of trials and now the demands of Sea Training.

An hour later and they were snugly swinging around their bridle. With everything secure, Jon decided to go walkabout. When they were at sea, he had very little time to be anywhere else but the bridge or the Ops room and he wanted to see how the rest of the ship was looking as well as having a chat with his lads.

He went down the bridge ladder and out of the door in the island to the flight deck. Although still not operational, he had been loaned two Mark Four Sea Kings from Yeovilton to act as HDS aircraft and provide the air link needed to get the staff on and off every day as well as collect stores and mail when needed. Both aircraft were being made ready to be struck down into the hangar and he watched in admiration as the aircraft handlers slickly attached the towing booms onto the tail wheel of each aircraft and manoeuvred them onto the two lifts, one aft and one forward by the island itself. As he watched Barry Thornton the Flight Deck Officer came over. Barry ran the whole 'roof rat' team as they were known. He was a Lieutenant Commander of vast seniority and experience. He had a grizzled weather beaten face from years of being blasted by the winds over various ship's flight decks and sported a bushy grey beard, presumably to keep his face warm. Jon knew he was lucky to have him, he had been an aircraft handler Chief Petty Officer on the last Ark Royal, the one with Phantoms and Buccaneers and was just the man Jon wanted to manage the deck when Formidable was crowded with aircraft starting in a few weeks time.

'So, it's an early secure Sir?' Barry asked. 'Ops told me to strike down the two cabs although they are both serviceable.'

'Yes Barry,' Jon replied. 'We're going to need half the deck space to accommodate the MEOs engine change over the next couple of days. Apparently, they arrive in very large boxes and we're going to have to put them somewhere.'

'No problem Sir but will this bugger up the programme? It seems Formid doesn't like the FOST staff. She behaved herself when we were doing our proper job the other week.'

'Now don't you bloody well start,' Jon retorted and then reigned himself in. Barry was old and bold enough to know the issues. 'Sorry Barry,' he continued. 'It's just that I don't want the lads always blaming the ship when things go tits up as both you and I know they often do. And to answer your question, we are going to bring the last harbour week forward. We'll be able to do most of what's needed while the engine is being changed. So you should still have your full outfit of aircraft arriving on schedule. That'll keep you busy then.'

The FDO was about to reply when the ships main broadcast started to blare out. 'FOR EXERCISE, FOR EXERCISE, FOR EXERCISE, FIRE, FIRE, FIRE. FIRE IN THE FORWARD HANGAR, FIRE AND EMERGENCY PARTY MUSTER IN TWO BRAVO FLAT.'

The FDO turned to Jon. 'Excuse me Sir it seems that the bloody FOST staff never miss a trick.' Without waiting for an answer he ran towards the forward lift which had just started to descend with the Sea King lashed onto it. 'Don't lower the lift you silly arses get it back up now!' The rest of his colourful language was lost in the distance but Jon had to smile to himself. He definitely had the right man for the job.

The rest of his tour was similar. Everyone he spoke to was in good spirits, although all too often he heard the ship being blamed for all sorts of silly issues. He made a decision to talk to everyone at the right moment. In fact, he would have 'clear lower deck' as soon as they were declared operational. It was the right time to do it. He was just thinking about going back to his cabin when the Commander caught up with him.

'Longroom have been on the blower Sir. The Queen's Harbour Master has cleared us a berth and would like us to dock at eighteen hundred.'

'Fine,' Jon replied. 'Set up an entering harbour brief for sixteen hundred and then we'll head on in.'

Two exhausting months later it was all over. The ship had managed a weeks leave between BOST and OST but that was all the time off anyone had had and the rest of the time had been frantic. While the training packages tended to focus on individual areas of the ship at a time before coming together in final overall exercises, they all required Jon's attention. He felt mentally and physically drained. At the same time, he was vastly satisfied with what they had achieved. The next two years would no doubt be hectic but now they could look forward to a measured programme and even some good runs ashore. In fact, despite wanting to sleep for a week, he realised he couldn't be happier. He was just musing on all of this when there was a knock on his cabin door.

'Come in,' he called from the arm chair he was relaxing in.

The Commander appeared. 'We're ready for you Sir. All mustered in the hangar.'

'Excellent Paul let's get on with it,' For Jon this was the occasion he had been looking forward to. Just him and his ship's company. No outsiders, no senior brass, no VIPs. He was dressed in his working rig, his standard 'woolly pully' dark blue jersey and was wearing an American style baseball cap with scrambled egg on the beak. The words FORMIDABLE stitched around the front in raised gold thread. At first he had balked at the idea of the caps. He didn't like following American tradition but the sailors loved them and actually they were far more comfortable than a full naval cap or its alternative, a beret.

He followed the Commander down to two deck and entered the hangar through the forward air lock. Despite being alongside they still used the two doors one after the other. The ship now had a full outfit of ammunition and fuel as well as eight Sea Harriers, two Sea Kings and a Lynx which were all ranged on deck at the moment. Safety precautions would never be relaxed now. He knew that the ship's company had actually come down on the lifts to get them all in place quickly.

As Jon entered the echoing space, the voice of the ship's Mater at Arms rang out loudly. 'HMS Formidable, ship's company HO!' There was the sound of over five hundred men standing crisply to attention. Not the large stamping noise the army would have produced but still a well ordered sound.

Jon turned to the Commander, who saluted him. 'Ship's company mustered and correct except for essential watchkeepers Sir.'

'Very good,' Jon said formally. 'Stand them at ease.'

Without waiting for the order, Jon walked up to raised dais at the front of the hangar and deliberately removed his cap.

He stood in front of the microphone. 'Stand easy everyone and break ranks, come up closer it will save me having to shout when WEO's microphone goes tits up.'

A small ripple of laughter came from the crowd as they all shuffled up towards the dais and formed up in a semicircle.

Jon looked at his men. 'First of all, let me welcome everyone from the Air Group who have joined us. It's been my first opportunity to talk to everyone as one team. Now, the first thing I have to say to you all is how proud you have made me.' He reached into his pocket and pulled out a folded piece of paper. 'This is a signal from FOF3. To HMS Formidable. 'Well done, you have successfully passed all your Sea Training, the overall assessment was very satisfactory. Welcome to the fleet.' Now, I don't need to tell most of you that that sort of assessment is not handed out with the Corn Flakes and is a reflection of how well we've done. It's a bloody good start. But it's only the start. Ahead of us now is several years of operating around the world and as we all know, despite what the politicians tell us, it's still a dangerous place and our job is to go to those places. There's one other thing I want to say. We've all been around enough to have heard stories of unlucky ships. This ship has had its fair share of problems. Let me make it quite clear. There is no such thing as an unlucky ship. The ship itself is an inert lump of metal, it's you, the people who make her what she is. All I can say is that if we continue to operate together as we have during our work up then this is going to be the luckiest ship in the fleet. Oh and on that note where is Able Seamen Mitchell?'

There was a moment's silence and then a hand tentatively went up near the back.

'I've got something for you Mitchell,' Jon said with a grin. 'If you'd like to come up here please.'

Mystified the young sailor came through the throng with a look of bemusement on his face and not a little trepidation at being singled out by the Captain in front of everyone. When he got in front of Jon, he stopped.

Jon reached down onto the shelf under the dais and carefully lifted out the birthday cake the Chief Chef had made for him. 'Happy Birthday Mitchell,' Jon said with a grin as he handed over the cake and then reached down for the case of beer that had also been hidden from sight. The Master at Arms had been horrified when Jon had told him of his intentions. Sailors were normally rationed to three cans of beer a day. Jon overruled him, he wanted his ship to have its own silly little traditions and this was one of many sorts of thing that would bind them together.

As the young man held onto his presents, Jon turned back to the microphone. 'Now, just to confirm all the buzzes that have been going around. I can now tell you that our programme for the rest of the year will consist of at least one major NATO exercise.'

A small groan came from the men.

'Yes, I know how everyone loves those but I forgot to mention that it will be a transatlantic one and on completion we will be doing an East Coast States trip. And I'm sure there are enough of us here who have done that before to tell those who haven't what a dreadful time that means we will be having,'

This time there was a much louder cheer.

'So, we have time for summer leave, which you all deserve and I'll see you here at the end of August.'

Chapter 15

The first thing Max Llewellyn was aware of was the smell. It was a foul mixture of excrement, urine and rotting blood. It was followed by intense pain from his head and left leg. In combination, they were enough to make him vomit, which only made the pain worse. He realised there was something lying on top of him which seemed to be blocking the light. Despite the pain, the panic that was welling up in him was enough to give him the energy to push whatever it was away. Immediately the light got brighter but sand started pouring in on his face. Coughing and retching he was able to force himself up and into daylight. His vision was blurred but he was able to see that the thing that had been pressing down on him was a corpse. He fell onto his hands and knees and crawled a few feet before collapsing. His breathing was ragged but at least he was clear of the sand and the awful stench had reduced.

Some indeterminate time later, his senses returned again. This time his vision was clearer and he was able to look around. The last thing he remembered was being in the mess tent having a quick meal with his colleagues after the Chinese man had left. He had absolutely no recollection of anything after that. There was no sign of the mess tent. In fact, there was no sign of anything although he was sure he was in the same place.

'What the fuck?' he muttered and immediately realised how dry his mouth was. He turned to look behind him and see what it was that had been confining him and almost retched again. The body of his colleague Peter Jones was lying half out of the sand. The problem was that half his face was missing. Max had been in the military and knew the effect of a gunshot wound when he saw it. He quickly did an inventory of his own body. There was some sort of wound along his left temple and he could feel dried blood but nothing worse. His left leg hurt like hell and the whole of his trouser leg was wet with blood. He ripped his shirt off and tied an impromptu tourniquet above where the blood appeared and despite the agony, saw the flow stop. He reached behind him and found that his knife was still in the leather holster on his belt. Using the blade, he hacked off the cloth of his trouser leg and examined the wound. It looked like a clean shot that had missed the bone. A small hole at the font of his thigh just above the knee and a far more ragged exit wound at the back. He bundled up the cloth he had cut from his trousers and then cut an arm off his shirt and used it to tie the bundle tightly around both wounds. The blood didn't start again but he knew it was a very temporary fix at best. He couldn't work out how he hadn't bled out while in the ground and could only assume that weight of his friend who had clearly been thrown in on top of him had somehow kept pressure on it.

Solving that problem was for another time. He crawled over and pulled the corpse away and saw several more arms and legs in the shallow depression, the bodies half covered in sand. It was clear there was nothing he was going to be able to do for anyone. There were five of them on the team and he could clearly see that there were the remains of four people buried in the pit.

Suddenly, he saw that there weren't just bodies that had been buried. Off to one side was what looked like part of one of their tents. He managed to get to it and gave it a tug. It slowly came free and below it was a mass of piled up equipment, all smashed to pieces. His eye was caught by one thing. It was a plastic water container the one that normally lived in their cooking area. Desperately, he reached for it. At first, he thought it was empty but then he saw some water sloshing around at the bottom. He unscrewed the plastic top and carefully, with shaking hands, tilted the container backwards towards his mouth. The taste of the water defied description but he had the sense to be careful and swill it around carefully before swallowing. Before he really wanted to, he put it back on the ground and refitted the cap.

Half an hour later, he knew he was dead. There was no more water in the pit that the soldiers must have dug. In fact, there was nothing of any use although he did find the remains of a first aid kit and managed to make a better attempt at dressing his leg wound. There was no food and no means of communication. He couldn't walk more than a few yards and from their surveys of the area, he knew there was no habitation for miles. He couldn't even end it all by blowing his brains out. He managed to rig up a bit of the old tent material for some sort of shelter and decided to finish the little water that remained in the container. It wasn't long before weak from the loss of blood and shock, he slowly closed his eyes.

It was with some shock, some indeterminate time later that he heard voices. Before he could even sit up and see what was going on, he found himself staring down the barrel of an AK47 with the grinning face of a very large black man behind it.

Rupert Thomas strode back into his office sighing mentally in frustration. He had just spent the last three hours of his life in a budget meeting that had achieved absolutely nothing. He didn't even know why he had been invited and it was quite clear he didn't need to be there except for the one simple fact that his job title was on the attendance list. He made a note to tell his secretary to reject any further calling notices. He didn't really expect that to work but it was worth a try. He grabbed himself a coffee and plonked himself down at his desk. At least now that he was relatively senior, he had an office overlooking the Thames. It might have been summer but obviously no one had told the weather that. The sky was grey and rain was pelting down. A strong wind was whipping up little white caps on the river. So, even the view today was depressing. Stuck in a world of paper pushing and endless meetings, he wondered what his friend Jon Hunt was up to now in his bloody great ship. Jon used to complain that the navy wouldn't let him fly anymore and then gave him a great big toy to play with. For Rupert, now that he was too senior and too old to work in the field there was no light on the horizon. For the thousandth time, he wondered whether it was time to quit. Maybe go and work as a consultant. That way, he could at least pick and choose his work.

Just then, Gina his secretary came in with a sheaf of paperwork. She was in her early forties but looked ten years younger. If Rupert hadn't been her boss he would have asked her out by now. He knew she was widowed and had a couple of kids. She dressed impeccably but always managed to find something that emphasised her figure. Rupert had never married and was never that fussed when the few serious relationships he had, had failed. But the more he worked with Gina the more tempted he was. Maybe if he resigned he could ask her out. '*Yet another reason to move on,*' he thought gloomily.

'It's not as bad as it looks,' she said with her usual smile. 'Just some routine files and the latest intelligence digest. I know how you like to keep in touch with the operational side. How was the meeting? Was it as bad as you expected?'

'Ten times worse Gina,' Rupert replied. 'Look, next time, could you accidentally lose the calling notice or even better arrange an important meeting for me off the premises?'

'I'll see what I can do Rupert,' she said brightly and turned to leave.

The tight woollen skirt emphasised her trim rear end and he almost cracked and called out to her to ask her out for the evening but managed to restrain himself at the last minute.

He reached for the files and spent half an hour flicking through them annotating the odd comment where necessary and then reached for the weekly digest. It was one of the few bits of paper the department produced that he looked forward to reading. It was a summary of all general intelligence from the field without any spin.

He started reading and soon his eye spotted something. All the articles were attributed to the relevant desk officer. He picked up the phone. 'Malcom, this is Rupert Thomas do you have a moment. There's a bit in the digest that you've written. I'd like to get a bit more detail if you wouldn't mind.'

Five minutes later, Malcolm Marks, the desk officer covering the western region of Africa came in. He was a young man who had done extremely well at Cambridge and was already making a mark in the department. However, it was unlikely he would ever be employed in field work. Not only was he painfully thin but his eyes hid behind thick pebble glasses which gave him an almost comical air, which belied his quick intelligence.

'What can I help you with Rupert?' he asked, as Rupert indicated a chair for him to sit in.

'Tell me about Ukundu Malcolm,' Rupert replied.

'What do you want to know?'

'Well to start with, a precis of its recent history and resources please.'

'Hmm, well after the First World War it was taken away by the League of Nations from its German masters and divided between Britain and France as a protectorate. In nineteen sixty the French part became independent and then the British bit merged in sixty one and it became a federation. Very stable politically but mainly because of Peter Bayan the President although the old British areas have tried for independence and failed. It's pretty typical of many African countries. Lots of oil and timber revenue and very little going to the general populace. Is that the sort of thing you were looking for?'

'So, Africa in miniature then?'

'Yes, that's a good way of summing it up. They tend to look to France for support rather than us but that's fine, we have no real interest there although there are quite a number of expats living in various places.'

'And minerals?'

'Oil, shared with Nigeria, which has led to trouble but it's all quiet at the moment. Not much else. There was talk of copper a few years back but that never came to anything.'

Rupert thought for a minute. 'So, what about this British geological survey team that you mention in your article?'

'Ah, that's what caught your interest. I'm glad someone has picked up on it. When I first suggested there might be a bit more to it in my department, no one seemed to see anything particularly sinister.'

'What?' Rupert exclaimed but then he realised you had to be fairly well up the organisation to be cleared to the issues that he was able to access. It was one of the purposes of the weekly digest after all. It was a way of ensuring just this sort of issue got the wider circulation it sometimes needed. 'Sorry, tell me more about them.'

'They were a small team of survey geologists, contracted by the government to do mineral assessment in the north east of the country. It's fairly inhospitable and the borders are vague. A legacy of some colonial civil servant in the last century with a ruler and no understanding of the ethnic boundaries at the time. The consequence is, that like many parts of Africa, there are all sorts of petty tribal warlords conducting themselves to their entire satisfaction with no regard to any central government. We see it everywhere, Somalia is the worst but is not the only place. Anyway, the Foreign and Commonwealth Office contacted us about them last week. I had a word with our Embassy resident but he knew no more than anyone else. They went into the bush and never came back.'

'Surely they had some sort of escort? They wouldn't have gone to such an area without military back up, especially under a government contract.' Rupert asked.

'That's where it gets murky. Yes, they took a platoon of soldiers with them.' Malcolm replied. 'When our man asked discreetly around, he couldn't find out if the soldiers had returned or not. No one was saying anything. And then there is the other issue. The government are now denying that they had a contract with the team at all.'

'How do we know they did then?'

'Simple, the company that employed them are based in Cardiff and I rang them. They have the signed contract. They faxed it over to me and it's quite clear. The only odd thing is that it's not signed by their Internal Develop Minister but rather by their Foreign Minister although that could be explained as it's a foreign company they're dealing with.'

'Right, thanks for that. Only one other question, did anyone mention any Chinese involvement?'

'What? No, that's never come up. Why do you ask?' Malcolm looked intrigued.

'Oh, just another line of enquiry sprung to mind but obviously it's not an issue. Thank you Malcolm, if I need more, I'll call you.'

Taking his cue, Malcolm left, leaving Rupert to ponder. It wasn't much but his internal radar said it had spotted something, possibly important. He had no idea what it might be but he knew when to trust his instincts and this was one of those times.

Chapter 16

'How many?' Jon asked, surprised at the number.

Before Wings could answer, they were both distracted by the roar outside the bridge as a pair of Sea Harriers shot up the ship's ski jump ramp one after the other and into the distance.

When both men were satisfied that the aircraft were well clear and climbing away, Tim turned back to Jon. 'Sixteen Sir and half could be GR7s as you suggested although obviously FA2s would be easier as the support requirements would be simpler.'

'I assume we would need a permanent deck park? Juggling that many airframes around our size of flight deck and hangar will be bloody difficult.' Jon remarked.

'Yes Sir, that's actually the limiting factor. I've been working with the Aircraft Control Officer on this and we think it's a jig saw puzzle that we can solve. We should be able to keep the three helicopters as well. The AEO is confident we have enough room for the extra spares. The other limiting factor will be aviation fuel. MEO and I have done some numbers based on three months deployed with six weeks at normal peacetime flying rates and a week at full combat and we will definitely need our own tanker in company.'

'Not surprised, one of the things about the design of this ship is that they didn't really make our tanks big enough, those Harriers seem to guzzle the stuff. What about weapons if we took some GR7s?'

'Not really a problem Sir, most are common to the two types although we would need some extra Sidewinder storage. The magazines should be able to accommodate the RAF bomb variants. AEO is looking at those issues now.'

'Good work Wings,' Jon replied. 'And what's your opinion on how the exercise is going?'

'Serviceability has been remarkably good Sir and the Yanks got a really big shock when they sent all those F16s out against us.'

Jon laughed. 'Yes, what was it that the Yank Admiral said? 'That's a dinky little airplane with one big dick radar.''

'Yes Sir, he said that after we shot down most of his aircraft with AMRAAMs before they even knew we were there. It a bloody good combination of radar and missile. As for the exercise, as you know the marines from the Bataan are just about ready to go in. We've taken over the duties of Combat Air Patrol over the whole fleet which means they can use their Harrier AV8bs in their primary role instead of having to use them to guard themselves as well.'

Jon looked out of the window at the massive American assault carrier, the USS Bataan just ahead of them. Her deck was covered in aircraft, ranging from her own ground attack Harriers to massive CH53 assault helicopters. It was particularly satisfying to know that his much smaller ship with its 'dinky little airplanes' was now considered capable of protecting the whole amphibious force from outside air attack.

'So, one last push for their marines and then we can peel off and head to New York, should be a good run ashore and the lads have all deserved it.' Jon remarked.

'Yes Sir and I'll be glad to get the aircrew out of the bloody wardroom for a while.'

'Oh God, what have they got up to now?' Jon asked, not sure he really wanted to know.

'Nothing serious Sir, it's just that there has been a bit of a contest between the 888 boys and the rotary lot.'

'Nothing new there Wings, that's been going on since Nelson's time.'

Wings laughed. 'Maybe not quite as long as that Sir but I get your point. The thing is, although we have only three helicopters on board, there are just as many helicopter aircrew as fixed wing. What with two full Lynx crew and three Sea King, the numbers are just about even.'

'I get that Wings but what's the issue?'

'Pigs Sir,' Wings said deadpan.

Jon looked puzzled. He knew the word was used as a derogatory term by the lower deck for officers but clearly it wasn't what Wings was referring to. 'A little more specific Tim, if you don't mind?'

'Pass the Pigs Sir. It's a game. They have these two little plastic pigs that they throw like dice and depending on how they end up you either get a score or lose the lot. First to a hundred wins. It's taken over from Uckers and they've been playing it in the ante room after dinner.'

'That actually sounds quite civilised. I seem to remember much more dangerous things in my time.' Jon responded with a grin.

'And me but it's not that, it's the bloody racket they've been making. Each throw generates a great cheer and cries of things like 'leaning jowler' or 'making bacon' it's been driving the ship's officers mad. Two nights ago, the Commander got so pissed off he told them to shut up or he would ban the game. Last night they all turned up and played without saying a word, they just held up bloody great signs with all the words on them.'

'How did the Commander take it?' Jon asked trying hard not to laugh.

'Quite well actually, at least it made for a quiet night but we really need a run ashore. We're all getting a little stir crazy if you ask me.'

'Yes, well that's just around the corner. A good standard pusser's visit to a foreign port. Cocktail party first night in then five days to unwind. I have to say, I'm really looking forward to it. I've never been to New York. Have you?'

'Yes Sir when I was at the Embassy in Washington I came up several times. The lads will love it. I suspect there will be a few American females who will as well. And before you ask, I will do my utter best to stop the aircrew monopolising all the totty at the cocktail party. I have a few ideas up my sleeve.'

Jon laughed. 'I wish you the best of luck with that one Wings. They'll have just as many tricks of their own.'

'I know Sir but I have to try. Sometimes, I really feel like a poacher turned gamekeeper.'

'I know just what you mean,' Jon agreed ruefully.

A week later and Jon was beginning to think that the cocktail party wasn't such a good idea after all. He was standing on the brow in his best uniform along with FOF3, Admiral Spencer, who had flown out specifically for the visit.

'How many invites were sent out Jon?' The Admiral asked looking down onto the jetty which seemed to be covered in people as far as the eye could see.

'Four hundred Sir, from the consulate but I've just done a mental count and there are at least twice if not three times that many down there.'

'Are they gate crashers? I know the Yanks like us but this seems a bit extreme.' The Admiral asked pensively.

'They should all have official invites Sir.' Jon turned to the Bosun's mate who once again was Able Seaman Jones. 'Jones pipe for

Lieutenant Commander Black please. He's the liaison officer for the visit Sir. We'll see what he has to say.'

Just then, the first visitors were allowed to climb the gangway and Jon and the Admiral had to devote their energies to smiling and shaking hands. A few minutes later, a harassed officer arrived and Jon took a quick time out to talk to him. 'Mathew, what the hell is going on? Why are there so many people here?'

He looked aghast at the waiting crowds. 'Absolutely no idea Sir. I sent four hundred invites ashore to the consulate. Give me a minute and I'll get on the phone.'

'You do that Mathew, I'm not impressed nor is the Admiral.' Jon hissed.

Jon returned to meeting and greeting but he could hear a muted conversation taking place behind him.

A few minutes later, Mathew Black came to him. 'I've spoken to the Consulate Sir and they say they received the invites but it appears one of the clerical staff wanted to try out their new colour photo copier and also get a few favours, so he decided to print more off. He got the settings wrong and ended up with about eight hundred more. Rather than throw them away, he passed them on. I'm sorry but there's no way to distinguish between the real ones and the copies.' He looked pensive as he spoke.

Jon immediately berated himself for losing his temper. 'Alright Mathew, sorry I snapped at you earlier. Now, what I want you to do is get the Commander and Wings warned off. The Admiral and I will hold the fort here for another thirty minutes and then I want them to come and relieve us. That should see the bulk of them on board. Also, warn the wardroom that they're going to have to get more booze up from store.'

When Jon was finally able to leave the gangway and join the party, he was amazed at how crowded the flight deck was. Most of the aircraft were struck below but two Harriers were parked at the bow and well roped off. He also did a very quick survey and wasn't surprised to see the number of guests who were female and under the age of thirty. It was going to be a happy hunting ground for the ship's officers and he expected many of the girls would be invited down to the wardroom after the official event ended. He suddenly felt himself wishing he wasn't the Captain of the ship but rather a young lieutenant with no ties once again. He didn't get the chance to follow up on the thought because he was immediately singled out by several guests and had to give them is full attention.

An hour later and all the guests had been moved off to one side of the flight deck so that the Royal Marine band that had been flown out especially for the occasion could beat the retreat. Jon remembered a previous visit in HMS Hermes, where a friend described it as the best way in the world for loosening American women's knicker elastic. Especially the last part where the Last Post was played and the White Ensign lowered and on that occasion he was right.

The band came up on the aft lift and proceeded to march up the deck playing 'Hearts of Oak', Jon didn't notice it at first but then he heard a distant bell ringing. The MEO who was standing near Jon did a double take and shot into the island. He came back a few minutes later.

He came up to Jon and talked quietly. 'We have enough of a list now Sir that several alarms went off in HQ1.'

'Jesus, are we safe?' Jon asked anxiously.

'Yes Sir, its only a few degrees but it just shows what putting almost twelve hundred people on one side can do. I've got my duty chaps monitoring it and we should be fine. Besides, there's not a lot we can do now.'

It was only after the bulk of the guests had finally left that Jon started to relax. The wardroom party was in full swing but his job was to entertain the Admiral. At the Admiral's request, they both changed into civilian clothes and left the ship for a quiet dinner ashore. As they walked down the now quiet jetty towards a waiting cab, the Admiral turned to look back up at the bulk of Formidable. 'Well done Jon. That could have been a disaster. It seems your ship has had its fair share of those.'

Inwardly, Jon winced at the remark but he managed to keep a straight face.

Chapter 17

They bundled Max into an old open topped truck. Through the miasma of pain, he was able to see the state it was in. The almost total lack of suspension didn't help his leg as they drove away from the site after spending ten minutes getting the machine started. His guards, if he could call them that, were all in their teens with the exception of the man who had first found him. He was clearly the leader and they all deferred to him with an almost comical reverence. They were all armed with the ubiquitous AK47 but Max noted they didn't seem to have much ammunition. Indeed they seemed to have almost no other military equipment at all. They were all dressed in ragged shorts and T shirts. He was also surprised at how gentle they were with him. They chattered like schoolboys but he couldn't understand a word. The dialect was so far from any that he knew. He wondered where they had come from. The briefings they had been given before they came out said that this area was generally unpopulated, a fact that had been confirmed as they had toured the area. In fact, thinking about it they hadn't seen any signs of life at all for the whole previous three weeks.

In the end, he had no idea how far they had gone as after a short while, despite the pain or maybe because of it, he passed out. When he came to, the sun was low in the horizon and there was no sign of the salt lake but that was because quite steep hills surrounded them as they pulled into what looked quite a large African tribal village. The truck was suddenly surrounded by chattering people all asking questions and peering at him. Whatever answers were given made no sense to him but seemed to make the people quite agitated and some of the looks he started to get seemed far from friendly. He was starting to get concerned when there was a woman's shout from the back of the throng and a middle aged lady forcefully pushed herself through the crowd. She was dressed in a curious mix of clothes with some sort of scarf over her head but a faded khaki blouse and shorts. Max suddenly realised she was speaking the local language but also swearing at them in English. In fact, her language was the most colourful he had heard in a long time and bearing in mind he had been sharing his life with a bunch of male toughs that was saying something.

She reached the rear of the truck and started shouting at his guards who all seemed quite nervous of her and immediately started to help Max out.

The big man came around and confronted the woman. She wasn't intimidated in the slightest even though she barely came up to his massive shoulders and whatever the exchange was about, he quickly gave in with a resigned shrug. He turned to the young men and said something and they carefully picked Max up and carried him behind her as she made her way through the curious villagers towards one particular thatched hut. She pushed the grass screen away from the entrance and motioned the men to take him in. Inside, it was unlike any native accommodation he had ever seen. On one side were two beds, one of which he was carefully laid down on before the men left. In the middle, was a small desk with a large locked cabinet behind it and on the other side a series of folding chairs set out in front of what could have been an altar or a school desk although the large crucifix over it made Max think it was probably the former.

The woman came over to the bed. 'So, do you speak English?' she demanded in a broad Irish accent.

Taken aback by her attitude but also impressed by the way the locals treated her, he decided that discretion was a good idea.

'Yes, my name is Max Llewellyn, I'm a geological surveyor. Who are you?'

The woman ignored his question. 'Oh bless me, a bloody Welshman as well as fuckin' land rapist, that's all we bloody well need. Right, let me have a look at those wounds.'

Without waiting for an answer, she first looked at the head wound. 'Right, that can wait,' she muttered and then took the amateur dressing off his leg with a surprising gentleness that belied her rough attitude. 'Hmm, you did a half decent job there Max. Now let's do it properly.' She went to the large cabinet and unlocked it with a key that was on a chain around her neck and soon returned with some clean bandages and several bottles. After inspecting both wounds, she carefully cleaned them and looked him in the eye. 'No anaesthetic out here lad. This is going to hurt. Let's see what you're made of.' Without waiting for a response, she started to stitch the wounds.

By this time, Max was beginning to get not a little angry with this tough looking, bloody minded woman and so lay back, gritted his teeth and let her get on with it. The front leg wound wasn't so bad but when she started on the one at the rear the pain was intense. Forcing himself not to scream, he passed out.

When he came to, not only was his leg throbbing but nothing like as bad as it had been but he felt a bandage around his head, She must have sorted that wound out as well. He looked around but there was no sign of the mysterious woman. It was clearly dark outside but an oil lamp by the bed cast a little light. There was a large pitcher of water by the bed and he managed to grab it and gulp some down. It tasted magnificent even if he did spill most of it down his front.

'Jesus, Mary and the Holy fucking Ghost, look at the mess you've made,' the voice came from behind the desk where she must have been sitting out of his view. She came over and wiped the worst of the spillage away and then poured the remaining water into a glass that he hadn't seen in his haste to get a drink. She handed it to him and this time he was far more careful. When he finished, he lay back and looked at her. He suddenly realised she probably wasn't quite as old as he had first thought. The African sun had clearly taken a toll on her skin but she was probably in her mid-thirties he guessed. 'So, are you going to tell me who the fucking hell you are? Or do I have to put up with the abuse for the rest of my stay here?'

To his surprise, she burst out laughing. 'Good, that means you haven't got an infection, at least not yet, otherwise, you wouldn't feel like that. My name is Sister Agnes and I live and work here. I'm the doctor, teacher and priest to these people.'

'What? You're a nun? What the hell are you doing out here? At one level Max wasn't surprised. The room seemed to have all the functionality of a Sick Bay, school room and chapel. Yet this woman hardly looked like a nun or any of the other roles she claimed for herself for that matter.

'Bloody men, always react like that. I've been out here for seven years as a missionary. I do what I can for these people and they seem to respect me for that. They even make an attempt to like my religion. Do you expect me to be in a black robe with a silly fucking hat in this heat? I do God's work whatever I'm wearing. Now, you tell me what the hell happened to you and what you were doing here in the first place.'

Max lay back and wondered what he should tell her. He needed to know just what the situation was that he had found himself in before he came completely clean. He decided on a simplified version. 'We were contracted to do a geological survey of this area of the country. Primarily, we were looking for copper but anything else was on the agenda. There was a vague hope of diamonds or gold even though we told them the area was the wrong sort of structure. We'd been out here for weeks. We had an army guard. We were all sitting down to dinner a couple of days ago and that's the last thing I remember until I woke up in a pit in the ground with the corpse of my partner on top of me. You must know the rest. Now, why did you call me a land rapist when we first met?'

Agnes's eyes narrowed. 'Ah, you remember that do you? This land belongs to these people not those crooks in the capital. If you had found anything do you think for one moment anyone here would benefit? Not a bloody chance.'

'Hang on, this still part of Ukundu isn't it?' Max asked puzzled.

She laughed. 'I suppose it could be considered that but no one ever asked the people who live here, the people who have farmed the land for centuries.'

'But they told us the whole area was unpopulated. How come we didn't see anyone when we were surveying?'

'Because we didn't want to be seen. We knew you were out there surveying but this village is well up in the hills. No doubt you could see it on a satellite photograph but who would bother to look? As far as the government are concerned we don't count. More to the point, you haven't told me the whole story, have you? What have you found?'

It was Max's turn to look hard at his interrogator. 'What makes you think we found anything?'

She laughed. 'Because it's quite clear who shot you all. It must have been your so called guards. Now, why would they do that unless you had found something and they didn't want you to report it back?'

Max felt like a complete idiot. He had been so focused on survival he hadn't even started to think things through. It must have been that bloody Chinese man Li. But if that was the case, how had he managed to make the local soldiers turn on them? More importantly, why had he done it? The events of the last few days suddenly caught up with him. Delayed shock overwhelmed him and he fell back on his pillows with his breath coming in short gasps.

Sister Agnes immediately realised that she had pushed him too hard and too fast. She went over to the medicine cabinet and took out some sedatives. She poured some water and got him to swallow them. Within minutes, his breathing had slowed and his eyes had closed. She would stay with him for the rest of the night while she thought through all the implications of what she already knew and what she dreaded finding out.

Zhang Li was amazed at how fast his masters in Beijing had reacted. They had already been making moves to gain leverage with the local government. An arms sale was part of the plan and already well underway but this was even better as it would tie the two countries together economically for years to come. Within a week, they had a full diplomatic team in the country to support him. As usual the selective application of large quantities of cash had opened doors and greased wheels. Li found himself in a whirlwind of meetings with his own people as well as local politicians.

Today, he was in the Interior Ministry with both the Minister and one of his aides, who Li actually knew was his second son. Nepotism was a way of life in most African countries. He had been authorised by his superiors to come clean on the discovery. They clearly had enough confidence now to confide in at least certain elements of the local hierarchy. His brief today was to look at the issues of extraction and its effect on the locality. A large map was spread on the table and he had been given enough detail by the engineers to know what would be required.

'Firstly,' he said looking at the two men. 'We will need a road to get the semi-refined material out. There is no way a rail line can be laid to the site as the terrain is too hilly and anyway it would take too long. The processing site will need to be quite large but the real problem will be pollution. To build a clean processing plant will take years and we don't think it is necessary. However, the quick solution will contaminate the land for some distance as we will need settling pools which will allow chemicals to sink into the local rock structure and water table. Even though the area is quite arid, there is still water deep down.'

The two men just shrugged. The Minister studied the map. 'If we do this, how long before we see revenue?'

'*Typical,*' Li thought. '*Straight to the cash question, why am I not surprised?*'

Keeping the thought off his face, he replied. 'Within a year, with full production a year after that.' He knew the figures. He had been well briefed. 'If we go for a fully clean system, it will take at least three years before we see anything.'

'Then that is what we must do,' this time it was the son who answered, although the look of greed on his face was identical to that of his father.

Li had to ask the next question although he knew it was for the record if this decision ever came out in public. His government would be able to deflect the blame.

'What about the people who live there Minister? What will become of them?'

The man just shrugged. 'There are very few Mister Li and trust me we will look after them.'

The answer was given with the total lack of sincerity that Li expected but he would make sure that it was written down word for word in the minutes of this meeting that he would be writing and getting the Minister to sign off.

Chapter 18

Rupert felt like banging his head against the wall in frustration. Despite all his efforts, he felt he was drowning in paperwork. There was a school of thought that he certainly subscribed to, that said that the more classified something was, the more boring it became. Now that he was so senior in the organisation, he was certainly privy to some momentous secrets, none of which actually represented a challenge to him in the current political climate. The only thing that was keeping his mind sharp was the results of the ongoing overview of what was going on in Ukundu.

Luckily for him, the country was within his area of responsibility so he had every reason to get his people to keep an eye on what was going on. The problem was that they couldn't find out anything. The disappearance of the geological team had given him some leverage with the Embassy in the capital but it had proved a complete dead end. The government was saying nothing and all enquiries had hit a brick wall. They had finally admitted that they had awarded a government contract but denied all knowledge of why the team hadn't returned, simply saying that it was not unheard of for people, especially white men, to go into the bush and not return. All requests to send in a search party had been flatly refused on the basis that the area had already been searched to no avail. A claim that Rupert completely disbelieved. He had even got the FCO to call in their ambassador in London but they only got the same story. Although it wasn't an unusual response, the complete lack of desire to enter into any sort of dialogue was only confirming Rupert's suspicions. The problem was that he had no idea what he was looking for. The obvious conclusion was that they had discovered something significant and the Ukundu government wanted to keep it secret. However, after talking that through with the men's parent company it didn't make much sense. The team had been primarily looking for copper and the consensus was that it was a pretty forlorn hope, the geology of the area was poor and the chances remote. Oil was in the same category. There was one large salt pan but that would hardly be significant. The survey company had made this all clear to the Ukundu government at the start but in a country starved of natural resources it was deemed a reasonable gamble.

Rupert had been about to put the whole thing down to his desire for any sort of operational work to keep his brain active when he got a report about a large Chinese delegation arriving. It hadn't been possible to find out exactly why they were there but there seemed to be a great deal of activity in various government ministries. He had authorised the secondment of two extra agents for the Embassy in the capital but even with the extra manpower nothing more had been learned.

It was time to call a meeting of his staff. As he entered the conference room and took the chair at the head of the table, he nodded to Gina who was sitting next to him to take any minutes and then the five other people seated around the table.

'Good morning everyone,' he said cheerfully. 'We all know why we're here. This isn't a formal meeting and Gina will only be taking action notes. That is if we are lucky enough to have any. The main purpose today is to decide whether to continue with this investigation or close it off and hand the Chinese element over to routine surveillance. As you are all well aware, anything that costs money comes under close scrutiny these days. I've managed to finesse sending our two chaps out to the Embassy but I won't be able to get away with that for much longer. The bloody bean counters will soon be looking over my shoulder unless we can come up with something significant.'

There was a ripple of amused agreement around the table. Financial pressures had built up steadily in recent years particularly after the fall of the Berlin wall.

'Malcolm, I'd like you to summarise please.' Rupert asked.

Malcolm stood and went over to the little lectern. He turned on the screen above it and activated a Power Point presentation. 'We all know the background so I'm not going to dwell on it. However, last night there was a significant development. Rupert, I'm sorry I didn't warn you about this before but I was getting the analysts to confirm my initial assessment.' He clicked the lectern mouse to get the next slide. 'This is the main military airfield just outside the capital.'

There was silence for several minutes as everyone studied the grainy black and white photograph.

A voice called out. 'The French support the government don't they. So presumably those are Mirage fighters?'

'Nope,' Malcolm said firmly. 'The Mirage family of aircraft have pure delta wings. Notice that these ones have a tail plane and these ones over here are normal swept wing variants.'

'Looks like a Mig 19,' someone said. 'Are the bloody Russians moving in as well?'

'Not a bad guess,' Malcolm replied. 'That one is based on the Mig 19 but it's actually a Chinese Q5 ground attack aircraft. The other is a J8 interceptor fighter not unlike our old Lightnings.'

'Oh fuck,' someone muttered.

'Oh fuck indeed,' Rupert said. 'How on earth did they get there and when for that matter?'

'No idea.' Malcolm answered. 'One moment the airfield had a few old French helicopters and some even older Mirage jets that hardly ever flew and then these turned up. We're not even sure when they arrived as the place is not normally under surveillance. I had to twist some arms just to get some satellite time for these pictures. The best guess is some time in the last two weeks and we think they came directly from China with air to air refuelling. If you look over on the other side of the airfield there's an Ilyushin Il-76 large transport which the Chinese also operate. It has an air to air refuelling capability.'

'How many Malcolm?' Rupert asked.

'Eight of each we think. The hangars are quite small and as we can't see any of their Mirage we assume they have been put away. We were surprised they haven't put them all under cover but think we caught them getting ready for a training sortie. We were lucky.'

'What the hell are they doing there?' Rupert mused. 'First, we have this missing survey team and then this Chinese build up. The real problem, of course, is that we have no credible link between the two things. Any ideas anyone?'

They discussed the issue for over an hour but without any further evidence, Rupert realised they were stuck. One point that came up was that the area the team had disappeared in was part of the old British territories which might give them some leverage with the current government Rupert wasn't too hopeful it would help but any advantage no matter how small might be worth pursuing.

He summed the meeting up. 'Alright everyone, I will go upstairs and seek authorisation for further funding. Meanwhile, I want our people out there to dig around further and try to find out what the hell the Chinese are up to, especially by deploying these aircraft there. Any link, anything at all, to the missing survey team is the other priority. Look to seeing if we can find out what their actual route was and I'll get one of our people out there to try and get some information on the ground.'

When he was back in his office, Gina brought in a coffee. 'Thanks Gina, sorry you weren't really needed in the end but it's always worth having someone there just in case.'

She smiled. 'There is one thing Rupert. I didn't really think it was my place to bring it up at the meeting.'

'Go on,' Rupert said intrigued.

'You probably don't know it but I'm a Catholic and our local church is heavily involved in sponsoring missionary work. It was being discussed the other day and there are apparently several of our parish out in Ukundu. I was careful what I asked but wonder whether it would be worth me looking into it a bit further. We might get some intelligence that would be impossible any other way.'

The question caught Rupert completely by surprise but he couldn't see why not. It couldn't do any harm and if Gina could contact someone already up country maybe it would give them a valuable new insight into what was really going on.

'That's fine Gina, just continue to be careful.' And then before he could stop himself. 'And how about going out for a drink tonight? You might be able to give me some more background.'

Chapter 19

The rolling hills of Dartmoor were plainly visible behind the roofs of the town which was fronted by the green of Plymouth Hoe as HMS Formidable carefully negotiated the breakwater that sheltered the massive Sound. Jon loved the sight, the backdrop for so many homecomings during his naval career. However, he didn't have exactly much time to appreciate the view before Amelie Smith gave the next wheel order to change the ship's heading to stay in the buoyed channel.

It had been an exhausting few months. The first exercise with the Americans had gone extremely well. The visit to New York and other ports had all been very successful, so much so that he knew that several of the ship's company were a little anxious that certain females might have flown over to greet them on the jetty when they got in. This was fine as long as their wives weren't there as well. Apparently, there were contingency plans in place. Jon had left that particular problem to the Commander. The next few weeks had seen the ship conduct a series of smaller exercises and visits down the eastern seaboard by the end of which everyone was starting to think of getting home for Christmas. Jon knew Ruth would be waiting for him and they had plans to go to London for the holiday period, which he was really looking forward to. He would also spend a few days with Brian, Kathy and the kids. The one thing that had really given him great satisfaction was the performance of the ship. Not one breakdown for the whole period. On top of that, the Air Group had shown how capable and reliable they were. In the bad old days of fixed wing carriers, a ship returning with the same number of aircraft on board as it had left with was extremely unlikely. To date, there hadn't been one serious incident with the jets or helicopters and for that he was really grateful. They had all flown off that morning to their various air stations. It always amused Jon how a squadron would struggle to maintain all its aircraft in a serviceable state but always managed it when it came to disembarking for leave.

An hour later, they were tied up. The Commander, Wings and Jon had retired to his harbour cabin for a final wash up.

'All good Paul?' Jon asked as Jenkins put down the inevitable tray of coffee.

'Yes Sir, leave will be piped in an hour. We actually had enough volunteers to man the ship over the period and they will all get second leave once the rest of us are back. You might be amused to see this.' He handed Jon a piece of paper.

Jon studied it for a second and grinned. 'How did you get this Paul? I assume they will be putting it up all over the place for when we all return.'

He handed the paper to Wings who looked at it in turn and laughed. 'Second Leave is Best Daily Orders, by the Second Leave is Best duty officer and all items on the list state that Second Leave is Best. Don't you just love sailors?'

Paul joined in. 'You might love them but the Master at Arms has his methods of finding things out and I don't always enquire too deeply. I told him to let them get on with it.'

'Fine, just don't let them go over the top when we return,' Jon said smiling. 'Now, more importantly how about the 'knickers'?'

The Commander grimaced. Ever since the ship had sailed, every now and then someone had said the word over the ship's main broadcast. It happened at various times of day and was said differently each time but not often enough to be anything other than quite funny. The Commander, WEO and Master at Arms had spent many fruitless hours trying to track down the culprit, to no avail. 'We've tried to analyse the timings against the watches that people keep and the technical ability to access the system but haven't been able to work out how the bugger is doing it Sir but I have a cunning plan. Over leave, one of WEO's chiefs who is staying on board is going to physically trace the wiring of the broadcast. The best theory we have is that there is a microphone somewhere in the bowels of the ship that we don't know about, possibly left over from build. Even if there isn't one, he should be able to see any physical signs of tampering.'

'Good plan Commander,' Jon stated, although personally he didn't think they would be successful and anyway his view was that this sort of prank was a sign of good morale not bad. But he also understood why the Commander saw it as a challenge to his executive authority and needed to be seen to be trying to stop it. Jon remembered back to his time as a midshipman in the old Ark Royal when for a time there was a reign of terror by 'the Phantom Crapper' who did more than leave verbal messages in some of the officer's cabins. That stopped being funny quite quickly.

He turned to Wings. 'Tim, how many girls are on the jetty waiting for Peter Yorrick?'

'Ah, you know about him do you Sir?' Wings asked.

'Well, I know he started out as a sheep's skull nailed to a piece of wood which the squadron used as a 'Grimmy Trophy' to give to the lucky officer who trapped the ugliest girl during any run ashore. But he seems to have a life of his own these days.'

'Indeed Sir, he has. He's had a least a dozen 'letters from America' I know that because there is a pigeon hole in the wardroom letter rack with his name on it. I'm pretty sure some of them are bills and I'll make sure the squadron pay them. He even managed to run up a mess bill before the Chief Steward stopped it. As to ladies in love with him, I've left the Squadron to sort that out.' Wings said looking amused.

'Good, then I'm going to leave the good ship Formidable in your capable hands Commander. Just because you live locally, don't waste too much of your leave on board please. The Duty Lieutenant Commander will keep her safe. I'll see you all after leave and have a good Christmas and New Year.'

Taking the hint the two men left, leaving Jon to contemplate what he needed to pack.

The holiday period passed in a blur. After stopping at Brian's for a couple of days, Jon headed to London and spent Christmas and New Year with Ruth in her house in St Johns Wood. They did a couple of shows and ate out nearly every night. At New Year, Rupert joined them and to Jon's surprise he had a rather pretty girl in tow. In all the time they had known each other Jon had never met one of Rupert's girlfriends, indeed at one point he did wonder whether he batted for the other side. But after a rather drunken night out some years previously Rupert admitted that although he rarely had girlfriends he very definitely was not gay. Jon was surprised to discover that Gina was actually his secretary and did mention this to Rupert in private.

'Yes, it is frowned upon Jon but to be honest I've reached the point where I don't really care and it's not specifically banned.' Rupert explained. 'To be honest I'm considering my future at the moment. It's alright for you, you can still play with the toys but all I seem to do is spend endless hours in committees.'

Jon was taken aback by the reply. He had always seen Rupert as a career man. That he was even contemplating such a thing was a total surprise and he said so.

'Surely there must some operational real time stuff to keep you occupied, not just budgets and paperwork?'

Rupert shrugged. 'There's something going on in Africa which could turn out to be significant but it's bloody hard to get any real information. But even if it comes to something I can't see the system letting me get involved except from behind my bloody desk. Come on, we're keeping the girls waiting. Now's not the time to talk shop.'

The two men went back upstairs to the first floor living room. Gina was just putting down her mobile phone. 'Rupert, remember I said I would ask my local priest about any of our people out in Africa? Well he's just rung me with some rather odd information. We have two missionaries out in the back country. One is a priest and the other a nun. Father Joseph, the priest, has access to the telephone system whereas Sister Agnes is with a community right up country. Apparently, Father Joseph has had a message saying that Sister Agnes is looking after a wounded man who they found in the bush. That's not particularly unusual but apparently the man is a mining engineer of some sort. He's quite badly hurt and she thinks it will be some time before he will be fit to travel. I've asked for more information but it sounds like we might have the breakthrough you were looking for Rupert.'

Jon looked at Rupert. 'Sounds like the goal posts just shifted old chum.'

'Too bloody right. Well done Gina. Er, I know its New Year's Eve but I'm sorry, I think Gina and I need to get back to the office.'

Jon and Ruth were disappointed to see the other two leave but they both understood why and Jon was pleased to see the spark re-ignite in his friend's eye with the news from Africa. They spent a quiet evening in a local restaurant before going home and seeing in the New Year quietly curled up on the sofa in front of the television before going to bed. Jon woke the next morning, suddenly feeling worried, quite why he had no idea but he couldn't get the thought out of his head that something was wrong. Scolding himself for being an idiot, he slipped out of bed and went downstairs to the kitchen to make coffee for himself and Ruth. They both liked to lie in bed in the morning when things were quiet and read, along with a coffee.

Suddenly, the phone in the hall range. Jon went to answer it.

'Sir, its Paul Taylor. You need to get down to the ship as fast as you can. We've a bad fire on board. It's being tackled now but you really need to get here.'

'Alright Paul, I'm on my way but it'll take me at least four hours so do your best. Use my mobile phone to keep me in the picture.'

Jon ran up the stairs calling for Ruth. His premonition had been right, it had all been going too bloody well.

Chapter 20

Paul Taylor had been called into the ship very early in the morning by the Duty Lieutenant Commander. It appeared that a small fire had broken out on five deck aft, in one of the ship's stores. Although any fire in a warship was nothing to be taken lightly, he hadn't been too worried. In fact, on the drive in, he was more worried about being stopped by the police and breathalysed. He had been very careful the previous night but one never knew. He also knew they were extra vigilant at this time of year. However, it was a risk he was prepared to take. In fact, he had made it to the dockyard gate in record time and had hardly seen another vehicle, with the exception of two fire engines with their blue lights flashing ahead of him as he drove into the dockyard. It was quite clear where they were heading and that hadn't been a good omen.

As soon as he mounted the gangway, the quartermaster reported that the DLC was in HQ1 and he wasted no time in getting there himself. The civilian fire crews were already getting out hoses and pieces of equipment on the jetty as he disappeared into the ship.

In HQ1 there were several people making up the state board which looked far too busy for a simple storeroom fire. The DLC looked relieved to see him. 'It's worse than we thought Sir.' He pointed to the state board. 'At first, I thought we could handle it with the fire and emergency party but it seems to have spread very fast, which is why I alerted the shore authorities. The first report was of smoke on five deck near the aft bedding store and that's where we went. The smoke was actually coming from there but only because of a fire in the next compartment which had heated the bulkhead up so much the blankets were smouldering.'

'What's in that compartment then?' Paul asked looking at the state board. He didn't recognise the space or what it was used for.

'Air conditioning plant Sir. There shouldn't be much in there to catch fire but there is a lot of electrical equipment. The Chief who's down there thinks one of the motors must have burnt out.'

'But why should that cause such an intense fire? That doesn't make sense.' Paul asked worriedly.

'That's what we all thought at first Sir. The only thing we can think of is a hydrogen fire.'

Formidable

'What? That only ever happened in old fashioned steam plants in the boilers. I should know, I was in HMS Bulwark when it happened to her in Philadelphia years ago. You need massive temperatures and lots of water to disassociate and make hydrogen. Where the hell would the water come from?'

'Just after the smoke was reported Sir, the automatic sprinkler alarm went off. All we can think of is that the heat set off the sprinklers in the compartment while whatever it was that burnt out was hot enough to start the reaction. Whatever is in there is burning bloody hot.'

'Right, have we turned the damned sprinklers off? That is literally like pouring petrol on a fire.'

'Yes Sir but they were on for a good ten minutes so there's a lot of water in there. My biggest issue is boundary cooling. If we can keep the compartment bulkheads cool enough it should just burn itself out.'

'Yes good thinking and getting the temperature in there below critical will also stop it. In the Bulwark it was in one of the boiler rooms and the entrance had an airlock which is how they managed to get back in safely. We're not going to have that luxury here. What about the rest of the ship?'

'We went to emergency stations about half an hour ago Sir but the reality is that nearly everyone aboard now is involved in fire fighting.'

Just then a civilian fireman came in escorted by one of the sailors. 'Need my help?' he asked cheerfully.

Paul looked at the DLC. 'Your call, you're more up to speed than me.'

The DLC turned to the fireman. 'Our priority is cooling the compartment from the outside. If we show you where to run hoses can your tenders supply us with water into the ship?'

'We'll try. But we don't know where to go,'

'Don't worry, my chaps will be with you. Chief Jones, take charge please.'

One of the Senior Rates nodded and left with the fireman.

'I'm going to call the Captain,' Paul said. 'You carry on for the moment and then I'll take over here and you can take charge at the scene.' He went over to one side of the compartment and picked up a shore telephone.

Once Paul had alerted the Captain and sent the DLC off to the scene of the fire to work with the Officer of the Day. He sat back and took a

Formidable

moment to consider the situation. The compartment supplied air conditioning to the aft half of the ship. He called over to one of the sailors by the state board. Petty Officer Brown isn't it?'

'Yes Sir,' the Petty Officer answered.

'What about all the inlets and outlets from the air conditioning plant itself?'

'All closed down Sir. They automatically close once the sprinklers come on.'

'Can we manually override them and get them to reopen?' Paul asked as an idea formed in his mind.'

Probably Sir but that would only make things worse,' the Petty Officer replied.

Just then the door flew open and Dave Johnson the MEO ran in. He looked as though he had literally run from his bedroom ashore because he probably had done just that. In normal operations he would be the man to take charge in this sort of emergency and Paul was delighted to see him.

'Just got the message,' Dave said. 'Can you give me an update?'

Paul explained the problem and what they were doing about it just as another alarm came on. 'Shit I recognise that from the cocktail party in New York,' Paul exclaimed. 'We must be listing with all the bloody water we're pumping into the ship.'

'You're right Paul,' Dave said and then turned to Petty Officer Brown. 'Have we rigged pumps Brown and if so how many?'

'Well ahead of you Sir. All the portable ones are already in use and the rear fixed bilge pump as well.'

'Right, talk to those shore firemen and see if they have any more with them or can get us more quickly.'

'Right Sir,' Brown responded and he picked up a telephone and started talking urgently.

'So, if we've already taken on a significant list, how long before we're in trouble Dave,' Paul asked worriedly.

'We're already in trouble Paul,' Dave responded. 'If we can't get the fire under control it will eventually melt through the hull and we probably won't sink because of our watertight integrity measures but that whole section of the ship will flood and God knows how much damage will be caused, particularly when more sea water hits the red hot fire in there. It will certainly cause an explosion of some severity.

Formidable

If we keep pumping boundary cooling water into the ship at the rate we are and can't get rid of faster we capsize. Fuck.'

'I've got an idea,' Paul stated firmly. When he finished, Dave didn't look convinced. 'It might have worked in Bulwark but this is a different matter Paul.'

'If we don't try something the ship is in severe danger of sinking Dave. Look, there will be a partial vacuum in there. All the oxygen was used up ages ago, it's only the water that's keeping the fire going. What's the danger of trying?'

'Dammit, you're right. Petty Officer Brown, contact the on scene officer and tell him to manually open as many of the compartment vents as they can but to be bloody careful as they do it.'

The Petty Officer looked as if he was going to argue for a second but saw the look on the two Commander's faces and picked up an internal telephone.

There was nothing else they could do. The two men waited in tense silence for several minutes then the telephone rang. Petty Officer Brown answered. When he finished he turned towards them with an odd look on his face. 'The Chief reports that they think the fire is out or at least the really hot part. As soon as they saw the temperature start to drop they shut the vents again and now the whole place is cooling quite rapidly. They've started to minimise any boundary cooling and we are now pumping out more than we are pumping in. Excuse me Sirs but how the hell did that work?'

Paul laughed in relief. 'Hydrogen fires need to be above about one thousand eight hundred degrees to be self-sustaining. At that temperature, water turns to hydrogen and oxygen and metal will burn. As you saw, water is the last thing you need. It is literally the fuel for the reaction. The same happened some years ago in Bulwark as I said earlier and they got it out by opening the boiler room access hatch and the blast of air going in cooled the compartment enough to stop the fire. We did the same here by reopening the compartment vents.'

'Bloody well done Commander,' Dave said. 'Frankly, I don't think I would ever have thought of that. Consider yourself an honorary MEO from now on.'

'I'm not sure how much of a compliment that really is Dave but now I've got to work out what the hell to tell the Captain when he gets here.'

Formidable

Three hours later, a flustered but relieved Jon had managed to get back to Devonport and hurry on board. As it was New Year's Day the roads were relatively quiet but he still couldn't get there fast enough. Luckily, the police seemed to all be on holiday as well which was good as he had completely ignored the speed limits. By the time he arrived, he knew everything was under control. Paul had rung him on his mobile phone to tell him that the fire had been extinguished and they were pumping the ship out. That didn't stop him fretting about the damage to his ship and the effect it was going to have on their future programme.

As soon as he climbed the gangway, the Officer of the Day met him and took him straight to HQ1 where the Commander and MEO were waiting for him.

'Sorry I wasn't there to greet you Sir,' Paul said. 'We're still not completely safe. The temperature has now dropped to almost normal. The civilian fire brigade had got thermal cameras and they have been monitoring the situation for us. We're about to open up and go in.'

'In that case you two stay here, I'm going down there now,' Jon said firmly and left before the two men could formulate a reply. Jon shot down the ships main passageway aft to the ladder leading down. He went past the wardroom and down two more ladders. The closer he got to the scene the more he could see what had been going on. Fire hoses snaked down the hatches and when he was almost at the AC plant room he saw several portable pumps in operation with hoses leading down into various surrounding compartments. A gaggle of men in grey fearnought, fire proof suits, were clustered around the main door to the compartment.

One of them turned and saw the Captain. 'Chief Peterson Sir. We're about to do a re-entry. Can I respectfully suggest you get the hell back. We're not totally sure what we're going to find in here.'

Jon realised the Chief was totally right and made his way clear. All the men looked exhausted and the last thing they needed was him getting in the way.

A voice called to him from behind. 'Over here Sir. It's Lieutenant Commander Duncan I'm the DLC.'

'Good morning Duncan. Sorry, I should have looked for you first.'

'Don't worry Sir, I completely understand. We should know the worst very soon.'

The two men looked up the corridor. Suddenly a spray of water appeared as the first hose man turned on his hose with the nozzle set to produce a circular fan of water called a water wall. It would provide protection for the next man who would open the door in case there was still a fire raging inside. The door was closed with a lever operated set of clips and it was clear that it was jammed. The next thing they heard was the dull clang as the lever was attacked by a sledge hammer. It suddenly started to move. The man with the sledgehammer was immediately replaced with another wearing full breathing apparatus who carefully opened the door. Nothing happened. Two more men, with another hose, pushed past him and entered the compartment. There was a loud hissing noise and what appeared to be steam or smoke came out of the door in a cloud but immediately dissipated. A few minutes later, the two men came out and removed their breathing masks.

All the firefighters relaxed and the Chief came down to the two officers. 'Fires completely out Sir. Sorry about being rude but we had to be careful.'

Jon laughed, he could see the Chief was extremely tired. He was amazed he hadn't actually been ruder. 'Chief, don't apologise. I should have checked in with the DLC first. Anyway, how's it looking?'

'Well, we won't be getting any conditioned air for a while, that's for sure Sir. It's cool enough now if you want a look.'

They went back down the corridor and Jon looked in. There was still some residual steam but he could see inside. The compartment appeared almost empty apart from a molten mass on the deck. Jon had never actually been in this particular compartment before but he was pretty sure it should be crammed full of machinery.

He turned back to look at all the fire party who were starting to remove their protective suits and sort out their gear.

'Well done everyone, that was a fantastic job.' He called out. 'Happy New Year and I believe the other thing to say is that Second Leave is Best.'

That got a cheer from them all.

Chapter 21

Max was starting to fret. His leg wound seemed to be healing well and he was keen to get away. Agnes, he refused to call her Sister, had gone away several days ago on a pushbike of all things and said she had passed a message on to the missionary people back in England that he was safe. The more he lay in his bed, the more angry he had become. The only reason he could think of for him and his men being massacred was to hide the fact of their discovery but when he thought deeply about that it didn't make much sense either. The contract they were working under was with the government even if that Chinese bastard was put in overall charge. That had been explained as an administrative issue as the Chinese were funding half of the contract. He hadn't been too surprised by that as everyone knew the Chinese were sucking up to lots of African countries. As long as he got paid and was able to do the job he loved he didn't really care about the overarching politics. Now he wished he had paid more attention although he couldn't see what good it would have done in the end.

Just then Sister Agnes swept in. Without talking, she lifted the bed clothes and inspected the wound. 'It's about time you were walking you lazy Welsh bugger,' she said in her normal forthright manner. 'Here, I got them to make you this,' and she handed him a rough wooden crutch.

Max lay back for a second and regarded her. She was slim and actually quite pretty under the almost permanent scowl. Her hair was blonde almost bleached white under the African sun although most of it was covered by her headscarf. Despite her coarse demeanour, he could see the care in her eyes. He saw it when she tended to the people of the camp as they came in and she treated them as well as she could with her limited medical supplies. He saw it when she held classes for the children or attempted to conduct a religious service. All this was done with him in his bed although she did give him the courtesy of pulling a screen around him when he asked.

'Why are you here Agnes?' he asked softly.

The question seemed to catch her off balance. 'Silly bloody question, you know why I'm here. I'm a missionary.'

'No, that's not what I asked. I know what you are. I asked why you are a missionary.'

'Someone has to care for these people. The British didn't do too bad a job for a while, the French were bloody awful and now the existing government ignore them. They have nothing except what they can get for themselves.'

'And your God tells you to boss them around?'

'I don't boss them. They would never let me do that. No, I try to guide them and bring them the word of God in the process. Now it's too bloody early in the morning for philosophy or religion. Are you going to get out of that bloody bed or what?'

As she said it, she leaned forward to help him up. She was wearing a light khaki shirt with the top button missing. Suddenly, Max could see right down the gap and she wasn't wearing a bra. Her breasts and nipples were there for his examination. The sight was as unexpected as it was delightful.

She saw where his gaze was locked and cuffed him around his good ear. 'And that's enough of that you randy sod. You can bloody well get yourself up. I'm a nun and don't you forget it.'

'Not going to forget that in a hurry,' Max muttered to himself as he sat back up and gently started to swing his legs to the floor. However, he did notice a red flush across Agnes's face and smiled inwardly to himself. Maybe she wasn't quite the tough, celibate woman she liked to think she was.

Two days later and his need to get away was becoming overwhelming. With the help of the crutch, he had managed to walk all around the village which was considerably larger than he had at first realised. The people seemed quite reticent around him and he wondered how they would have treated him without Agnes's presence. That was all, except for the small children who seemed fascinated by him and followed him chattering and laughing whenever they could, until either their parents or Agnes shooed them away. Strangely, it was the surreptitious sight of the nun's naked chest that was catalysing his thoughts. Their very untouchability made him realise how much he was missing his own version of civilisation, which often included young women. He very much felt cut off and alienated in this strange place.

He found Agnes in her hut conducting a surgery and patiently waited for her to finish. When the last family had left, she turned to look at him from behind her desk. 'You want to go home.' It wasn't a question.

'You can read minds as well as talk to God,' Max replied sardonically. 'Yes, I want to go bloody home as you put it. I usually spend a couple of months on survey trips and then it's back to sunny Wales. This isn't my place and I need to talk to the British authorities about what went on.'

'No you don't. You want revenge don't you?'

The question caught Max off balance. Of course he wanted revenge but it was only when Agnes stated it so baldly that he realised it fully himself. 'Those bastards murdered my colleagues and tried to do the same to me. It was cold blooded murder. Of course I want fucking revenge. I also want to know why they did it. And then I want someone held accountable.'

'I haven't asked you this before Max but what did you find? Why do you think it was so important that they decided to wipe you all out? Don't forget that you were found because we could hear the rifle fire. We may be behind these hills but whatever you discovered is close enough that it could affect us all. You owe it to me to tell me.'

Max thought about it. Why shouldn't these people know? If he had the geography of the area right, then the salt pan was part of their local area and part of their economy. He knew that one of their sources of revenue was selling salt to other tribes. At the very least, if the lake was exploited for its riches that line of commerce would stop and he very much doubted that any subsequent wealth generated would filter down to these people.

'Lithium, we found the richest source of Lithium on the planet. The salt lake probably has more than the rest of the world's resources combined. Whoever controls it will be able to hold the rest of the world hostage.'

Agnes looked perplexed. 'I don't understand Max.'

'Lithium is used in batteries. Everything from these new mobile phones people are using to much larger applications. I won't go into the physics but it revolutionises battery technology. Once news of the find gets out, all hell will break loose. It's the reason they tried to remove us from the equation, I'm sure of it although there are still elements of that explanation that I don't really understand.'

'What will it mean for these people Max?'

'Nothing good I don't suppose. In time, this whole area is probably going to be industrialised. As a minimum, they will have to build roads into the site and build an extraction plant. It will take several years but from what you've told me I can't see anyone caring much about any locals. Sorry Agnes but you did ask.'

She sat back and looked hard at Max. 'This could be done properly with minimum impact couldn't it?'

'Of course, but what chance is there that the government will do that? I think you need to prepare these people for the worst. If we could get the UN interested I suppose there's a chance a supervised approach could be taken but don't forget the Chinese are already in bed with the government over this and they sit on the UN Security Council. By the time that lot stop talking in New York it will be far too late.'

'You could help us Max.'

'I don't see that I could do much Agnes. Help me get away and out of the country and I will inform anyone who will listen about what is going on. I don't see there's much more than that I could do.'

She nodded her head in acknowledgement. 'You're right but just getting the word out is going to be a start. Will you come with me and we'll go and talk to the chief about all this? He needs to know. After that we'll see about some transport.'

The next day Max and Agnes sat together in the cab of the old truck that had brought him to the village. It was a tight squeeze with the driver there as well but far better than sitting in the back. Max's thigh was pushed up hard against Agnes's and the jolts of the truck made for a good degree of almost intimate contact. He wondered how she was taking it but concentrated on the view ahead. They stopped at the ambush site. It was clear that Jackals had made inroads into the burial pit. There were human bones scattered around it. Agnes had brought her old camera and allowed Max to shoot one of her precious rolls of film for evidence and then it was another four hours to get to the nearest town to meet with the resident priest.

Max was totally surprised when he met Father Joseph. Yet another cleric who didn't dress in any way as he expected. Tall and very thin with almost no hair, he was wearing shorts and khaki just like Agnes and there was no sign of a dog collar. He also looked to be in his seventies although Agnes had explained that he was, in fact, only sixty one. He had been in Ukundu for over twenty years and, like Agnes, the toll of the African climate had aged him prematurely.

What surprised Max even more, was his welcome or rather lack thereof. After a very quick introduction, he was hustled into Father Joseph's house, an old, single story, adobe building and taken to a desk with a telephone on it.

'The line's not that reliable but after I spoke to home, things started to get very interesting. The next day I got a call from a man who identified himself as being from British Intelligence. He didn't say that exactly, it was clear he was worried that the line wasn't secure but I got the message. He wants to talk to you Max as soon as he can. I have his number here.'

Chapter 22

Jon looked up at the massive Cold War jet, the Sea Vixen that was displayed outside the headquarters of Flag Officer Naval Air Command at Yeovilton. The modern office block had been built on the opposite side of the main road that cut through the air station and had originally been surrounded by playing fields. It was now itself surrounded by new buildings as part of the MOD's continuing attempt to move out of expensive real estate in London.

The twin tail boomed aircraft looked exciting and Jon wondered what it was really like to fly. He knew that they had had their share of mishaps particularly the earlier versions but that was expected at the time. Accident rates like that would not be tolerated these days. Putting such thoughts out of his mind, he entered the double glass doors and there waiting for him was an old friend. Paul Glaser was a Captain like himself and Chief of Staff to the Admiral. He had been Jon's instructor all those years ago when he had first been learning to fly. Jon found it a little odd that they were now both in the same rank although Jon knew that Paul was soon to retire.

'Welcome Jon,' Paul boomed. He had never been a quiet officer. In some ways he reminded Jon of his friend Brian Pearce as they were both navy rugby players and built accordingly but Paul had almost no hair now and peered at Jon through quite thick glasses. 'The Admiral has asked me to give his apologies but he's had to go up to London so you'll have to put up with me today.'

'That shouldn't be a problem,' Jon laughed as he took Paul's proffered hand.

'Right, come on up to my office and we'll have a chat and then I'll do the introductions.' He led Jon up the wide carpeted stairs to a bright office that overlooked the air station in the distance. A pretty young girl came in with coffee and then left without a word.

'So, how's the steamer Jon?' Paul asked. 'I've read the Board of Enquiry report but it's always worth hearing things from the horse's mouth.'

'We're good to go Paul. The fire did remarkably little damage to the rest of the ship. There was some water damage and we had to write off some stores. I'm sure the Supply Officer had a great time rationalising his inventory.' Jon said this with a smile.

'Hah, just like when Atlantic Conveyor went down in the Falklands. I've heard tell that if you weighed the amount of stores she was supposed to have been carrying it would have sunk her three times over.'

Jon laughed in agreement. 'I heard that too. There's nothing like a good disaster to make sure all your missing stores items are accounted for. But seriously we've cleaned her up and the engineering staff and FOF3 have declared us operational. We're not going to replace the air conditioning plant until our first refit. The other plant and chilled water systems are sufficient to keep our electronics going. If we go somewhere hot it will be uncomfortable but there's nothing new in that. We've both been to the Gulf in un-air-conditioned ships as have most of my men. We can live with it.'

Paul nodded. 'So we can get on with our planned little experiment then?'

'Yes but can you explain the command and control? I'm still a little confused.'

'Simple, we at FONAC are leading on the policy which means liaison with everyone and making sure everything will work from logistics to which regulations to follow. Once at sea, you come under the Operational Command of FOF3.'

'That's as I saw it but it's good to have it confirmed Paul. So, where are we all meeting up?' Jon asked.

'Downstairs in the main conference room.' Paul looked at a wall clock. 'I said eleven o'clock and that's now so let's go and see everyone.'

When the two Captains entered the conference room it was crowded. The one major difference that stood out starkly was that the majority of officers in the room were wearing light blue. At the front was an Air Commodore. Jon had been warned that this might happen. The RAF always seemed to want to have the most senior man they could at any meeting and preferably one more senior than any other service present. There were also two Group Captains and five Wing Commanders. The dark blue in the meeting, apart from themselves, were three naval commanders from FONAC staff and Pete Moore the Commanding Officer of 888, who was the only Lieutenant Commander present. *'This is going to be fun,'* Jon thought to himself while keeping a neutral expression on his face.

Formidable

Paul went to the lectern. 'Good morning everyone. I'm glad to see you made it down from High Wycombe and Wittering in time. I assume the traffic wasn't too bad or you came down last night?'

There were several nods from the assembled officers. 'Good, I would like to introduce you all to Captain Hunt the Commanding Officer of HMS Formidable and the man who will have overall responsibility for making the next four months a success.'

Jon noticed a few sour looks on the faces of the more senior officers. He could understand why. Passing operational control of some of your key assets to another service was never going to be popular. However, he wasn't going to let that affect any of the key decisions that needed to be made today.

Paul continued. 'Now, in a minute, Jon will give a quick brief on the ship. No doubt you will all have heard that there was a small incident on board over the New Year but I'm happy to say that all is well and the ship is operational. I would point out that it clearly makes the point about why we were so insistent that any of your people going to sea conduct the basic fire fighting and sea survival training as a prerequisite. After that, Air Commodore Smith will give us an overview of where we are with aircraft preparation and particularly aircrew training to operate off a ski jump fitted ship and also some general points about the capabilities of the Harrier GR7. Then we will break up into working groups for the rest of the day to ensure that all key areas have been properly covered. Tomorrow, we will all go down to Devonport and visit the ship. A Jetstream has been arranged to fly us down to Roborough in Plymouth. Jon over to you.'

Jon thanked Paul and took his place at the lectern.

By the end of the day, it was looking good. Jon was pleasantly surprised by the attitude of the RAF officers. Operating from a ship was very much out of most of their comfort zones but they all seemed genuinely keen to give it a try. He did wonder how they would feel after several months away from friends and family. While it might be the norm for naval personnel, it wasn't something the RAF ever really had to put up with. Jon was staying overnight in the wardroom as were most of the officers who had attended the meeting so the mess had put on a special dinner for them. Once the drink had flowed a little and everyone was relaxing Jon took the opportunity to talk to his two squadron Commanding Officers. He had especially asked to be seated

Formidable

with them for dinner. Wing Commander Bob Everrett was the CO of 88 Squadron RAF. He looked surprisingly young for such a rank with thick dark hair and penetrating blue eyes. He obviously kept himself fit. There wasn't an ounce of fat on him. Jon had already had a brief chance to talk to him earlier and so far was very impressed.

'So which joker gave your squadron that number?' Jon asked him as they filled their port glasses after the meal and speeches had finished.

'Coincidence Sir, honestly,' Bob Everrett answered. 'We stood up in the middle of last year before we even knew we were going to get this task.'

'Well, if we ever end up going on combined operations we can call ourselves 88888 Squadron, that should confuse everyone including the enemy,' Pete Moore observed wryly.

'Look Sir and Pete there's something I would like to sort out right at the start,' Bob said in a slightly concerned tone.

'Yes go on Bob,' Jon answered. 'We're in the mess and rank tabs are off if that's what you're worried about.'

'That's the point Sir. The two squadrons will be operating together for some time. I know space is limited so we will have six aircraft and only four of Peter's but I'm senior to Pete. I really don't know how we square that.'

Jon was actually relieved that this was out in the open so early. He had been wondering how to manage the issue as well. He had already decided on an approach and was grateful that Bob had brought it up. 'It's quite simple Bob, as far as I'm concerned you are both equal. You both command your respective squadrons and you both answer to Wings and then to me. As far as interaction in the ship, you are a rank above Pete and I'm sure he'll have no issues with that but as far as the important element goes I will make no distinctions.'

To Jon's surprise, Bob frowned at the reply. 'That's not quite what I meant Sir. When it comes to tactical decisions do I take charge of all the aircraft?'

Jon was puzzled by the question and then the penny dropped. Before he could reply Pete got in first. 'Sorry Bob, we don't get to make the tactical decisions, that's the Captain's responsibility. He will look to us for advice but in the final analysis we are just a weapon system in the ship that he deploys as he decides. Another way to look at it, is that in a warship the Commanding Officer is the final authorising officer and responsible for fighting the whole ship which includes all of us.'

'But I'm the authorising officer for my aircraft,' Bob protested.

'Not at sea you're not,' Pete replied firmly. 'You don't leave the deck unless the 'clear to launch light' goes green and that is a command decision.'

Jon could see that Bob was far from happy with that reply although it was absolutely correct. However, he also understood the problem. In the RAF, the Squadron CO had far more direct tactical responsibility and freedom to act as they were a fighting unit in their own right.

'Bob, let's not get bogged down in semantics. You are correct in one sense and I expect you or your delegated officers to authorise individual sorties just as you do now. I also expect you to provide me with tactical advice on how you would deploy and fight your aircraft but Pete is right. The final decision on how and when to actually deploy you is mine and mine alone. I expect you and Pete to work together as a team, despite the difference in rank. That's the point I made earlier. I look on you both as specialists in your own rights. After all, the aircraft may be Harriers but one is a quite sophisticated fighter and the other is designed for ground attack. And you have yet to operate at sea which can be quite a different issue. Pete has been doing it for years and I'm sure he will be able to offer a great deal of practical advice.'

Jon could see the answer wasn't what his new Squadron CO expected or wanted but there was no getting around it. He deliberately steered the conversation to other matters but secretly worried that the coming months could be difficult unless the situation was resolved and accepted quickly.

Chapter 23

Rupert was sitting at his desk going through the paperwork that had been provided by the Welsh geographical survey company. There were the details of the contract with the Ukundu government but more importantly as far as he was concerned was the personnel record of the surviving man. His call to the priest had yielded that one piece of vital information.

He was just thinking about going out to lunch when the phone rang. It was the switchboard, they had a call for him from abroad. He listened for a few seconds his hopes rising as he did.

'Mr Max Llewellyn, I am very glad to be able to speak to you at last,' he said. 'Where are you?'

As the man at the other end spoke Rupert looked at the map that was to one side of his desk. It was the same phone that the priest had rung in from earlier. That was good because it meant it was still up country. He had been worried that they might have gone further back towards the capital. Rupert was also very glad to confirm who the man actually was and getting this person was the jackpot.

'Mr Llewellyn, let me stop you there. This line is not secure and I really don't want to say any more until we can talk freely. Are you prepared to stay where you are for the next two days and then I can get some secure equipment to you?'

They talked briefly for a few more minutes and then he agreed to call again in two hour's time. Next he dialled another number. Contingency plans for just his sort of situation were already in place. He spoke to his boss for a few minutes and got the authorisation he needed and then set the wheels in motion. He suddenly realised he hadn't felt this alive for ages.

Precisely two hours later, the phone rang in the priest's room and Max grabbed it. He listened for a few minutes and then told the other end to hold on. Putting his hand over the receiver he turned to Father Joseph. 'Do you have a map of the area Father, one with latitude and longitude on it?'

Father Joseph opened a desk drawer and pulled out a very old, folded map. 'Will this do? I've used it for years. It's probably a bit out of date.'

Formidable

Max opened it out. Although quite faded from use and time, it did have latitude and longitude scales. He picked up the phone and listened again. 'Hang on, let me write it down and check it,' he replied and then using a pen wrote down a series of numbers. 'OK, I'll just talk to my colleagues.'

He quickly plotted a position on the map and called his two companions over to look at it. 'They're proposing an air drop of some equipment at this position in the early hours of tomorrow morning. What do you think? You two know the area better than me.'

Father Joseph nodded. 'That would be alright. It's pretty remote there but the terrain is fairly rough. If they moved two miles or so to the east they would have a flatter area and you would be able to watch from this ridge and make sure no one else saw it without giving yourself away.'

Max nodded. 'Good advice Father. You aren't ex -military by any chance?'

'French Foreign legion my son but that's a story for another day.'

'Hang on Max,' Agnes interrupted. 'Did they say how large a drop it's going to be?'

'No but it's going to be a Hercules. You know one of those large transport planes.'

'Ok tell them I could really do with some more drugs and medical equipment, also some more bibles. If they argue, point out that keeping the local people on side will be to their advantage.'

Max nodded, amazed by Agnes's quick thinking and put the receiver back to his ear. The debate was quite short although he had to get Agnes to be more specific about exactly what supplies she wanted. They promised to do what they could.

Twelve hours later, Max and Agnes were sitting on top of a low ridge overlooking a long deep valley. The same old truck was parked several hundred yards behind them with the driver fast asleep in the cab. They knew that because they could hear the snoring even from such a distance.

'At least that bloody noise should scare away any lions,' Max observed as he looked towards where the horizon was barely visible. It was a partly cloudy night and there was no moon so it was very dark.

'Not many of those around here,' Agnes replied. 'I love this time of day, just before the sun comes up and God gives us another day.'

Max snorted derision. 'You mean before the planet rotates on its axis and the terminator reaches us.'

'You are such a cynic Max Llewellyn. There is no poetry in your soul.' Agnes sounded sad.

'Pragmatist my dear. So tell me, you clearly weren't born a nun, so when did you get bitten by this God of yours?'

'I wasn't bitten and it's none of your damned business.'

'No. I'm actually serious. There must have been something, some incident that convinced you? I would really like to know what it was.'

She heard the sincerity in his voice and decided to tell him. Maybe he would understand, maybe he would see the logic. 'Eleven years ago, I was happily married and had a husband and two little children. One evening there was an accident on the M25. A Polish lorry driver fell asleep at the wheel of his HGV and didn't see the queue of vehicles that were stopped ahead of him and ploughed into them at fifty six miles an hour. Forty tons of lorry at that speed is a massive amount of energy. My family were in the rear car. I never identified the bodies, it was impossible, they had to use DNA matching.' She said it all as though it had actually happened to someone else.

Max was dumbstruck. Not because of the tragedy, that was bad enough but at its outcome. 'And something like that turned you to God? I'm sorry that just doesn't make sense to me.'

'Nor me at the start. I was desperate to lay blame. The lorry driver was killed too so I couldn't get revenge on him. I started to try to make sense of the whole thing. A vicar called on me soon after and I threw him out of the house. Then, one day, a few months later I was walking past a church and for no reason at the time, I went in. I had been brought up a Catholic and this was a Catholic church. I knelt down at the back and suddenly realised that there had to be a reason for what had happened. And if there was a reason then there was only one person who could have planned it. It was a comfort in a way I find hard to describe and once I had made the leap and acknowledged his presence, in time all the rest started to make sense. Several years later, I came out here to do his work.'

Her statement was met with silence. A band of gold was starting to appear on the eastern horizon. 'Surely you see the beauty Max. Who else could give us that?'

Max finally laughed but it was a sad sound. 'Seven years ago, I had been married for two years and my wife was expecting. The baby she gave birth to was deformed and brain damaged. None of the doctors could explain why and nothing had shown up on the scans. He died nine months later. My wife and I couldn't cope and eventually we separated. Now, you tell me why a loving God would do such a thing? Why he would invent cancer and Downs Syndrome and Mosquitos that bring malaria to millions. And your religion wants me to bow down and worship such an entity? Well he can fuck right off because he clearly doesn't give a toss about me or any of us. Sorry Agnes, I can follow the logic of some sort of creator but if I ever get to meet it, it won't be love or worship it gets from me.'

It was Agnes's turn to be silent as the dawn slowly broke. Eventually she spoke. 'Funny isn't it how two almost identical tragedies have led to two people coming to two totally opposing viewpoints?'

'Just don't tell me it's all some sort of fucking plan lady.'

'No Max, I wouldn't do that. We all have to live our own lives.'

The conversation was interrupted by a low growling sound to the north. Several minutes later, the outline of a large, four engine aircraft appeared very low over the hills. Within what seemed like only seconds, it roared down the valley and was gone. Behind it was the mushroom shape of a large green parachute which was already collapsing as the load underneath it hit the ground.

They ran back to the lorry and within minutes were at the load. It was a large square green container with metal clips down one side. Max immediately went to bundle up the large parachute.

'We'll keep that,' Agnes called. 'It will come in useful for all sorts of things.'

They then loaded the crate onto the back of the truck. It took the three of them to lift it. 'It's all those bloody bibles,' Max grunted as they finally slid it onto the bed of the truck.

Agnes decided to say nothing.

Two hours later, they were back at her hut. Agnes had managed to get the curious locals away with a mixture of threats and promises and they were finally alone. Inside the crate were several large boxes of medical supplies. They took them out first and she put them to one side but she was pleased to see antibiotics and other malaria drugs amongst them. Someone in England had a good idea of what she would need. There were indeed bibles. Two cases of twenty four each which was more than she had expected. And in total contrast, some sort of rifle and a pistol along with green metal cases of what must be ammunition. While she was looking at these, Max had taken out a large green fibre glass box which he opened. Inside, embedded in black foam was a curious device. It looked like an overlarge mobile phone with a very large aerial on one side. Max found a sheet of instructions and sat down to read while Agnes started to catalogue the medical supplies.

After a few minutes Agnes called over to him. 'What is it Max? Some sort radio?'

'More than that, it's an encrypted satellite phone. I've heard of them but never seen one,' he replied. 'Give me a minute and I should be able to call whoever it is that sent it to us.'

He fiddled with the device a little more while referring to the instructions and then held it to his ear. It was answered immediately.

'Max, my name is Rupert Thomas and I work for MI6. Now we can talk safely.' The voice at the other end said.

'That was quick, you must have been waiting for me,' Max responded.

'You've no idea. Now just to confirm, you are the Max Llewellyn who until some years ago was a Sergeant in the Royal Marines and latterly a member of the Special Boat Service?'

Max felt his heart sink. He knew he shouldn't have been surprised but he had held out a vague hope that they wouldn't find out. 'Yes, that's me but I'm retired from all that.'

'Sorry old chap but you are still on the emergency reserve list and I'm authorised to activate that in times of national need. And this is one of those times.'

Chapter 24

'It's not going to work Sir,' Wings said to Jon as both men looked out over the flight deck which was crowded with aircraft. They were standing together in the Flying Control position that jutted out from the side of the island known as 'FLYCO'.

'Go on Wings. Why not?'

'Not enough airframes Sir. Serviceability has been pretty good but we don't have enough FA2's to maintain a full time Combat Air Patrol and if we keep pilots on deck at high alert they still get knackered and the reaction time is severely degraded. We need the full squadron as we had in the American exercise last year.'

Jon privately agreed with the assessment but wanted Wings to make his case. They needed to be on the same hymn sheet for this one. 'So why not use some of the RAF machines in that role, they carry Sidewinders don't they?'

'Two problems with that Sir, they have cannon as well but both are dog fighting, visual range weapons. AMRAAM and radar on the SHARs give us area protection and secondly what do we do when we need the 7s for their primary role? That's likely to be when the threat is the highest and they will be needed elsewhere.'

'Good points all,' Jon conceded. 'So what's the answer?'

Wings smiled because both men knew what it was. 'If we are needed in an autonomous role without any other air support, then we need maximum overload Sir. Sixteen cabs.'

'I agree,' Jon said as he watched a GR7 in the distance as it turned downwind and lowered its undercarriage. 'We've been at sea for a month now and both squadrons are fully worked up day and night so I think we are in a position to start putting words on paper for our Lords and Masters. I would like you to get a first draft ready for us all to discuss.'

Wings grinned. 'Already started Sir. Fuck, that doesn't look right.' He turned to Lieutenant Commander (Flying), commonly known as Little 'F', who was controlling the aircraft in the landing circuit. 'F, what's that cab doing? He's far too low.'

'No idea Sir, he's not made a call. Hang on,' said Little F as he turned towards the radio microphone in front of him. 'Whiskey Tango confirm finals and you are too low, increase power over.'

Formidable

For a second nothing was heard. The aircraft was almost alongside the stern of the ship now and still sinking slowly down. It was already at the same height of the flight deck and it was quite clear it wasn't going to make it and nor would it be possible for it to transition back into forward flight. Little F didn't wait for any further response, he grabbed the microphone and shouted 'Eject, Eject.'

There was a gout of fire and smoke from the Harrier as the pilot ejected and the rocket pack on the bottom of the seat fired him upwards and clear. At the same time Little F hit the 'crash on deck' button and a loud warning blared over the ships broadcast. Everyone on the flight deck reacted instantly. They all knew exactly what to do.

The aircraft still had a little forward momentum and maybe because of the loss of weight as the pilot and his seat left it actually started to level off and roll to port before ploughing into the stern of the ship. There was a loud explosion which could be heard from behind the armoured glass windows of FLYCO. The noise was accompanied by a small blast of flame as the wrecked machine fell into the ships wake and started to sink.

Jon ran the short distance back to the bridge and called to the Officer of the Watch. 'Launch the sea boat then turn us towards the man in the water.' He realised that he was actually too late as the OOW was already doing just that.

Jon was once again in that strange position of being almost helpless. He knew Wings and the flight deck team would be handling any issues on deck and that the standing sea fire party were already mustering below decks aft to manage the situation there. The OOW was doing a fine job in getting the sea boat launched and he didn't want to interfere unless something went wrong so all he could do was take his seat on the bridge and listen to what was happening and wait.

He didn't have to wait long. Wings came in to speak to him. 'Burnt paint on the stern Sir, nothing worse.'

'Good, who was the pilot?'

'Bob Everrett Sir, 88's CO.'

The ship was turning hard now and both men could see the ship's sea boat, a large RIB, blasting across the sea towards a bright orange dinghy, which could only mean that the pilot was at least conscious and able to do his survival drills.

'Shame we can't have a permanent helicopter plane guard like the old carriers did,' Wings observed.

Formidable

'Well, we always knew that this design was a compromise,' Jon replied. 'And let's face it aircraft are far more reliable now. Mind you I'd love to know what happened to that cab. It seemed to be on full power, so why couldn't it maintain a hover?'

'It's going to be difficult without the wreck to examine Sir. We're in over a thousand metres of water out here and its long gone by now. Hopefully, Bob will be able to tell us.'

Half an hour later Jon made his way down to Sick Bay. Bob Everrett was lying on a bed with a brace on his neck. Jon took the doctor aside. 'How is he doc? He doesn't look too sharp.'

'There's normal ejection seat damage Sir,' the doctor replied. 'But his head took a bad knock that's why he's in a neck brace. Something must have gone wrong with the ejection sequence.'

'Can I talk to him?'

'Yes, but don't be too long. I'm about to try and X-ray his back and neck.'

Jon nodded and went over to the bed. 'Told you that naval landings can get you wet old chap.'

Bob grinned weakly. 'Sorry about that Sir. Bloody aircraft just wouldn't hold its height even with full throttle and water injection on. I got so side tracked with things getting so bloody busy so fast I didn't even have time to make a radio call. Not very professional I'm afraid.'

'None of that is an issue Bob. The doc is going to X-ray you now and then I expect we'll get you ashore. I've cancelled all flying for the moment and signalled FOF 3 that I intend to return to base. The first phase of the trial was just about complete anyway so we've lost nothing there. Your number two can take over. You just concentrate on looking after yourself.'

The doctor came over and hustled Jon out of the way.

Three days later Jon and his command team were in Devonport conducting a hot wash up with FONAC and FOF3 staff before going up to High Wycombe the next day for the full debrief with the Air Force.

'The latest on the CO of 88 is that my doc thinks he may have a fractured neck vertebra,' Jon said to the assembled officers. 'The best guess is that the canopy didn't fracture properly and he clobbered a bit in the way out. They may have to replace him.'

'How was overall integration Jon,' someone asked.

'Frankly, I was extremely impressed with how well the RAF guys settled in, especially the lads. They took a great deal of stick from the sailors of course but gave as good as they got. Our mess decks are better than most but even so it must have been quite a culture shock. I've got a three badge AB who is quite a useful sounding board and even he said they're good lads. Can't think of a better endorsement. On the flying side, once they got the idea of being part of the ships overall weapon system everything was fine. But you've all seen my preliminary report, the mix of aircraft wasn't optimal and if we ever had to deploy for real then I would really want eight of each. I know it's far more than we were designed to take but we can make it work.'

Jon was about to say more when a young lieutenant put his head around the door and called one of the FOF3 staff officers away. He returned a few moments later with a white sheet of paper in his hand. He looked up from the signal to the assembled officers. 'Not quite sure what this is all about but it looks like the Captain of Formidable might just get his wish.'

Chapter 25

Rupert was amazed at how fast things had escalated. The key factor had been the conversation with the surviving surveyor. Once it was clear that a massacre of British nationals had definitely taken place and that a Chinese national had been involved in some way as well, all hell had broken loose. The Foreign and Commonwealth Office had immediately become involved and almost immediately the issue had gone to the Cabinet. For the moment, the party line was to wait and see how the situation developed. The Prime Minister would need hard evidence before making any formal protests but once the discovery of the Lithium was made public all bets would be off.

However, the Defence Secretary wasn't prepared to sit on his hands and had gathered the Defence Chiefs to discuss options. Memories of doing nothing until it was too late in nineteen eighty two were still fresh in people's minds. For the duration, Rupert had been given overall charge of the intelligence operation and had formed a core team of staff to work with him.

They were all gathered together for a progress meeting which Rupert had called. 'First of all what have we got on this Zhang Li character?' he asked.

One of the analysts spoke up. 'A little and none of it good. We got some intel from Mister Llewellyn. Zhang speaks good English and is clearly well educated. We dug around university records and found him. Son of a government official, very much a party man and well up of the greasy pole of Chinese politics. His degree was in geology which is probably why they gave him the task of overseeing the mineral survey. I suspect he is highly ambitious and even more highly motivated now that he's in the middle of this situation. Having said that, any decisions for deploying military assets will be way above his pay grade and no doubt taken in Beijing. However, on that subject, we've had our assets in China ask around and there is an indication that it's possible that the aircraft have actually been sold to Ukundu as a first tranche of military support. It seems that the French were approached last year and declined any further arms sales so they turned to the Chinese. If that's the case then they are there to stay. However, our assessment is that this had nothing to do with the

Lithium find, its just happenstance. The timescales are all wrong for a start.'

Before anyone could answer there was a knock on the door and a man came in carrying several photographs. 'Sorry to interrupt but we've got some interesting satellite images that have just come in.' He spread them on the table in front of Rupert.

'What am I looking at Ted?' Rupert asked as he studied the black and white photos.

'This is the main port of the country. It's also where the tiny Ukundu navy operate from. It's just a coastal force of a few small patrol boats. Because of the alert, we decided to have a good look at all their military facilities and we spotted these. They weren't there a week ago.'

One of Rupert's team identified them at once. 'Those are two Type 37 Chinese missile boats and they're parked up alongside a support ship. We wondered where they had gone. They were being watched but only on a casual basis. They rarely leave the Pacific. We thought they were just trying to expand their reach a little. It seems likely that they have been sold to Ukundu as well, the timing would be right.'

Rupert sat back and thought. 'So it's not just aircraft now. They have an effective little navy as well. And then there is the question of who is manning these aircraft and planes. I seem to remember that in the Korean War most of the Migs were actually flown by Soviet pilots.' He sighed. 'They must know that we know at least something of what they are doing even if they haven't realised that we know about the Lithium. This sort of overt posturing is something new.'

'We know the policy in Beijing has changed recently, maybe this is the first manifestation,' Malcolm offered. 'Maybe they're testing the west's resolve to intervene in Africa.'

'Well, one thing we must do is talk to the French,' Rupert said. 'They still have a great deal of influence in the area. I have some contacts with their security people. I'll try and see if they have any inside line on what is going on. It will be difficult though as I don't want to give the game away about the find unless the cabinet approve it. Alright everyone, the priority is to find out more about these ships and aircraft but more importantly what the Chinese real intentions are. We'll meet again this time tomorrow.'

Zhang Li was sitting at his desk in the Embassy also wondering what on earth was going on. Despite his success in keeping the major discovery secret and getting a cast iron agreement with the Ukundu government for joint exploitation, the situation seemed to be escalating with the arrival of the military. He knew that the sale of the aircraft and ships had been underway for some time and training had been going on back in China over recent months. His plan was to bring in the civil engineering people and start building the extraction plant as soon as possible. Indeed, ships were already loading with men and equipment and should be here within a fortnight. Once the extraction plant was up and running then the rest of the world would only be able to look on in admiration as the two countries reaped the reward. His country's stock in Africa would soar and opportunities elsewhere would open up. He wanted to be able to take all the credit for himself.

There was a knock on his door and an aid came in. 'Li, this just came in, I thought it would be of interest to you so brought it straight in.'

'What is it?' Li asked testily. He hated having his thoughts interrupted, especially when they centred around his forthcoming success.

'Sorry, it is a telephone intercept between their Interior Minister and someone up country. We've not been able to identify who it is he is talking to but the meaning of the conversation is quite clear.'

Li knew that all the telephone lines of the Ukundu government were routinely monitored but it was unusual for an intercept to be brought straight to him. 'Give it to me,' he ordered. He glanced down at the words and then ordered the man away. When he had gone, he read it again, not sure whether the message was a problem or not. It seemed they did not want to use the army for this operation, presumably so they could deny things if they became too public. However, there was serious risk in using a local semi-terrorist group even if the monetary rewards being offered were so high. He sighed there was not exactly much he could do.

Max was woken up by a single gunshot, then screams and the revving of diesel engines. He could tell it was just dawn because there was a faint light filtering in from the gaps around the door. He sat up quickly. There was no sign of Agnes who normally slept on the other side of the hut. He had continued to use the simple hospital bed as it was the most comfortable around. He grabbed his shorts and shirt and rushed to the door only to be almost knocked over by Agnes as she flew in from outside.

'What's going on?' He asked.

'Soldiers, or at least that's what I think they are. They're not in any uniform I recognise. They arrived a few minutes ago and told everyone they had to leave. The Chief tried to argue so they shot him. Fucking bastards. They're rounding everyone up now at gun point. This has got to be something to do with the lake hasn't it?'

'Shit I don't know, let me think. Yes, I can't think what else it could be. We have to get away.' He turned and pulled the telephone case out from under the bed. 'London need to know about this.'

Agnes rushed over to her medical cabinet and started stuffing supplies into an old grip. 'What are you doing girl? You don't need those.' Max shouted when he saw what she was up to.

'Who said I was going with you Max? You need to get away now and use that telephone and tell the world what's going on. I'm staying with my people.'

'But, you silly sodding nun, you don't know what they're going to do. They could be bent on genocide. It won't be the first time on this fucking continent.'

'Then you'd better get on that bloody phone fast and get the word out hadn't you?'

'You had better take this then,' Max said firmly and tried to hand her the Browning nine millimetre pistol that had come in the air drop.

Agnes looked at it as though it was a venomous snake. 'Not on your life. I will never use such a thing, ever. Laugh if you wish but now is definitely the time to trust in the Lord. Take care Max.'

To his surprise, she gave him a quick peck on the cheek and then turned and hurried out. In her haste, she didn't see Max drop the gun into the open top of the grip.

Max grabbed the SA80 assault rifle that had also been in the air drop and the suitcase for the telephone, there was no time to take anything else. He carefully looked out of the entrance. All the noise was coming from the centre of the village. If he had been in charge of such an operation he would have ensured that the whole place was surrounded before moving in. He had no faith that whoever these people were they had that much sense but he had to assume the worst. He carefully made his way in the opposite direction away from the noise. At one point, he saw a man with an AK47 but no military insignia, herding people up between a gap in the huts but was easily able to hide. Within minutes, he was at the edge of the village. He dropped to one knee and looked around carefully. 'Silly buggers,' he muttered to himself before settling into a jog and heading up into the hills.

Rupert was in the Operations room that had been set up once the situation in Ukundu escalated when the call came in.

'Where are you Max?' he asked when Max had told him about the raid on the village.

'In the hills above where the village stands. They didn't have enough trucks so they are making everyone walk and I'm shadowing them.'

'What do you think their intentions are?'

'Good question. At the moment they're just being forced to walk to the east. My thoughts are that if they were going to commit some sort of genocide they would have done it by now.'

'And what of Sister Agnes? Has anything happened to her?'

'Good question, I can't actually see her but there are hundreds of people. If she's got any sense at all she will try to keep in the crowd and out of sight. Hang on a second. Give me a few minutes, something is happening up ahead.'

Rupert sat and waited. He knew better than to badger Max for information. Five minutes later Max came back on the line. 'Another group of people have joined the main group from the east. Not as many but clearly the population of another village. Look, I'm going to have to limit my calls. The battery on this thing is already showing half a charge and I've no way of recharging it.'

'That's fine, call me this evening or if anything else significant happens.' Rupert heard the line click dead.

As soon as he had finished, Rupert grabbed another phone. 'Get me the Secretary of State for Defence,' he ordered.

Chapter 26

Jon looked around the bridge of Formidable. Everything was quiet and familiar, unlike the last hectic forty eight hours. The ship had been stored and her fuel bunkers topped off before going to a buoy and taking on a full load of weapons and ammunition. Her magazines were completely full. They were now steaming into wind in Lyme Bay waiting for the first aircraft to re-embark. The two Sea King Mark 4s and the Lynx Mark 8 from Yeovilton were expected first, then the eight Sea Harrier FA2s and then last of all eight GR7s from further away. As soon as they were all on board they would join up with their escorts, the Type 23 Frigate HMS Hampshire and the Type 42 destroyer HMS Swansea. Jon was glad to have them both, not only because they would give him the anti-submarine and anti-air capabilities that his ship lacked but also it was good to have his old friend Brian Pearce along for the ride. A tanker and stores ship would be setting out from Gibraltar to meet up with them off the African coast.

Jon decided it was a good time to talk to the ship's company. There hadn't been any real opportunity since their emergency sailing order had been given.

He picked up the main broadcast microphone. 'D'you hear there? This is the Captain speaking.' He knew that just about every member of the ship's company would be listening intently to what he had to say. 'Firstly, let me apologise for not being able to tell you all what this is all about before, although I'm sure that Able Seaman Jones has kept you all entertained with his theories. We are going to the west coast of Africa. Some British nationals have been attacked in Ukundu, some have been killed and some may be in need of rescue. However, at this point in time we are only going there as a contingency force. There is also a significant military presence in the country from the Chinese which complicates matters further. But as I said we are not deploying for a fight merely to have our own powerful presence in the area. At least that's what the politicians have told us. On that basis, once we have the full Air Group on board this ship will work up to full war status. Once past Gibraltar, when our tankers join us we will go to defence watches. We can hope for a simple solution to this but we will damn well prepare for the worst. If we have to, let's show what Formidable can do. That is all.' He put the microphone down, hoping he had caught the tone right. One thing he was absolutely sure of was that despite what any bloody politician or senior staff officer told him, he was not going to be caught with his trousers down. He knew exactly how fast things could escalate.

Ten minutes later, the three helicopters appeared and landed on to be struck down into the hangar straight away. The rest of the afternoon was hectic, not just recovering the jets but also stowing them according to the plan they had carefully worked out previously. Jon was pleased to see Bob Everrett climb out of the last RAF Harrier to land on. He hadn't been looking forward to a new and untried CO taking the reins in what could quickly become a shooting scenario. As it was, there would be several new aircrew who would be getting a crash course in deck operations over the next few days.

The Commander appeared at Jon's elbow. 'That seemed to go down well Sir,' he said. 'At least it will stop all the buzzes now.'

Jon snorted a laugh. 'Never, Paul. Sailors will always find something to generate a good buzz, you know that.'

'True enough Sir. Anyway I think we're all settled now. The only accommodation problem was the Special Forces guys.'

'Ah yes how many were there in the end?'

'Fifteen Sir, plus one Captain of Marines. He wasn't a problem but his lads were. However, the Regulating Chief did a minor miracle and managed to free up one mess deck for them. Of course being SF maybe we should have let them sleep on the upper deck somewhere, without camp beds just to make them feel at home.'

'Oh no, the ones I've met all like to make themselves comfortable when they can. Mind you, they don't particularly like ships I seem to remember. 'Floating coffins' one called one of my ships in the past. Mind you, he was SAS and all these lads are SBS I understand?'

'Yes Sir all died in the wool Royal Marines. I understand the chap who is in Ukundu is an ex-Marine as well. Their Captain mentioned that he was well known at one time.'

'Yes, it was a bit of luck if you can call it that. I wouldn't be surprised if our first job is to get him out so we can speak to him directly. Could you look around the corner into FLYCO and see if Wings is about?'

Formidable

'No need Sir, I'm already here,' came the cheery reply as Tim Malone appeared on the bridge. 'All safely on board Sir, all stowed as planned and we can start training for the new aircrew within the hour.'

'As long as we generate the right wind Tim,' Jon replied. 'Our priority now is to get south as fast as we can and if that means curtailing flying then we will have to accept that.' Jon then called to Amelie Smith who had the watch. 'Signal the Hampshire and Swansea Amelie and get us heading south at twenty four knots as planned.'

She nodded and turned to give the necessary orders.

Jon looked back at Wings. 'As I was about to say to Paul just now Tim, I want you to work up a plan to get into the country to retrieve this chap ashore. It's a bloody long way and we may have to do it completely covertly but my thoughts were that the Lynx with an overload tank and maybe a Sea King acting as a re-fueler might make it possible.'

'Hmm, something like that could work Sir. I'll get the lads onto number crunching straight away but that might be the easy bit.'

'What do you mean?'

'Well, a one man extraction is one thing but what if we have to get the SF guys in to do a more serious piece of work, like forcibly extracting our remaining nationals?'

'OK look at it but my thoughts were that if it came to that, then we would be looking at an air drop and evacuation to somewhere like Nigeria which is much closer and ostensibly a friend.' He saw the frown begin to form on Tim's face. 'Alright, the plan never survives the enemies first shot, bloody hell I should know that. Do it as well and brief me when you have some answers.'

The next day, with all three warships well into the Bay of Biscay and a reasonable flying wind, the day was taken up with flying training for the new RAF boys and re-familiarisation for the naval aircrew who had not been able to deploy on the last trip. The three helicopters conducted training as well which included emplaning and fast roping exercises for the SBS troop. The Mark 8 Lynx was fitted with an M3M half inch cannon in the cabin door which was a great improvement over the machine gun used previously. The ship towed a splash target astern and the Lynx and then the Harriers had great fun in trying to shoot it to pieces. Jon wasn't surprised to hear that Able Seaman Jones had convinced one of the ship's new junior sailors that the target, which consisted of a wooden cross with water scoops at its extremities to shoot plumes of water into the air to make it visible, actually needed a coxswain to drive it. The poor unsuspecting lad had toured the ship getting all sorts of clearances from various departments to allow him to do the job, including getting a special flight deck surcoat with 'splash target coxs'n written on the back. It was only when he reported to the quarterdeck and saw the reality of what he would have to do that the penny dropped. To his credit, he didn't get angry, although there were muttered words about getting his own back on that 'fucking Welsh git'. Jon wished him luck. Jones had seen it all before.

Flying went on well into the night. Meanwhile, the Commander and the engineer commanders had started the process of getting the ship ready. This included removing anything that could clog up a fire pump such as chair covers or any loose material. Everyone changed into action working rig, which they would now wear at all times. Action Stations were practiced. The first few times, at a slow pace to ensure everyone knew exactly what to do. The ship's company had done it many times before but the new Air Group personnel were on a steep learning curve. When satisfied, they tried it unannounced and timed it. The Commander was not satisfied and nor was Jon so they continued over the next few days to repeat the process. Jon kept his council because he knew that when they heard the alarm for real, the response would be faster than could ever be achieved during a peacetime practice.

As they passed the south of Portugal, the two Royal Fleet Auxiliaries joined them. One was a tanker, RFA Olna that had enough ship and aviation fuel to keep them going for several weeks, the other, the Fort Grange carried stores and just as importantly to Jon had a large flight deck and hangar. She had two Mark 6 anti-submarine Sea Kings embarked. 'One could never have enough helicopters', was a mantra that Jon wholeheartedly subscribed to.

While in the area, the two Mark 4 Sea Kings were kept busy flying into Gibraltar to pick up essential stores and a few replacement personnel.

As the last Sea King departed to the airfield at North Front, Amelie Smith approached Jon with a signal in her hand. She had never managed to shrug off the job of ship's PR officer and once again was having to fulfil the duty. She knew her Captain was going to be less than happy when he read the signal.

'As you know Sir, Fleet have insisted that we take five members of the press on board for this trip and the Sea King will be collecting them. I've just got a list of the names.' She handed him the signal.

Jon caught an odd tone in her voice and quickly scanned the list. 'Oh fuck,' he muttered before he could stop himself. 'Sorry Amelie, I didn't mean to say that out loud.'

'That's alright Sir, I quite understand.' She replied sympathetically.

'I have just one thing to say about this Amelie. Keep him away from me. Totally, alright? I don't want to see hide nor hair of Mister Simon Gross if that's at all possible.'

Chapter 27

Sister Agnes was finding it hard to keep her faith in the Lord strong. The crowd of refugees had grown over the last few days and still none of their captors would say what was going on. They had been given water and a little basic food but there still had been no explanation as to what was going on. She had managed to stay hidden in the crowd who all seemed happy to help with her concealment but she knew it wouldn't last.

Then, she realised she knew where they were. They must have travelled in a large circle as she recognised the place. It was a stone's throw from the salt lake. As they rounded a bend in a twisting valley, they were all ordered to halt. In front of them was what looked like a refugee camp. Rows of scruffy tents were pitched in roughly straight lines and there was a crude wire fence around the whole area. They were herded in at gun point. She could see that there were others there before them but before anyone could react, a man stood on the back of a truck and called through an old fashioned megaphone. He instructed all the men between sixteen and fifty to move to one side. At first no one moved and a muted grumbling began. The man held up a rifle and fired a short burst into the air. Silence descended and he repeated the order. More armed men started to move into the crowd and roughly pull out any men they encountered. A few scuffles broke out but rifle butts were used. A few shots were fired although they were aimed in the air.

Agnes was wearing a traditional shawl and dress like the other women. Someone had kindly given her the clothes at the start of the trek. However, it didn't look like it was going to help as the armed men were inspecting everyone, presumably to ensure that no men were masquerading as women. A young thug approached the group of women that she was standing with and started brandishing his AK47 and yelling for them to remove their head scarves. Agnes desperately looked around but there was nowhere to go. The young man was getting even angrier and stalked over to her and wrenched the scarf away. The look on his face when he realised that she was clearly a westerner would have been funny if it wasn't such a desperate situation. He pointed his rifle at her and then grabbed her arm and pulled her away towards the man on the truck. Desperate not to lose her medical supplies, she clutched her grip in her hands.

The man on the truck looked down at her as the young man dragged her up. He didn't seem at all surprised. 'Take her to the others,' was all he said before she was dragged away and marched to one of the tents near the middle of the camp. This tent had an armed guard at the opening. He opened the flap and motioned her inside. The flap closed behind her and initially she couldn't see anything it was so dark compared to the bright sun outside. Then she could make out several figures starting to stand from the camp beds they had been sitting on.

A man came out to her. He was clearly not a local and spoke to her in French. Seeing the look on her face, he switched to accented English. 'Hello, I am Francois and I think you must be Sister Agnes?'

They were left alone for several hours. Agnes found that she was with all the medical and missionary people who had been working in the area. There were seven others in all. Two were doctors and five others missionaries like herself. She knew that she wasn't alone in the area but communication was so rudimentary that she hadn't realised how many others there were. The doctors were men, one was French and the other was Dutch. The five missionaries were all women from Belgium but not nuns. No one had any idea what was going on and all had similar stories. Agnes told them about the mineral discovery at the salt lake and they all agreed that it probably had something to do with what was happening but the detail was still unclear. She decided to keep her knowledge about Max to herself for the meantime. She didn't want to give these people false hope. She was about to show them the medical supplies she had managed to grab but when she opened the bag, the first thing she saw was that damned gun. She realised that Max must have dropped it in when she wasn't looking. Not really knowing why, she pushed it to the bottom, vowing to herself that she would get rid of it as soon as she could.

Evening was approaching when the tent flap flew open and silhouetted against the glare was the man who had been standing on the truck. He was very tall, with unusually long, straight hair which was tied off in a ponytail. Agnes put his age around fifty but knew she could be off by a decade either way. He had a large hooked nose and hooded eyes. He smiled but his expression remained cruel and his eyes were bloodshot. He was one of the most savage and frightening men she had ever seen.

He looked around at the eight people. Before he could speak, Francois the Doctor stood and confronted him. 'What are you doing?' He shouted angrily. 'We are accredited medical staff. Accredited by the Ukundu government. You have no right to detain us.'

The man said nothing for a second and then without warning, he back handed the doctor hard across his face. The doctor's head flew sideways and he stumbled back but was caught by one of his colleagues.

'I didn't ask you to speak,' he said coldly in perfectly accented English. 'You are being held here because I say so. As you are medical staff, you will be permitted to attend to these people but that is all. Otherwise, you will be kept here at my convenience. Do you understand?'

Without waiting for a response, he turned and left.

'Well, that went well,' Agnes observed sourly.

The tent flap opened again and an armed man came in with several bottles of water and some bread. He left without a word.

They were left alone for the rest of the night. Despite talking through various options no one could come up with any ideas. Agnes was glad none of the men knew about the pistol. They were fired up enough to probably try to use it in an attempt to escape and she knew how that would probably end. And anyway, she had no intention of trying to escape. Her people were here and needed her more than before.

In the end, they all agreed that they might as well rest. There were only five camp beds and they had seen better times but the men insisted that the women take them.

Sometime later in the night, someone shook Agnes by the shoulder. Groggily, she came awake and saw the craggy face of Max smiling down at her. He was holding a finger to his lips. Luckily, she was at the end of the line of beds and all the others seemed to be asleep.

'How on earth did you get here?' she whispered.

'This fucking lot couldn't find their ass with a map. They're not soldiers by any stretch of the imagination, I reckon they're just a bandit group of some sort but they must be working to someone's orders.' he whispered in reply. 'Now, I was going to try and talk you into coming out with me but I see you've got friends. What's going on?'

Formidable

'I wish I knew. We've been told we will be used for our medical skills. There are two doctors here but everyone has medical training.'

'Shit, this changes things. I take it you won't want to leave them and there's no way I can get eight of you out.'

'I told you I wouldn't leave my people Max. Nothing's changed.'

'Stubborn cow. OK, do you have the others names and nationalities? I need to report this back.' He listened as Agnes gave him the details she had. 'My priority now is to let London know about this development. This could make an enormous difference. Look, I'd better go.'

'Yes but do you know what's going on outside?'

'The men are in a separate camp over by the salt lake about five miles away over the hill on the right. My guess is they are going to be used as forced labour and their families will be kept as hostage to their good behaviour. Look, I really must go. If you don't hear from me for a while, don't worry. I'll sort something out.'

Before Agnes could say anything further, Max disappeared. Suddenly a ray of hope was there, something she realised she had just about given up on.

Max left the confines of the camp with the same ease that had entered. Nearly all of the guards were asleep and anyway there weren't enough of them deployed to cover all the access points. He made his way back into the bush where he had been living quite comfortably for the last few days. His knowledge of the country and his Special Forces training had made his life relatively easy. His thoughts though, were troubled. Eight western hostages were going to be a real problem. They might be used in the short term to provide a medical capability but there was no way they could be released if what he was pretty sure was going on, actually took place. His trump card was that no one knew about him. He needed to talk to London as soon as he could. Something would have to be done and quickly.

Chapter 28

Formidable was dead in the water, totally, eerily, silent. All sorts of things could be heard rattling in lockers and elsewhere as her ponderous roll across the Atlantic swell shook them loose. Jon was fuming inside but trying to keep a calm external demeanour. It was proving hard. He knew his people were doing all they could and that anything he did or said would just get in their way. In the past, he had served under enough Captains who continually questioned and interfered to know that this was a time when the only thing he could do was trust the experts to get on with the job and keep out of their way. In the near distance, his escorts were circling around the ship protectively but there was nothing they could do either. Despite all his words to the contrary, Jon was starting to wonder if the ship really was jinxed in some way. Not that he would ever admit it to anyone.

They had made good progress south and the Air Group were as well worked up now as he could have hoped. All they needed to do was get into theatre and once again Formidable was proving she had a mind of her own.

Then, with no warning, fans started up and a blast of air caught Jon in the face from an overhead vent. The distant growl of a large diesel engine could be heard. Formidable was coming alive again.

'Permission to come on the bridge?' a voice called using the traditional request. It was the MEO.

'Yes, of course Dave,' Jon responded. 'Now what the hell was that all about?'

'Simple air lock Sir. The machinery control room were switching fuel tanks and when it happened, instead of a new fuel supply, all we got was air. Both main engines stopped and also one of the diesel generators. It happened so fast the other generator that was on line couldn't take the sudden load and tripped and we lost everything.'

'Jesus Dave, how the fucking hell could that happen?' Jon decided that just for once he didn't need to play the nice guy.

'Sorry Sir,' the MEO responded sounding subdued. 'We're not totally sure as we've never actually swapped tanks in this exact sequence before but it looks to me like yet another build issue. The lads are doing a physical fuel line inspection but we're all pretty sure that the fuel lines are not as per the ships manuals.'

Formidable

'Right, well bloody well find out and more importantly make sure it can never happen again. I want a full written report when you've got to the bottom of the issue.' Jon snapped.

He was about to say more when something was said over the main broadcast. A deep gravelly voice slowly intoned the word 'KNICKERS.'

The two men looked at each other. Jon tried not to grin and found his voice first. 'We really shouldn't laugh Dave but that just about sums thing up. I still want that bugger caught but he hit the spot that time. And I'm sorry, I didn't mean to snap at you back then. I know you and your team did everything you could.'

'That's alright Sir. I do understand. It must be bloody frustrating. I'll get you that report as soon as I can.'

The next day, with the Formidable Group finally in position, Jon was called to the Main Communications Office. They had a secure satellite system now which made communications ashore much easier. A conference call had been set up between the ship, FOF3, and MI6.

Rupert was on the line and started off. 'Formidable this is Rupert Thomas, we've had a communication from the man ashore. The situation just ramped up. We now know of eight foreign nationals being held in a camp close to the original salt lake where the mineral deposit was found. We think the people in the local area are going to be used as forced labour with their families being held as hostage. However, we've lost communication with the chap. His batteries have given out. Before we lost him, he gave us a position where he reckons he could be picked up without alerting anyone. He says he can wait there every night from midnight to dawn.' Rupert then read out a latitude and longitude. 'Of course, the question is can you get there?'

'Hang on,' Jon said and turned to one of the ratings present. 'Pipe for the navigator and Commander Air to come to the MCO and also ask for the navigator to bring a chart of Ukundu with her.' He went back to the handset. 'We'll check that Rupert but we have already worked up some contingency options for doing that sort of operation. However, what the hell are we going to do about diplomatic clearances and the rest? This could escalate into an international incident very quickly.'

'Good point Captain Hunt,' another voice broke in. 'This is Captain Johnson, Chief of Staff to FOF3. We are liaising with the MOD, FCO and Cabinet as we speak. As you say, this could get very nasty but if we can get hold of this Mister Llewellyn then we will have an eye witness to the murder of British nationals and possible outside interference by the Chinese. Without him we've got nothing. We can't see a request to the Ukundu government being considered for a moment so if we are to do anything it will have to be a covert recovery.'

Just then, Wings and the navigator came in. Jon gestured them over. He addressed them while holding the telephone handset clear. 'Amelie, plot this position and Wings tell me what you think are the chances of a covert extraction of one man from there.' He put the handset back to his face. 'I've got two of my staff plotting that position now, if you can hold on a couple of minutes please.'

Jon conferred with his two colleagues and they all looked at the map. He listened to Wings carefully and asked a couple of questions then picked up the handset once again. 'Yes, we can do it. As I said, we've already considered that this might happen and with the two Sea Kings and the Lynx we have a couple of options. It will take too long to give you all the detail now so I'll send it all in a signal in a couple of hours. I assume you'll want to consider it and feed it up the chain. Its mid-afternoon here and even if you told us to go now it's just about too late but we could be ready for tomorrow night.'

'Fine Jon, thanks for that,' Rupert replied. 'That should be enough time to get a decision.'

'Jonathon, this is Captain Johnson again. We'll look at your plan but you are the man on the spot. If you think it's feasible then we'll back you up, good luck.'

Jon returned the handset to its cradle and looked at Wings. 'Let's get everyone we need together for a planning meeting in the main briefing room straight away. Looks like we have a real job to do.'

Two hours later, with the ships aircrew briefing room full of the helicopter crews, engineers and ship's staff, Wings stood to sum up the plan.

'So this is what we'll do. One Sea King will be stripped of any gear not required for the plan to give it maximum endurance. Even so, the pick up point is almost at the maximum range of the aircraft and that's allowing for cutting the corner and flying across Nigerian territory for some of it. The first cab will go straight for the pick up and then

Formidable

return. The second aircraft will carry an underslung fuel bladder and land approximately a hundred miles inland. It will dump the fuel in a suitable place and return to the ship. If it needs to, then the first cab can land and take enough gas to get back to us. Either way, we leave the bladder where it is. The only radio call for the whole mission will be to give the coordinates of the fuel dump. The whole trip will be low level, on night vision goggles and radio silent except for that one call. As a contingency, we'll also have the Lynx on standby with its internal ferry tank fitted. It hasn't got the load capacity to carry the underslung fuel but will have the range to get to the pick up and get back at least two hundred miles so the fuel drop will have to be further up country. Let's hope we don't have to use this plan as we all know how bloody noisy a Lynx is and we don't want to alert anyone in the area that we were there. Any questions?'

There were none and the room quickly emptied. Jon grabbed Wings before he left. 'Talk to me Tim. I know the aircraft and likely terrain as well as you but you know the guys who will be doing the flying better than me. Are they up to it?'

Wings gave Jon an odd look. 'They're all well trained Fleet Air Arm pilots Sir.'

Jon barked a quick laugh. 'Well said and that's put me in my place, thank you Tim. Sorry I asked.'

Chapter 29

The African country side was eerily quiet. A large, slightly yellow coloured moon was just rising above the horizon. Once again, for the fourth day now, Max sat with his back against the same small tree and waited patiently. He had no idea when or even if, he would get picked up. His last call before the batteries in the phone went dead had loosely arranged this rendezvous. He had picked this place as it had a good clear area for a helicopter to land in but there was also a good valley for it to fly up, which would conceal its approach both visually and from the noise of its rotors. He knew that there were ships on the way but that was about all. Quite what he would do if no one turned up, he had no real idea. Living off the land had been quite easy, not the least because he had the rifle but it wasn't something he could do indefinitely. Not that he could really do anything about the plight of the people by the salt lake either. His only real hope would be to make his way to the coast somewhere, either that or get across the border into Nigeria which was meant to be a friendly country. Either way he would be abandoning Agnes, her friends and all the local people. No, he would stick it out here for as long as he could, it was his and their only real hope.

He knew how far from the coast he was and from his past military experience how long it would take a chopper to get to him if they left after dark and realised that it would be several hours yet before any possible pick up. He made himself more comfortable and prepared to wait.

The sun had set and Formidable was approaching the coast. They would stay out of territorial waters but Jon wanted to get as close as they could to reduce the flying distances. The aircraft were ready to go and would be manning up in a few minutes. Jon had decided on one last walk about before the operation started. The go ahead had been given only a few hours before. He wondered just how much debate there had been at various MOD and government levels to get the approval. The risks, not to just the aircrew involved but all the people being held hostage were considerable. And a cynic might add the risk to his own career but Jon had no qualms about that. He had a job to do.

Inside the ship there was considerable bustle but once he closed the door from the island behind him and he stepped onto the darkened flight, deck everything was calm and quiet. He knew it wouldn't last. In just a matter of minutes the three helicopters would man up and the flight deck would be bustle and noise for the few minutes it would take to launch the machines. Then it would be hours of nervous waiting until they returned. Jon thought back to nineteen eighty three when he had launched in a Sea King Mark 4 from Illustrious to go into the unknown above the Arctic Circle. This was a similar situation, except this time it would be he that was waiting anxiously for news rather than getting involved directly. He suddenly realised what it must have been like for his old Commanding Officer that time. Ducking past the wing of a parked Harrier, he walked aft. The ship was steaming gently into wind and although there was a moon, he had to be careful not to trip over one of the many lashings holding the aircraft securely to the deck. At the back end were the brooding shapes of the two Sea Kings ranged on the aft two spots. The sleeker shape of the Lynx was off to one side and would only actually take off if there was a problem with one of the bigger machines.

It was moments like these that Jon felt at one with all Fleet Air Arm pilots over the years. Waiting quietly on the flight deck of a carrier or small ship for that matter, knowing that in a few moments they would be strapped into a vibrating, roaring machine that would take all their concentration just to get clear of the ship let alone fly away and fight an enemy.

He could hear the whisper of the water streaming down the side of the ship and smell the acrid diesel fumes from her funnel, Formidable was going to do her job.

Suddenly he heard a strange grating, scraping noise. For a second, he was surprised and wondered what it was. Stories of the 'phantom chockhead' who dragged his chain lashings over the deck and woke people trying to sleep on the deck below sprang to his mind for an instant. He smiled to himself, he had been woken by just that noise on more than one occasion when serving in the Hermes. He turned and indeed it was an aircraft handler dragging chain lashings but he was real and not a ghost and was being joined by several others as they removed the lashings from the Sea Kings and replaced them with the lighter nylon ones that would be used until launch. His time of reflection was over. It was now time to get to the Operations room and get ready.

Max's head jerked up as he realised he must have nodded off. He looked at his watch which was just visible in the light of the moon that was past overhead now. It was just past midnight. Depending on when they launched they would either be here soon or not at all. If not, it would be another hot, boring day waiting and watching until the sun went down again. He decided to get up and walk about, not the least to get the cramp out of his leg muscles and the pain in his arse from being in the sitting position for too long. He reflected back to his days in the marines. Although the SBS were primarily required for work at sea or on the beach, they took pride in being able to conduct all sorts of Special Forces operations. 'Like the SAS but wearing flippers' was the standard line but to a large degree it was true. He had done time in Northern Ireland and other theatres of war. This time it was different, he wasn't part of a team, he was on his own. He suddenly realised just how much he wanted to get away from here.

Without warning he heard it and his heart leapt. A sudden, faint, distant growl to the south, exactly where he expected it. With no radio or any other way of contact he knew he would still have to give them some indication of where he was. The position he had given was reasonably accurate but still had some margin of error. From previous experience, he would expect at least one of the pilots to be using night vision goggles and knew that shining even a relatively weak white light at the helicopter could cause the goggles to white out. He certainly didn't want to be the cause of his rescuers crashing just as they came to pick him up. His solution was simple. He turned to the small fire he had started as dusk fell. It was only embers now but that was as he had planned. Earlier on, he had emptied the cordite from half a dozen of the rounds from his rifle and mixed it with some dry grass. He blew on the embers to make sure they were glowing and waited.

The growl was getting louder. He recognised the sound, he had heard it so many times before. It was a Sea King. Then he spotted something black moving against the almost black sky. It was very low and heading straight towards him. He grabbed a handful of the grass and threw it on the embers. There was a brief noise and then a flash of light as the cordite lit off. The fire was briefly burning brightly. He

Formidable

grabbed a blanket and held it in front of the fire and then moved it rhythmically away and back again. From the aircraft it should look like a flashing beacon.

In what seemed like seconds, a massive, roaring monster appeared in front of him and flared into a landing. A blast of noise and gravel heralded its arrival as the downwash picked up anything loose on the ground. He was tempted to run in under the rotors but held back. He could just see that whoever it was at the main cargo door was pointing a rifle his way and he could hardly blame them for their caution. He threw the blanket over the fire and then walked slowly forward with his hands held high. Another figure appeared at the door and jumped down. He was also carrying a rifle but had a bag over his shoulder. Max waited patiently.

The man quickly reached him and while still pointing his rifle, yelled over the noise of the gas turbines and rotors. 'What's your name?' He pulled his helmet to one side to hear the reply.

'Max Llewellyn,' he shouted back. 'And you've come to pick me up and take me to Formidable.'

The man visibly relaxed and dropped the muzzle of his rifle. 'Get your gear and let's go.'

Max turned, picked up his bag and rifle and followed the man under the whistling rotors. As soon as they were on board, it immediately lifted, spot turned and headed back the way it had come.

Jon hadn't slept and had spent the night in the Operations room waiting for some indication of the success or not of the mission. The Sea King with the fuel had made a successful drop and returned some hours previously. Everything had gone well at least until then. Now they couldn't know the exact time for the return of the other machine as the wind inland could vary and there was no way of knowing how easy it would be to find the rendezvous point in the African wilderness. Even so, they should have seen something on radar or had a radio call by now. He was just beginning to think about what he would have to put in a signal to home when an excited call came from the radar plot. 'Link track from Swansea Sir, contact over the coast.'

Jon knew this meant that the Type 42's more powerful area radar had picked something up and shared it with the force over the data link system they all used.

Before he could respond, a single word was heard on the HF radio. 'Beaverbreath,'

He hadn't liked the code word but knew it had some humorous connotation with the aircrew so hadn't vetoed it. Now he was delighted. It meant mission accomplished.

Chapter 30

Simon Gross was an unhappy man. He had been unhappy ever since his editor had insisted that he join this bloody ship. He had tried to get out of it but it was pointed out that he had made a crusade out of following its Captain and so he would be going or be fired. He went. Simon hated ships and it was quite clear the ship didn't like him much either. He was hardly surprised. They all seemed to know about the Culdrose incident as well as the article he had later penned about their brush with a certain dockyard wall. The other journalists hadn't been sympathetic either. The only saving grace was that he had managed to dig up some more dirt, particularly when all the electrics failed the previous day which he should be able to use when he finally got home. That and his secret weapon, something that no one board knew he had, his satellite phone. He was keeping that in reserve.

He quite liked the pretty young officer who was acting as their liaison. She, at least, was being professional. The rest of the wardroom were a different matter. Most wouldn't talk to him at all. Those that did were either rude or took great delight in winding him up. A few days after they had joined the ship, one of the aircrew officers, who for once seemed to be prepared to be friendly, invited him for a game of snooker. It had taken him hours to discover that the 'gyro stabilised snooker table' was a fiction. The laughter behind his back had only made his temper worse.

He had managed a few interviews with some of the ship's company and got some good background. It seemed that the ship's habit of breaking down was continuing but everyone only spoke highly of the Captain. He hadn't been able to get anyone to say anything bad about him at all. In fact, when he had pressed one of the seamen, a Welshman called Jones, he had discovered just how well liked the man was as he dodged a fist that would have laid him out. Such a thing happening a second time would not have been good. Luckily, the girl officer had stepped in in time. A further problem for him was that he was actually quite impressed with what he had been shown. Watching flying operations from the sanctuary of FLYCO had been an eye opener but so had their tours of the machinery and operational spaces. Simon had had no idea just how complicated the ship was or how professional her crew seemed to be. However, he had no intention of saying so in any copy that he produced later.

However, today it looked like they would at last be getting some serious input as they had all been invited down to the squadron briefing room to be told about the events of the previous night. All the journalists knew so far was that there had been some sort of operation overnight but had no idea what was really going on. In fact, they only had a rough idea of where they even were.

Amelie Smith ushered the five of them into the room. The walls were covered in complicated charts and other arcane aviation runes but at least the seats were comfortable.

Jon entered with the man Simon recognised as the quaintly named 'Wings' who he knew ran the aviation department.

'Gentlemen, thanks for coming,' Jon said, looking at them all one at a time. 'I'm sorry that we haven't been able to keep you fully in the picture so far but I'm sure you'll understand that we have a situation on our hands and that has kept us all pretty busy. However, we've now had clearance from our command ashore to bring you up to date. Commander Air here will give you all the detail so I'll leave that to him. I hope you understand that this is all in confidence for the moment.'

For some reason, Simon felt that that last remark was particularly aimed at him as he felt the Captain's gaze boring into his. The Captain then left and Wings took his place.

Jon didn't go back to the bridge as he normally would have done. The man they had rescued had already given a general debrief during a conference call to London and a signal with all the detailed information had also been sent but Jon wanted to get to know the man a little more and had arranged lunch in his harbour cabin for him and a few guests. It would be a better way to judge his worth and the quality of his information. Jon also suspected that he would be needed in the near future and he really needed to get the measure of him.

Max was waiting along with the Commander and Captain Tony Shaw, the Royal Marine and SBS detachment commander. 'Good morning everyone,' Jon called as he entered. 'No don't stand. Sorry I'm a little late, I was just talking to the journalists. Wings is giving them the full story now and then he'll be joining us.'

Formidable

Jenkins appeared with a coffee for Jon which he took gratefully and they all sat around in the comfortable arm chairs. Jon looked at his newest guest. 'So, Mister Llewellyn, did you manage to get any sleep?'

'Please call me Max and yes I've had a couple of hours. Have you had any word from London yet? Something will have to be done and the longer it's left, the more risk there is to the people ashore.'

Jon was immediately pleased to note that Max's first concern wasn't for himself. He looked a tough and competent man and that was borne out by his recent story. Tony Shaw had also asked for his service record to be sent to the ship but several of the SBS troop on board knew him from the past and had nothing but good things to say about him. 'Not yet Max I'm afraid. We have been told to stay in the area for the moment and that's all. You can't expect much for a few days at least I'm afraid. Oh and we've had those photos you brought with you developed. You can have a look in a minute. They don't make good viewing as I'm sure you know.' Jon indicated a large envelope on the table. He was about to speak again when his words were drowned out by a rising whine followed by a roar, which was repeated again after a few seconds. 'So we keep on with our normal business for now. If you hadn't gathered, that was a pair of Harriers taking off. We'll be conducting flying operations to keep ourselves busy.'

Max nodded. 'Sorry, I realise that these things take time. But wouldn't it be a good idea to at least brainstorm some thoughts on what we could do?'

'Excellent point,' Jon agreed. 'And I'm already ahead of you. After lunch, I'd like you and my command team to do just that. However, one thing you may not know about yet is that we have good intelligence that there is a significant Chinese military presence in the country now and we will have to take that into account.'

'Why am I not surprised? I'm pretty certain it was the Chinese bastard who ordered me and my people to be murdered.'

'Max, I'm sorry but revenge is not on the agenda, there are bigger fish to fry. By the way you should be aware that although we know they are holding French, Dutch and Belgian nationals as well, there is little in the way of help coming from any of those countries for the short term at least. The best we can hope for is one or two small warships. The only other aircraft carrier we could hope for is one of

Formidable

the French ones and they are committed elsewhere. In fact, a betting man would put his money on this going to the UN now. With your testimony and the photos, there is a good chance that we could embarrass the Chinese enough for them to put the Ukundu government under pressure to stop what they are doing. I suspect that this is what the thinking in Whitehall is at the moment. But I always plan on the worst case scenario and that's where I want your input as soon as possible. Just in case they want you back in the UK soon.'

As if on cue there was a knock on the door and Petty Officer Jenkins was handed a sheet of paper which he then took to the Captain. Jon studied it for a moment and then looked up. 'Well who needs a crystal ball? We've been ordered north to Port Harcourt in Nigeria where there will be an aircraft waiting to take Max back to the UK tomorrow morning. So I would really appreciate your input into our planning this afternoon before we lose you. Oh and there is a second thing here. They say that your emergency reserve status was invoked when you were ashore and that this still stands. So welcome back to the Royal Marines, Sergeant Llewellyn.'

Simon Gross's was sitting in his cabin with his head spinning. The account they had been given of the operations ashore was staggering. Anyone who could get it out first would have the scoop of the decade. So, now he had a decision to make. He could phone in some general copy and make some hay out of the failure of the ship's power the previous day, all along the 'Captain Calamity' line he had used before. However, there were two problems with that. Firstly, it wasn't much of a story anymore and the ship had dealt with it pretty quickly but far more importantly it would give away that he had a means of communication. Once it was known that he had talked to London, he knew he wouldn't get a second chance. Of course, he could wait and see what happened next but from what the Commander had said, it was expected that the whole incident would be passed over to the diplomats and maybe the UN. That could drag on for months. The story would have slipped through his fingers.

He made his decision. This was probably the best chance of his career and he just couldn't let it pass him by. He had already scouted out the ship and knew exactly where he would be left alone but with a clear view of the sky so his phone could lock on. He grabbed a sheet of paper and started writing. He needed some simple coherent words and a good headline before he made his call.

Chapter 31

The phone next to Rupert's bed interrupted a rather good dream. He felt Gina's warm buttocks against his back as he leant over and looked at the clock before grabbing the receiver.

'Rupert Thomas,' he said blearily. 'Jesus, you do know it's only five in the morning? This had better be good.' He listened for a few moments. It was the duty officer back at the office. 'Why the hell wasn't there a D notice out about this?' he asked angrily. 'Sorry, don't answer that, it's not your fault. Contact the paper and tell them one is on its way and not to send out any more copy. I'll be in, in less than half an hour.'

By this time, Gina was also awake and looked anxiously at him. 'What's the matter Rupert?'

'One of those fucking journalists on Formidable had just blown the gaff. It must be that moron Simon Gross because it's his paper. God knows how but he's got the story to his editor and they've plastered it all over the front page. The whole bloody, thing including the mineral discovery, the murder of the survey team and even what's going on ashore now. Once the Chinese and Ukundu government get wind of it, if they haven't already, I don't give a flying fuck for the lives of those ashore. They'll just dispose of them and deny the whole thing.'

'What? Even with the evidence we have?'

'Had we been able to go through diplomatic channels then we probably have been fine but can you see them accepting this in public? Come on girl, we've got work to do.'

Zhang Li heard the story only an hour later. An emergency meeting had been called at the Embassy chaired by the Ambassador. The military brass were also there. When it was over, he had been given the task of liaison with the Ukundu government who had also heard. No one seemed to know what to do. It wasn't helped when Li discovered that a British Task Force including an aircraft carrier had been off the coast for several days and it was this force that had managed to rescue a man he thought was dead. Initial talk of a diplomatic protest over invasion of Ukundu air space quickly died when it was pointed out that their response would be to point out they were rescuing someone who was the sole survivor of a massacre carried out on Ukundu soil. Not only that but the murdered people were meant to be working under a contract from the government itself.

It only got worse when the Ukundu Interior Minister confirmed that not only was a British missionary being held illegally but there were French, Dutch and Belgian captives as well. Why hadn't the idiots told him at the time? In fact, the full extent of the round up of local people only came clear at that point. He had assumed that it was just a few locals. No, it seemed that they had cleared a very large area. And then he dropped a second bombshell. They hadn't used official troops merely bribed one of the many local warlords to do the job.

By the time he got back to the Embassy, Beijing was demanding answers. They were answers they didn't have. Then the blame game started and it all started falling on Li's shoulders. It had been his idea to remove the survey team once the discovery had been made. He pointed out that he had been praised for the decision at the time. He also pointed out that the action had been taken solely by Ukundu soldiers. He wasn't even there when it happened. There was no solid link back to him at all.

As the day wore on, several things started to come into focus. The Ukundu military were clearly mobilising but were not telling their Chinese colleagues anything. There were enough trained aircrew and maintenance staff to fly the new jets they had purchased even though it had been intended that they would share the burden for some time with their Chinese trainers. The two ships were already fully crewed by Ukundu naval staff. On the diplomatic front, the Ukundu Ambassador in England had been summoned to Whitehall and demands made that any British or other European personnel be immediately released. Similar actions had been taken in Paris, Belgium and Brussels. The government's response had been to deny any knowledge that anyone was being held captive. Their line was that anything happening so far up country was clearly the work of local terrorists who were probably trying to take over the Lithium discovery for their own ends. Bearing in mind what Li now knew, that statement was probably quite factual. When Britain offered, on behalf of all the European countries, to provide military support to rescue the captives, the Ukundu government dismissed the offer out of hand even though they knew the strength of the naval force only a few miles off their coast.

An emergency meeting of the UN Security Council had been called and as usual it resulted in very little. By that time, the British delegation had been able to produce some photographs but without the testimony of the man who took them who was still travelling back to the UK they were of little value. In any event China, would have used its veto had a vote actually been called.

Late in the afternoon, a final meeting was called in the Embassy. Li summed up the situation for everyone. 'We have admitted that we helped the Ukundu government with the managing the geological survey but as none of our engineers or mining and refining equipment has sailed from home yet we can say we never knew about the Lithium find. Then, with all honesty we can also say that we are as much in the dark as to what is going on up country as anyone else. We have been asked and have admitted that we have sold the aircraft and ships but that was part of a long standing agreement between the two countries and nothing to do with this situation. So as far as China is concerned this is nothing to do with us.'

Heads were nodding around the table. Then someone asked, 'and what will the Ukundu government do? Have we heard anything?'

Li answered. 'Yes, they admitted to me in private that they 'contracted', if that's the right word, some local militia to do their dirty work. If they've got any sense they'll tell them to let the locals disperse until this is all over.'

'And the western hostages?'

'They'll have to disappear is my guess.'

Agnes and her colleagues never left their tent. Despite the original instruction that they were going to be used to give medical help they had been left totally alone. Once a day, a guard delivered some meagre rations and water. Apart from that, they were left totally to their own devices. The biggest problem had been sanitation. After the first day, Francois the French doctor accosted the guard when he delivered food. The guard appeared to speak French and the doctor demanded some sort of toilet facilities. An hour later, they got three buckets. The next time the guard appeared, they made him take them and they were returned later empty. Even so, the smell in the tent would stay with her for the rest of her life. Francois and one of the other men had tried to get out one night and see what was going on. Agnes had shown him the small slit that Max had made to get in on the first night but they were soon back via the main entrance with two guards. Both had been beaten. No one tried that again. She then decided to tell them about

Max and what he might have been able to do but as the days wore on, even that hope started to fade.

Then one morning, everything changed. The first thing they heard was shouting and then several gunshots. Very soon it became eerily quiet. No one came to them and their morning ration of food and water didn't appear. Around midday, the man who had originally spoken to them came back.

'Listen to me,' he said immediately. 'We will be leaving now. You people will come with us. Things have changed and you are now our hostages. I will not answer any questions. Do as you are told or we will shoot you.' He turned and left without another word.

Within half an hour, they had been blindfolded and loaded into the back of an old truck.

Chapter 32

Within twenty four hours, a small area of a remote part of Africa was taking everyone's attention. Rupert and his team had started to gather as much intelligence as they could but it was an uphill struggle. The most they could do practically was to look at satellite photos. They had some from a few days ago and now Rupert was studying some taken that morning.

'Something's changed that's for sure,' he observed. 'Where's everyone gone?'

'They've either cleared them out or just let them go.' Malcolm Marks replied. 'They must have had word from someone in the capital. They certainly won't have newspapers up there and we've managed to keep it out of the broadcast media for the moment.'

'Hmm, probably not for long,' Rupert replied. 'But I agree someone must have tipped them off. The big question is, where are our doctors and missionaries? Alright, we haven't seen any army infrastructure in the area and Mister Llewellyn's assessment wasn't that the people who did this were definitely not trained soldiers so we're looking at a local militia or terrorist group, any ideas?'

'There's one tribal group who operate in the area although they are also active in Nigeria as well,' Malcolm suggested. 'Not much is known about them but there is a rumour that they have a very strong leader, possibly well educated, at least by local standards.'

'Are they Muslim or do they have some sort of revolutionary aims?' Rupert asked.

'Neither that we know of. Like we often see in this part of Africa, it's probably just a group of thugs out to get what they can. I assume they had some connection with somebody in government and were doing their work for them. Until now that is.'

'There's a chance that they've kept them as hostages then?'

'More than a good one. If their boss is that well educated he will know their value. So even if he's been told to make them disappear, he might well hang on to them. For the short term at least.'

Rupert suddenly had an idea. 'I've been studying the terrain and its pretty barren to the north and west but back inland there are several settlements. What was the name of that priest who contacted us at the start of all this?'

'Father Joseph,' Mark answered. 'Do you want me to try and get hold of him and see if he has heard of this guy?'

'Yes because in the short term it's our only lead.'

Formidable had turned around. An urgent signal from the UK had ordered the Task Group back to their station off the Ukundu coast. It had also informed Jon why and ordered him to find out how the leak had occurred and make damned sure it couldn't happen again. Jon was seeing red. He had immediately ordered all the journalists to come to his cabin although he was one hundred per cent sure who the culprit was. The Commander and Wings brought them in.

Jon didn't stand on ceremony. He was trembling with rage. 'Gentlemen, yesterday you were brought up to date by myself and Commander Air. Today the story has been splashed all over one of the UK's tabloid newspapers. Your paper, Mister Gross. Do you have anything to say?'

The other four journalists turned and gaped at Simon open mouthed. He decided to tough it out. 'Yes of course. You know it was me. It was my paper. But you didn't say we couldn't pass the story back home. I expect you didn't know I have a satellite phone and so was in a position to use it.'

'What? You fucking moron,' one of the other journalists said before anyone else could speak. 'We've all got them, you're not the only person with access to the new technology but we weren't stupid enough to think we should do something like that.'

'Thank you Mister Brown,' Jon interrupted. 'On that point, I will want any long distance communication devices any of you have turned in immediately. You can have them back once the situation is resolved.'

'Now look here, that's my personal property.' Simon blustered. 'You can't treat us like your bloody crew.'

Paul Taylor could see that his Commanding Officer was about to do something rash. Jon's hands were clenched and his knuckles were turning white. He decided to interject. 'Mister Gross, your actions have put the lives of the people ashore at severe risk. They could even be dead by now. If by any chance they are still alive there is a good chance we are going to have to risk our people and even these ships in getting them back. The situation was under control and we had every

Formidable

chance of sorting it out until you decided to tell the whole world what was going on.'

'Well that's my job. I'm sorry if you don't like it.'

The Commander's fist came from nowhere and caught Simon on the jaw. He dropped like a sack of cement.

Paul turned to an astonished Jon. 'Sorry Sir but it was my turn. You might remember that I told you that my son was on the Uganda and that I owe you one. Have that one on me.'

There was a moment's silence and then one of the Journalists spoke in a deadpan voice. 'Goodness Captain Hunt, you really should get that carpet fixed. Look Mister Gross has just tripped over it and knocked himself out.' The other three grinned acknowledgement at the remark.

Completely taken aback, Jon could only nod in acceptance.

'I think that maybe we should take our colleague back to his cabin now.' One of the other men said. 'Maybe you should lock the twat up then for his own safety.'

Minutes later, they left escorting a groggy Simon, who was dazed but walking. Jon called the Commander back. 'Paul, I don't know what to say. But thank you, because if you hadn't done that then I'm afraid I would have and twice would have been a really bad idea.'

'Exactly Sir. Anyway, it never happened. I'll ensure that Mister Gross spends the rest of his trip in Formidable staring at the deck head in his cabin. He won't bother you again.'

Jon was about to reply when the ship's main broadcast broke in. First with a raucous siren and then the words. 'ACTION STATIONS, ACTIONS STATIONS, ASSUME NBCD STATE ONE, CONDITION ZULU, CLOSE ALL WATER TIGHT DOORS.' It then repeated the message but Jon wasn't hearing it as he sprinted for the Operations Room.

He was there in record time. The ship had already been at defence watches and the reports were already coming in confirming that the ship was closed up. Jon had to smile briefly. That must have been at least twice as fast as they had achieved in any practice. He grabbed a headset as he sat on his command chair.

'What have we got PWO?'

The duty Principal Warfare Officer answered over the command loop. 'Two fast movers Sir. The Sea Harriers on Combat Air Patrol picked them up about the same time as Swansea did. Low level, sub sonic and heading straight at us. We've no ESM on them but are vectoring the CAP in for visual confirmation. They are about fifty miles out and will be here in a few minutes.'

Jon thought for a second. 'Make damned sure the Force stays weapon tight PWO. I suspect this is the Ukundu military or their Chinese pals paying a visit to make a point.'

'Agreed Sir but should we illuminate with targeting radars?'

Jon considered the point. Swansea and Hampshire would need to lock their respective fire control radars on to the targets to obtain a firing solution which could be needed in an instant. Even his own ship would need to do so if her point defence guns needed to fire. The problem was that locking systems on could be seen as a hostile act and he didn't want to escalate the situation.

'Do the Harriers have a firing solution?'

'Yes Sir, they are well within AMRAAM range.'

'Very well, only point defence radars. Tell Swansea not to lock up at the moment. Frankly from the intelligence we got the other day I'd be surprised if these aircraft can actually detect any of our radars at all but let's not take the chance. What are the Harriers doing?'

'We're vectoring them in Sir. Luckily they won't have to chase as they were just about overhead us at the time.'

'Right carry on with that but I want them to try to get close behind the targets without being seen. Let's try and give these buggers a fright.'

In the lead Harrier, Pete Moore was grinning hard inside his oxygen mask. He and his number two had picked up the targets on their Blue Vixen radar even before they had crossed the coast. As soon as they had, they reported in, they immediately turned towards them and manoeuvred to obtain a good AMRAAM solution. However, the ship had then ordered them to get down and identify the incoming aircraft. While firing a long range missile was fun, fighter pilots really wanted to get up close and personal. Pete wanted to see what he was shooting at. Both aircraft dropped their noses and headed for the deck. With a closing speed of over twelve hundred miles an hour they had to be careful not to overshoot and end up in a long tail chase. Suddenly, they could see their quarry in the distance while they were still well above them. Both Harriers continued their dive but started a high G turn in order to slot in close behind their targets. As they did so, Pete called Mother on the radio. 'Foxtrot Mike, this is Blue leader, targets identified as two Chinese built Alpha Five attack aircraft. Unable to see any ordnance yet.'

The ship immediately came back. 'Roger Blue leader, expect they will overfly us before you can catch up. Let them past and get them on the turn, over.'

The next thing Peter heard was a call on 'Guard' the international emergency frequency that all aircraft monitored. He recognised his Captain's voice. 'Unknown aircraft approaching British Task Force, this is Warship Formidable, I am operating aircraft, please remain clear of my circuit, over.'

Silence was the only response.

In the Ops room they could see that the track of the two incoming aircraft was unaltered. An excited call came from the bridge. 'Alarm aircraft, red nine zero.'

'All weapons remain tight,' Jon ordered. Suddenly, there was a muted roar that could easily be heard within the depths of the ship.

'Ops room, this is the Bridge, they've just flown past, below flight deck level and incredibly close. There was no ordnance on their wings. Hang on, they're in a tight turn, looks like they're coming back.'

Jon pressed the transmit button on the Guard frequency again. 'Ukundu Alpha Five aircraft, this is Formidable on Guard. You have encroached my aircraft operating circuit and under international law you are endangering my ship and my aircraft please leave the area.' Jon looked over at the aircraft direction plot and grinned. 'Ukundu aircraft, I suggest you look behind you.'

Someone else came on the radio just as the roar of returning aircraft could be heard. 'Actually, I suggest you just look up.'

Mystified Jon called the bridge. Whoever it was that picked up the microphone, he was having trouble speaking for laughter. 'Sorry Sir, we were just watching a four aircraft fly past. I think our Squadron CO has been watching Top Gun too many times.'

'What? What did he do?'

'Not just him Sir, both Harriers flew over the top of the other two jets and stayed there in very close formation. The only thing was they were both upside down.'

Chapter 33

Agnes and her co-prisoners were locked up in an old adobe building of some sort. If the tent had been bad, this was ten times worse. The smell and heat were appalling but so was the noise. There seemed to be incessant rap music being played outside. Their captors, when they rarely saw them seemed to be half stoned. The first evening, Francois the doctor was taken away. He returned later in the evening.

'The place is a dump,' he announced. 'Most of them seem to be having a party and are drunk or on drugs of some sort although there are few who are sober enough. They wanted me to treat a couple of them. One had a broken arm but the other seemed to have overdosed on something, probably heroin of some sort. He didn't make it but no one seemed to really care. The only person I spoke to, who seemed even half alert was the man who brought us here. He calls himself Jamar and I don't trust him an inch. He said he was giving his men some down time after the last few weeks. There were some women around as well but they seemed as bad as the men. At least I got a promise of water and food but he wouldn't be drawn on why he wanted us or why they pulled out.'

'I have a theory about that,' Agnes said. 'The British already know what's going on from Max Llewellyn but I suspect something has brought the situation out into the open and the Ukundu government didn't want any signs of what they'd been up to. This Jamar character clearly saw his chance and decided we might be valuable to him.' She looked hard around at the others. 'In some ways we may have been lucky because I'm damned sure the Ukundu government would rather we had just disappeared.'

'So, do you think that your government will negotiate to get us released Agnes?' Francois asked.

Agnes frowned. 'They say they never negotiate in hostage situations but we don't know what these people actually want. My guess would be that its money to release us. But I don't suppose the Ukundu government will be that keen on the idea. All we can do is pray and do our best to survive.'

The next morning Zhang Li, called another meeting. In the face of accusations from various European countries, the Ukundu government had maintained a steadfast denial of any involvement. They had also continued to refuse any offers of military help saying that it was an internal problem and that they would deal with it. The Chinese policy was still to deny any involvement and keep out of it as much as possible. Then Li was called to the telephone. When he finished he turned to the room with an odd look on his face.

'That was them,' he announced to the room. 'Their leader is called Jamar Hashem and he is clearly no fool. Of course, we know they were told to just disperse the locals but remove the problem of the westerners in a more permanent way. Instead, they've taken them somewhere and he's demanding money for that task otherwise he will trade them to the west.'

'Why is he talking to us about this?' the Ambassador asked. 'He should be talking to the Ukundu government and anyway, how do we know he's not bluffing? We don't know where he is and for all we know he's actually done the task and is just trying it on.'

'I asked him all of that,' Li replied. 'He was quite honest. We have more money and he clearly knows that we are in partnership on this project and would not want to be embarrassed further. Damage limitation he called it. I'll talk to the Minister. We need this situation resolved fast. Frankly, my recommendation would be to pay the man. It will be a tiny fraction of the gains we will make and we really don't want any more bad publicity. I'm sure the government will be able to sort him out later when all this has settled down.'

It was only after he had ended the call that Li wondered how on earth the man had got his telephone number and even more strangely how he had made the call in the first place.

Rupert Thomas was under pressure from all sides. Little word was coming out of Africa although he had been made aware of the fly past of Formidable the previous day. Everyone agreed with Jon Hunt's assessment from sea, that it had just been macho posturing on behalf of the newly empowered Ukundu military. Whichever way he thought about the problem, he came up against a brick wall. They just didn't know where the hostages were being held and in such a vast landscape that was a complete showstopper. The UN would no doubt talk for more days but the one thing they didn't have was time. He had even managed to talk to the Jesuit priest, Father Joseph but once again had drawn a blank. He was staring out of his window in frustration when there was a knock on the door.

Gina came in. He smiled at her but realised by the serious look on her face that this was something important. She had a sheet of paper in her hand.

'This just came in from GCHQ Rupert. You need to read it.' She didn't say any more just handed the paper over.

Rupert studied it and realised immediately that it was a transcript of a conversation between the Chinese Embassy in the capital which had been under special scrutiny for obvious reasons and the people holding the hostages. At last, he had a name which could be significant. Far more importantly though was that the man had suggested that he was prepared to trade for them. This could only mean that he would be probably trying to contact someone from the west as well and soon.

He grabbed the phone and rang the FCO. He warned them about what could soon happen. The obvious place for the man to make contact would be the British Embassy in the capital. He strongly requested that any approach should be given apparent consideration, even though it would never actually be allowed to succeed. Time was what they needed and to dismiss it out of hand could have immediate fatal consequences.

He then got straight on to GCHQ and requested special surveillance explaining what he thought was going on. After that, all he could do was wait. In the meantime he called in his team and got them working on finding out all they could about a certain Jamar Hashem and the group he was part of.

An hour dragged by and then the phone rang. It was GCHQ. He talked for a few minutes and then put the phone down with a look of satisfaction on his face.

He turned to the assembled team. 'Got the bastard. He rang our Embassy as we thought and demanded ten million dollars for the release of our people. He was told we would consider it and he gave us until noon tomorrow their time. That's two in the afternoon here so we have twenty six hours to think of something. But the most important thing is that we have his location. He was using a satellite phone and because we were expecting the call GCHQ were able to pinpoint the location. I'll get straight on to Number Ten, you lot start working up some options.'

Chapter 34

The main briefing room in Formidable was full. Jon had called a full planning meeting. All relevant ship's staff were there as well as the COs and Ops officers of each Harrier squadron, the Flight Commander of the helicopter crews and the OC Special Forces.

'Captain,' the Commander called out loudly as Jon entered. They all started to stand but Jon waved them back down.

'No time for that gentlemen.' He strode to the front of the room. He was holding a sheaf of signals. 'Some of you know some of what's been going on but this meeting is to make sure we're all fully in the picture and look at options.' He nodded to the ship Ops officer who unfolded a large map of Ukundu which he proceeded to hang in front of the aircraft state board at the front of the room.

'Let's keep this simple,' Jon said. 'We know where the hostages are being kept and its here.' He pointed to a position well south of the place where they had conducted the recent rescue. 'Apparently, it's an abandoned mining camp. Mister, sorry I should now say, Sergeant Llewellyn has actually been there. Surveying the old mine workings was part of his remit when he was with his geological survey. He can go into the detail of the terrain and infrastructure later on. We should also be getting updated satellite photographs very soon. So, we now have a potential target. It's about three hundred miles away and therefore within range of our Sea Kings and if necessary our fixed wing aircraft. With luck, we also have a reserve fuel dump ashore, courtesy of our last little trip inland. That's the good news. There is plenty of bad news. Firstly, we have a deadline of noon tomorrow. Intelligence from home indicates that there is a very good chance that if it is not met, the terrorists will cut their losses. Their leader clearly has his eye on the main chance but he's no fool and he has other options. So that means the UN won't be able to help, not in that timescale. The Ukundu government had made it clear that they will not accept any outside help and are sticking to the line that it's nothing to do with them and will be dealing with it. Likewise, the Chinese have clammed up. One thing is clear, it's in both their best interests if the hostages are never found. We have intelligence that elements of the Ukundu army have mobilised and are heading into the area but we're pretty sure they don't know exactly where to search and we do. It's a

Formidable

massive place so the chances of them getting there first are pretty slim.'

'So what's our government's position?' a voice called.

'That's the sixty four thousand dollar question,' Jon replied. 'And of course it's also the question for the French, Dutch and Belgian governments as well. Although they haven't any military assets here and we have. At the moment we've been told to get ready for an assault tonight. We will have to wait for the go ahead but let's not get caught unprepared.'

Bob Everrett raised his hand.

'Yes Bob,' Jon responded.

'The military threat Sir. We know they have A5s. The CO of 888 has seen them up close.'

'But upside down,' a voice called and there was a smattering of laughter at the remark.

Bob continued, although he was smiling as well. 'The A5s are actually attack aircraft but they also have these J8 fighters and they could be more of a problem.'

Pete Moore joined the debate. 'Yes, we've been boning up on them. They're quite capable but they don't have the weapon range capability that we have. If you got into a close encounter they could be a problem especially for a GR7 with only Sidewinders but the FA2 should easily be able to sort them out.'

'Right, you two get together with Wings as soon as we're finished here,' Jon said, 'and give me ideas for dealing with them if they get involved. One thing is certain. Initial rules of engagement will be that we cannot fire on anyone unless fired upon first. So you might just be quite close and personal before that happens. Please take that into account. I also want contingency for the Harriers to work in support of any ground action. Before you say it, I've asked for a tanker to give us air to air refuel capability but whether they can get one on station at such short notice I've yet to be informed. It will almost certainly have to stage through a friendly African country but the diplomatic hassle may make it unavailable in the short time we have.'

'Fine Sir,' Wings said. 'We'll work on the worst case as usual.'

'Good. Now I want the Sea King crews to get together with the SF chaps and Sergeant Llewellyn and work out a plan of attack. Plan for the standard three in the morning insertion. We've no real idea of how many terrorists we will be up against but from the Sergeant's intelligence, it is probably less than fifty and none are regular trained forces. That said, even a kid with an AK47 can do a great deal of damage. If we get to that stage, the only priority is rescuing the hostages, understood?'

There were determined nods around the room.

'Very well, I'll leave you to work out your plans. Feel free to be creative. It's now just past midday. I want your proposals by sixteen hundred. We'll all meet up in here then. Good luck chaps. Would the Commander, Ops officer and navigator come with me to my cabin please.'

Without waiting for an answer, Jon left them to it and headed back to his cabin.

Once the four of them were seated in Jon's sea cabin he outlined what he wanted. 'Once that lot are on their way, assuming we get authorisation, then we need a plan for the ship. However, I have a question. When the Ukundu Air Force paid us a visit the other day. How did they know where we were?'

The question was met with silence for a second and then the Commander spoke. 'Good point Sir. It's not as if we were in our normal position as we had only just turned back from heading towards Nigeria.'

'Correct,' Jon said. 'And it's a big sea out here. Those Chinese aircraft don't have much range and they came straight to us. Sorry, I should apologise. I got on to FOF3 afterwards and I've just had a response. Their best guess and its mine as well is that the Chinese are keeping an eye on us. Not surprising really. They may not want to be seen to be getting involved but supplying covert data on us is totally deniable. We know they have good satellite coverage and I think we must assume that our position is being monitored. Whether this will mean anything is a moot point at the moment but we should plan on that assumption.'

There were nods from the others.

Jon turned to the navigator. 'Amelie I want a detailed navigation plan. The first priority is to get to the launch positon but outside their national limit please.'

Amelie nodded. 'There's an uninhabited island about fifteen miles offshore, we could use that to give us a bit of a radar shadow even if they know where we are it will make pinpointing us that more difficult. It shouldn't hamper our surface picture because we will have airborne radar if we need it.'

'Good, work on that,' Jon agreed. 'Commander, I will want us at Action Stations well in advance, I would suggest from dusk onwards so please look at getting everyone fed and rested as much as possible beforehand. I also want you to work with the MEO on damage control contingencies. Those A5 attack aircraft could do us some harm as well as the two missile ships if they put to sea. Ops, please arrange for a Sea King Mark 6 from Fort Grange to be on surface search from dusk onwards, you can also use our Lynx or one of the escorts cabs to provide fill in cover when they are in transit. Work up a rota please but I want one Lynx to be on permanent alert fifteen with four Sea Skua.'

'I suggest we use Hampshire's cab for that Sir,' Ops replied. She has a Mark 3 and can carry four weapons for longer. The other two are Mark 8s but they could have two and still do the surface search work with the Sea Kings.

Jon nodded. 'That makes sense. For the escorts, I'll want Hampshire up-threat in a goal keeper role with her Sea Wolf and Swansea where she is best able to keep her Sea Dart arcs open.'

Ops nodded while making notes on a pad. 'What about Olna Sir? We'll need Fort Grange with us but Olna could be sent clear?'

'Good point, make it so but not too far away as she does offer us a spare deck if we need it. Alright, any other questions? Otherwise, let's get ready and hope that the bloody politicians have some backbone for once.'

Rupert Thomas was wishing he could sit down as his back was starting to ache. He had been standing in front of the great and good in Cabinet Briefing Room A, or COBRA as it was normally called, briefing and answering questions for quite some time now. He was starting to get fed up with answering what was effectively the same question over and over again. He decided he needed to try and draw the matter to a head. 'Prime Minister, we have clear, incontrovertible evidence of an atrocity committed to a number of our nationals. We have clear incontrovertible evidence of hostages being held in a known location, in the same country that committed those original atrocities and extremely strong evidence that unless we act before midday tomorrow those hostages will be murdered. There are only two choices left us. Do nothing, which will result in the death of eight innocent people or send in a rescue mission using the assets we have who are more than capable of doing the job.' Rupert was doing his best to keep a moderate tone but he let his anger show as he finished his last words.

'Thank you Mister Thomas,' the Prime Minister said with a note of asperity. 'I think we have all got the message.' He turned to the man on his left. 'Foreign Secretary, what will be the international ramifications of a rescue attempt?'

The Foreign Secretary thought for a moment. 'That depends on how well it goes. If the hostages are rescued and there is no collateral loss of life, at least other than to the terrorists, then I would think we would be seen as being totally justified. If the Ukundu military get involved in a shooting match, I agree with Mister Thomas that they would lose badly but that could bring us some approbation from certain quarters. However, I already have assurances from the French, Dutch and Belgian governments that they would support us in any debate in the UN. The worst case would be if we lose people and the hostage are not rescued. However, there is another way of looking at this. What if we do nothing? The press already have half the story and although they don't know about the hostage situation yet, there is no doubt they will do at some stage and then how will we look? May I remind you there is an election in eighteen months? There is a direct parallel here with Margaret Thatcher in eighty two. Can you imagine what would have happened to her if she hadn't taken the risk?'

Rupert could see that shot hit home, although once again he was amazed by the skewed logic of politicians. It was clear that the argument about winning elections was far more effective than stopping people being murdered.

The Prime Minister had inwardly flinched when Thatcher's name came up. The last thing he wanted was to be compared to her and found wanting and the point about the election was absolutely on the nail. He turned to the other outsider in the room. 'Admiral, what is your assessment of the likely success of this mission?'

The Chief of the Defence Staff had been well briefed as well. 'We have one of our finest commanders, with a track record of success over many years in command. We have our latest fighter and attack aircraft, sufficient troops of the highest quality in the world and excellent ships. We can do it Sir.'

The Prime Minister thought again, realising that this was his 'Thatcher moment'. 'Do it.'

Zhang Li put down the receiver of the secure telephone to London and thought for a moment. There could be only one reason for the British Cabinet to all be in Whitehall that afternoon. The big question was not what they were discussing but what decision they had come to. There were probably only two options. He would call the Ukundu government and warn them to be on the alert. He would also advise that maybe the Ukundu military could need some help. It was all he could do.

Chapter 35

'ACTION STATIONS, ACTION STATIONS, ASSUME NBCD STATE 1 CONDITION ZULU' The ship's main broadcast blared out its alarm but this time it was no surprise to anyone in the crew as they had all been warned they would be going to the highest condition of preparedness at eighteen hundred. Everyone had had time for a good meal and were aware of the situation with the exception of one major fact.

Jon waited ten minutes until all the reports had come in that the ship was closed up and picked up the main broadcast microphone. 'D'you here there, this is the Captain speaking. By now we all know that we have a hostage situation ashore and we are getting ready to do something about it. However, things have now changed, we are no longer just preparing for a contingency action. Half an hour ago, I received authorisation to go ahead with the mission. Our task is to send aircraft ashore with troops to rescue eight European hostages. At the same time we have to be prepared for the shore side military to try and stop us. Quite if or what that might mean, we don't know. What we do know is that they are well equipped and as we saw the other day, when two of them paid us a visit, they know we are here. We always plan for the worst but if all goes well, we'll be heading home tomorrow morning. It's going to be a long night but let's show what Formidable can do when she's really needed. That is all.'

He put down the microphone and looked around the Ops room. 'Any sign of anything ashore? We've been warned that they may be up to something.'

The on watch PWO answered. 'All quiet Sir, the first Sea King is just launching from the Grange. However, we have no reported extra radar activity from ashore and no unusual radar traffic at sea.'

'Very well, maintain radio and radar silence except for the surface search aircraft. I'm going to the bridge. I'll be back later on. Instruct the force to start making slow passage to our launch position and take up the designated dispositions.'

When he reached the bridge, Jon nodded at the Officer of the Watch and sat in his chair. The sun had set but only just and there was still enough light to allow him to see the forward part of the flight deck. Four Harriers were visible spotted on the starboard side and he could

Formidable

easily see that two were fighters and two were the attack variant. In a minute he would go back to FLYCO and talk to Wings about how the air department were getting on with ranging and spotting the aircraft in the right order for tonight's fun and games. He already knew that serviceability was good, two of the FA2s but only one GR7 were unserviceable and luckily both Sea King Mark 4s were also good to go. However, he knew how quickly, complicated naval aircraft could let you down. In a pinch, one Sea King could do the job but it would then be very tight. Wings had suggested that one of the anti-submarine Mark 6s could stand in. The problem with that was they didn't have the endurance of a Mark 4 in which case the need for the fuel that had been deposited ashore would be paramount. Despite the probability that it hadn't been discovered they couldn't be sure.

'Penny for them Sir?' a female voice interrupted his train of thought.

Jon turned to Amelie. 'Calm before the storm pilot. This isn't the first time I've been in this situation but it's the first time I haven't been part of the direct action. I'm going to have to trust a large number of people to make the right calls when they are well over that horizon there.'

'I expect there are quite a few people back in UK who feel the same Sir,' she replied.

Jon snorted agreement. 'Good point, at least I have a finger on the pulse here it must be far worse for them.' He was about to say something more when the sound of the Crash on Deck alarm blared out and he could hear shouting from FLYCO around the corner from the bridge. 'What the fuck?' he muttered. 'We're not even at flying stations yet.'

He vaulted from his chair and shot around the corner. Wings and Little F were both staring down out of the windows at something below them. Jon joined them and swore. The forward lift was half way down, with a flight deck tractor on it. That wasn't the problem it was the fact that attached to the tractor by its towing arm was a GR7 which still had its main wheels just on the flight deck, resulting in the aircraft being nose down by over forty five degrees with its tail pointing up to the sky.

Wings turned to Jon before he could ask anything. 'They were just spotting the aircraft when the lift started to descend on its own Sir. I don't know anything more.'

He was just about to continue when a voice over the flight deck loop system started to speak. 'FLYCO, this is the Flight Deck Officer. The aircraft is reasonably safe for the moment and wasn't carrying any ordnance. I'll let you know why the lift went down but I can tell you that the lift controller wasn't operating it and the safety key was in place. Fuck knows what this bloody ship will do next.'

Jon winced inwardly at the remark but kept his council. He was thinking hard. 'Wings can we launch the other aircraft with the deck fouled like that?'

'According to the rules, no Sir. The clearance width between the edge of the lift and the deck edge isn't enough. However, some time ago I got the FDO to do some measurements and then talked to the squadrons. It can be done but they'll have to be bloody careful not to drop an outrigger into the hole or clip the edge of the deck as they go past. Recovery won't be a problem of course as we only need the rear half of the ship for that.'

Jon nodded. 'First launches for CAP were due in what, an hour and a half?'

'Yes Sir, I'll get on to the engineers now and get you a SITREP as soon as I have one.'

Jon took the hint. Once again there was nothing he could do and all he would do was cause delays if he interfered. 'Good, I'll be on the bridge.'

An hour later after getting increasingly frustrated but managing to hide it under an apparent air of calm, Wings and the AEO came onto the bridge.

'The Harrier is secure Sir,' Wings said. 'We think we know what happened to the lift, sort of.'

'Go on,' Jon said.

The AEO carried on. 'As you know Sir, it's hydraulically powered and there is a safety interlock at flight deck level and in the hangar. Both have to be made before the lift can operate. In this case both were made to safe but the damned thing decided to move on its own. It appears to be a fault in the wiring so what we've done is isolate the whole system. It can only be made to move now by physically operating hydraulic valves. It means that we will need extra precautions and people to operate it but it won't be able to do its own

Formidable

thing again. That will get us through the operations tonight and then we can sort it out on the way home.'

Good, well done, so the flight deck will be fully safe? I didn't want to take the risks that Wings was offering.' Jon saw a look pass between the two men. 'Alright, what is it?'

The AEO was looking worried. 'We still have to get the Harrier off it Sir.'

'Can't you just raise the lift now and get it back on deck?'

'Yes Sir but the angle of the towing arm is so acute it will almost certainly break the nose wheel undercarriage as it comes back up, particularly as it comes up to the edge of the flight deck. If that happens the whole aircraft could fall into the lift on top of the tractor, God knows what could happen then. It's full of fuel for a start.'

'Shit, so what do you propose?'

'We tie another tractor on to the rear and pull backwards as the lift comes up, that will relieve some of the strain on the nose wheel and act as an anchor if it does break. However, the chances of getting it back on deck and not damaging it badly or even righting it off are pretty small. And that's not the half of it Sir.'

'I think I know where this is going but go on.'

Wings took over. 'We've got half an hour before we need to launch. With this many aircraft on board it's like a Chinese puzzle moving them around and getting them into the right place with very little room to spare. This one was meant to be the last one in the forward deck park. If we can't manoeuvre it properly once it's back on deck it will delay everything. There's only one thing we can do. There isn't time for anything else.'

Jon nodded and turned to the Officer of the Watch. 'Pipe for Wing Commander Everrett to come to the bridge please.'

A few minutes later, Bob Everrett appeared. 'Bob, are you aware of what it is that's being suggested to free up the lift and the flight deck as well?' Jon asked.

'Yes Sir and I'm not that happy as you can imagine. I don't want to lose one of my aircraft before we've even started.'

'Do you or any of your team have a better idea?'

Bob looked pensive. 'Not really Sir, your people are the experts but how do I account for it back with my Command?'

Jon laughed. 'Welcome to the wonderful world of naval aviation Bob. You don't account for it. I do. I explained right at the start that aircraft are just part of this ship's main armament. So, I'm making the decision. We get it back on deck and then over the side. Sorry, anything else will jeopardise the whole mission. This will drop us down to six of your aircraft which is still more than I need to do the job.' Jon turned to the two Commanders. 'As fast as you can please gentlemen.'

Half an hour later, exactly on time, there was the roar of Pegasus engines and two Sea Harriers shot up the ramp at the front of the ship and into the night sky. Jon felt only relief. The GR7 had been cleared and the lift was flush with the deck. As the AEO had predicted, the nose undercarriage had sheared off when the lift started to raise but the tractor at the rear had held the weight. Jon made a mental note to ensure that the driver of the tractor at the front who had volunteered to stay in it to try and limit the damage be given an award. But now they had bigger fish to fry. It was going to be a long night.

Chapter 36

Agnes couldn't sleep. Nor could any of the hostages. The raucous music and laughter from outside was only getting louder as the evening drew on. The Belgian girls were huddled in one corner. Agnes had tried talking to them but they only spoke German and a little of the local dialect which, to her embarrassment, she herself wasn't particularly fluent in so communication had been rudimentary to say the least. Three of the women were middle aged but two were in their twenties and quite pretty. Right from the start, Agnes and Francois had both discussed the danger that it could put them in and had managed to make them understand to keep as well wrapped up and out of sight as possible.

Her eyes turned towards her bag which for some unaccountable reason she had been allowed to keep. In fact, none of them had been searched the whole time they had been kept captive and all of them still had some personal possessions. She put it down to either arrogance or incompetence but couldn't decide which. Whatever the reason, there remained the burning problem of what to do with the contents of the bag. She had been totally correct when she told Max she wouldn't consider using the pistol but hadn't been exactly straight with him when she explained why. Many years ago, she had been with the Metropolitan Police in London and had been fire-arm trained. One dark night in Soho, she and about twenty others had been involved in a raid on a drug dealer's premises. It hadn't gone well and ended up with two drug dealers and one policeman dead. She hadn't had to use her weapon but had seen the results of what they could do. The next day she tendered her resignation. Five years later and her family were gone and she turned to God. Now she was terrified that she might be forced to go against all she held dear.

Just as she was trying to resolve the conflict in her mind, the door flew open and two men swaggered in. They were both armed and both were clearly half stoned. Wearing ragged jeans and not much else, they stood in the centre of the room and started shouting at them. One of the men went around and inspected them all one by one. When he got to the Belgian girls he started pulling off their head scarves. With a cry of delight, he pulled one of the younger girls to her feet. She started to struggle and he casually back handed her across the face.

She screamed but kept struggling. The other man seeing that the two doctors looked like interfering pointed his rifle at them and made it quite clear what would happen if they did anything by firing a round just above Francois head. The noise in the confined space was staggering and plaster dust filled the air where the bullet struck. The other man pushed the girl out of the room and a few seconds later, he returned and grabbed the other young one. The look of appeal and terror on her face as she was roughly forced out almost broke Agnes's heart. Before anyone could do anything more, the door was forcefully slammed shut. Cheers could be heard outside and few seconds later, the screaming started.

The agony of being helpless and the continued sound of rape and laughter almost drove them all mad and it seemed to go on for hours. In fact, it was probably less than two when all noise outside suddenly stopped and the two girls were almost bodily thrown back into the room. They were both naked and showed marks of having been beaten. The others immediately helped them as much as they could. They had enough spare clothes between them to get them decently covered up. As Agnes looked through her case for her few spare clothes her eyes settled on the gun. Looking over at the poor huddled girls in the corner, she made her decision. She reached into the bag and carefully looked at the weapon for the first time. It was a Browning nine millimetre which she was familiar with from her police days. She clicked the magazine release and withdrew it. Pressing down on the top round she could tell that it was fully loaded. She slipped it back into the pistol grip and being careful to ensure that no one saw her, tucked into the waist of her shorts at the back and pulled her shirt out to cover it. She wasn't actually sure why she wanted to conceal it from her companions. Maybe she didn't trust them to accept they might need it.

Taking her spare clothes, she went over to the two girls. One was almost catatonic, simply curled up in the foetal position. The other one was more coherent. She was saying something to Francois as she approached.

The girl was speaking in German which she knew Francois could understand a little. When she finished, Francois turned to her. 'She's hard to understand but from what I can make out the man Jamar came and got angry. He said he had ordered that we were to be left alone until midday tomorrow. He's told them to stop the party. She's not sure why but he said something about the army.'

Agnes sat back and thought. 'It seems that my idea that we are being ransomed was right but also that maybe someone is trying to stop it. If Max made it to safety then maybe Britain has sent some forces here. Nigeria is friendly they might have deployed there. If Jamar is stopping the party he must be worried about something. We just have to sit tight and hold out as long as we can.'

She sat back in the corner and started to pray.

Rupert Thomas wasn't a praying man but maybe it was time to start he pondered. It was going to be a long night. They had moved permanently into their Operations room and were in direct contact with the Ops room at Fleet headquarters at Northwood. When the message about Formidable's jammed lift had come in, he had worried for his friend and his ship but it seemed they had dealt with the issue swiftly enough.

His team in country had been deployed and it was clear the Ukundu military were up to something. They were either trying to find the hostages or prevent others finding them, probably both he realised. A convoy of military vehicles had left the capital earlier and were seen heading north east. Unfortunately Rupert didn't have the resources to follow it but was hoping for some real time satellite images soon. Activity at the airfield seemed to be ramping up as well. Many of the new aircraft that had been delivered were out on the hardstanding but none had taken off yet. One of his men was in a good position to watch. Then another call came in and as soon as he had taken it he was directly on to Fleet. He spoke to the duty Commander. 'Just got a message in from one of our men who has been watching those two missile boats. They've just sailed. No idea where they are going but I think you need to warn our guys. I can't think of another reason for both of them to leave now.'

Chapter 37

Sergeant Max Llewellyn was sitting strapped into a loud vibrating helicopter yet again. He was amazed just how quickly he had fallen back into the old military ways. He knew several of the team from his past service and they all seemed glad to have him back. Captain Shaw the OCRM had been very supportive and they had spent most of the afternoon reviewing the terrain and likely methods of approach. However, while they were pretty sure where they needed to go and what to expect there in terms of cover, they had to assume that there would be serious resistance. In the end, they had settled on a drop several miles clear so that the noise of the aircraft would not be heard and then a covert approach. Some of the more aggressive types had pushed for a fast roping, direct assault supported by the jets if necessary. However, without knowing what sort of resistance to expect, the Captain rightly deemed it unnecessarily dangerous. Max had agreed wholeheartedly. If they had called in the firepower of the Harriers they would have no way of knowing whether they would hit the hostages. However, he had to acknowledge that there were only seventeen of them. Eight of them were in one aircraft and nine in the other.

It should have been quite spacious as the aircraft had seating for twenty four but there was a great deal of equipment loaded as well. They were carrying some serious firepower. As Special Forces they were all allowed to take personal weapons of their own choice. In Max's case he was happy to stick with his SA80 rifle but had added to it with a nine millimetre pistol, a marine knife and six hand grenades. Many of the others favoured the American M16 rifle. However, one of the team was a sniper and had his specialist weapon with him. Three others were a mortar team and everyone was carrying extra rounds for the weapon. Also, nearly all of them had been issued with a LAW 60 millimetre anti-tank rocket which during the Falklands War had proved as good at emptying buildings and trenches as damaging armoured vehicles. Looking at his comrades, he just hoped his level of fitness or his still not totally healed leg wouldn't let him down. They didn't have packs, only their fighting order as they should only be on the ground a matter of hours but would still be carrying some serious weight.

The one thing that Max had not encountered in his previous time were the night vision goggles they were all wearing. He had used the same technology on the sights of his rifle before but had never had them available to be fitted onto his helmet. Everyone was wearing them, although apart from the aircrew flying the helicopter, they were all clipped up out of the way at the moment. Once on the ground, they would give an enormous advantage especially as the moon was due to set just after midnight.

Ten thousand feet above the two Sea Kings, two Harriers were keeping top cover, flying a racetrack along the route the helicopters were flying below them at fifty feet. One Sea Harrier and one GR7 were in loose formation. So far everything seemed quiet. The ESM equipment in the aircraft stayed silent except for a couple of air traffic control radars well behind them. They had another hour on station and then two more aircraft would relieve them. The marines should be able to call for air support at any time. The GR7 was loaded with an extra drop tank and three one thousand pound iron bombs. Although it could be carrying much more accurate Paveway laser guided bombs, it had been decided to keep things simple as there was no guarantee that a laser designator for the more accurate weapons would be available on the ground where they would be needed. The Sea Harrier was carrying four AMRAAM long range anti-aircraft missiles and a similar extra drop tank.

Suddenly, the radio broke the quiet of the night. 'Alpha Charlie, this is Whiskey Echo over.' Pete Moore who was flying the Sea Harrier knew the call was for him from the lead Sea King. There was meant to be radio silence but it could be broken in an emergency. Clearly, something had happened.

'Whiskey Echo go ahead,' he replied.

'Roger, we have a military column heading in roughly the same direction as us but with a hundred miles to go. Estimate ten troop lorries and four armoured cars of some sort. We flew over them and they didn't react probably because we caught them unawares but if they've got any sense they'll know what we're about and see the direction we're going, over.'

'Whiskey Echo that's all copied,' Peter replied I'll relay that to Mother over.'

Pete then did just that using his long range High Frequency radio and received a curt acknowledgement.

In Formidable's Ops room Jon was having to think carefully. He had already been warned that the Ukundu army were on the hunt as well and it looked like they had been given a bit more help unwittingly by his own aircraft. If he was the commander on the ground he would assume that the aircraft had a good idea of where they were heading. Luckily, he would not know how far he needed to go.

Jon turned to the Ops officer who was also the on watch Warfare officer. 'What sort of speed do you think a convoy of trucks could do on open terrain?'

'Twenty five maybe thirty,' Ops replied. 'I wouldn't think they could do much more especially at night.'

'Hmm and the moon goes down shortly. I'd be very surprised if they have NVG capability so let's say twenty five maximum. That gives our guys four hours and they'll be on the deck in less than an hour.'

'Yes but then they were assuming an hour to yomp in and another hour to recce and get stuck in.' Ops replied grimly.

Jon mulled it over. 'It's going to be cutting it fine and once our chaps go in, it will be a beacon to follow. We need to slow them down or stop them somehow.'

Jon was still thinking hard. Before he could put his thoughts into words the radio came to life. It was the Sea King on surface search. 'Delta Victor Four Three this is Bravo Two Charlie Six, Contact, two fast moving surface contacts have just come out from the coast, heading north west towards you, range from me fifteen miles at one five zero, over.'

The air controller acknowledged the report but before anyone could say anything more a data link track from the Hampshire came up. With her more capable ESM equipment she was detecting something. Ops called out, 'we have a racket on that bearing identified as Square Tie radar. Almost certainly it's the two missile boats Sir, the bearing ties in with Sea King's contacts. They are currently ninety miles from us and within engagement range of their SACCADE missiles. They must have sneaked up right against the coast and have now turned towards us.'

'Well, it seems the commander of that troop convoy was quick off the mark,' Jon said. 'Does that radar on the missile boats change modes to launch its missiles?'

'No Sir,' Ops said. 'They're like Exocet. They fire them on inertial guidance and they turn on their own seeker head when much closer. Each one of those ships has four of them.'

'Ops room, this is the Communications Office,' a voice broke in. 'Sir, we have a Flash precedence signal. Intelligence from ashore says multiple aircraft launches from the military airfield. At least eight aircraft have taken off.'

Jon acknowledged the call. It was clear that the Ukundu military were well awake now. It was time for Formidable to show her teeth. 'Ops, launch all alert aircraft including the Lynx. Plan Bravo please. Lift Emission Control, all radars on, let's tell them we know what they are up to.'

The roar of Harriers getting airborne lasted for several minutes. Jon just hoped he hadn't jumped the gun too early. Despite the posturing going on, no shots had been fired yet. His ROE were quite clear. He couldn't fire unless fired upon first. He understood why but it effectively tied his hands behind his back. If the first shots fired at him were effective it could tip the military balance before he could retaliate properly.

Ops broke into his thoughts. 'Sir, this all seems very well thought out. Combined use of aircraft and ships. It looks like they had a well thought out plan and were ready to use it at the drop of a hat.'

'Good point,' Jon responded. 'My guess would be they are getting some help from their friends in terms of operational planning. As you say, this has all the hallmarks of a well thought out response. So the question is, if they intend to start ramping it up, where will they strike first?' As he said it, the answer struck him.

Chapter 38

Cruising at six thousand feet up ahead of the force, the crew of Sea King Bravo Two Charlie Six felt very vulnerable. Despite all the ships now transmitting on all their radars, they were still the eyes of the force in the direction of the threat. The two missile boats the observer in the rear of the aircraft was tracking were still heading towards the British ships but had slowed down considerably. A few minutes ago they had picked up the transponders of three Lynx heading out their way. At least they wouldn't be on their own and they knew that thousands of feet above them two Sea Harriers were somewhere about on CAP. Even so it wasn't a comfortable place to be especially now there was the risk of enemy fast jets about as well.

In the cockpit, the two pilots were concentrating. The left hand pilot was flying but rather than relaxing, his friend in the other seat was keeping very alert. He was watching the Orange Crop ESM receiver. On his kneepad were the details of the threat radars they might face. Just as he was looking down for the hundredth time, a chirping noise came over his headset and three LEDs lit up on the Orange Crop receiver. Heart pumping, he moved the cursor over the LEDs and read out the details that the receiver had analysed. 'Type 208 sector radar fifteen degrees to starboard and a strong signal. Shit, he must be close,' he shouted, adrenalin coursing through his veins.

The observer had nothing on his radar but it wasn't designed to see small fast moving air targets so he wasn't surprised but this was the one they were worried about. This was the targeting radar in the nose of a Chinese F8 fighter. The observer immediately put out a radio call back to the force.

A new voice immediately came over the radio, it was one of the CAP Sea Harriers. 'This is Delta Three, confirm. I have the same racket on a bearing of one two five and radar contact.' He then gave a position. The two Sea King pilots exchanged glances as the observer broke in. 'Bollocks, that's only ten miles away from us. Has the ESM changed?'

The right hand seat pilot answered. 'Shit yes but he's turned it off. Why would he do that?'

'Because he's not going to use his missiles, he's got cannon and he knows where we are now,' the observer replied. 'Time for some of that pilot shit you two.'

Without waiting, the flying pilot dropped the collective and pushed the nose of the helicopter down. Just as he did so there was a tearing noise and a stream of yellow glowing balls shot overhead. It was followed by a blast of air that threw the massive helicopter around like a leaf. Twin spears of flame shot over their heads.

'Mayday, Mayday this is Bravo Two, we have been attacked by an unknown aircraft. He missed but we're taking evasive action.' The pilot wrenched the Sea King around in a turn that its designers never expected it to be capable of and they caught sight of the afterburners of their attacker in a hard turn back towards them. 'Delta Three is there another one?' the pilot called.

'Affirmative but the idiot is staying clear. Your problem is the first one. We're on our way, over.'

The Sea King pilot had no time to reply as he had lost sight of the afterburner plumes which could only mean the bastard was now heading back directly towards them.

A new voice came over the radio. 'All stations, all stations this is Delta Victor. Weapons free, I say again weapons free.'

'Fuck, I hope that's in time.' The Sea King pilot muttered as he prepared for another gut wrenching turn to keep out of the fighter's bore sight. Without being able to see his attacker he could only guess but when he judged the moment right, he pulled a hard turn to starboard and dropped the collective to the bottom. This time their attacker was well clear and above them. They could see his cannon fire clearly. He must have been having the same problem as the Sea King crew. It was one thing to sneak up on an apparently unsuspecting target and quite another when it was evading as only a helicopter could.

'Fox Four, Fox Four,' was suddenly called over the radio. The crew in the Sea King knew exactly what that meant but continued to head for the sea as fast as they could. They were passing through a thousand feet when a bright yellow star lit up over their heads followed almost immediately by another one a few miles ahead of them. Two AMRAAM missiles fired by one of the Sea Harriers had done their job and slammed into the two fighters whose pilots probably didn't even

Formidable

know they were under attack. The Harriers had fired from forty miles away.

The Sea King levelled out and started to climb back. The crew were shaken but knew they still had a job to do.

In Formidable's Ops room there was a sigh of relief when the Sea King reported that their attackers had been splashed and they were fine. Jon was now worried about the missile boats. Their radars were still transmitting. He needed that Sea King back on task to know exactly what they were doing.

'Get me a report on the Corvettes as soon as you can Ops.' Jon ordered. 'And tell the two Harriers on CAP to look out for more incoming. Also, make sure that the escorting aircraft inshore know that there are bandits about. The message was that eight had got airborne. We've only accounted for two.'

'Aye aye Sir and do we authorise the airfield raid?'

Jon thought hard for a moment. The attacking aircraft had come from there and from the intelligence there could be more. 'Yes, tell them to get on with it.'

'This is Bravo Two, be advised the two missile boats appear to have increased speed and are heading towards you again, over.'

Jon had a real problem now. He had no way of telling if they launched their missiles unless they were seen doing so visually. After that, the next thing they would know was when the seeker heads in the missiles turned on and that was far, far too late.

'Ops, where are the Lynx?' he asked.

'Closing fast Sir, our Mark 8 will be within visual range with her PID shortly.'

'Good, I want eyes on both of those ships permanently. Tell them to set up for plan Leopard. They are to stay weapons tight unless they see any indication of hostile intent.'

In Formidable's Mark 8 Lynx, the observer was watching his targets intensely. The large TV screen in the centre of the dashboard was displaying a grey and black picture of the helicopter's Sea Owl Passive Information Device or PID. Using powerful optics and infrared sensors, it could see the two targets as though it was daylight. The pilot was concentrating solely on his flying. One peculiarity of the system was that the picture from the PID was horizon stabilised. The

Formidable

pilot was having to use his instruments and the last thing he needed was to be confused over whether the horizon was at an angle or not. When the ship had ordered plan Leopard, the Mark 3 aircraft from the Hampshire, which carried four Sea Skua had departed and was making its way around the targets to make sure that if they did attack, the missiles would come in from two different directions. The Mark 3 didn't have a PID but his radar was quite up to the task now that the targets were identified.

Suddenly, the PID screen turned almost white with a streak of something coming from the left hand ship. The plume could also be seen in the distance with the naked eye. The crew in the Lynx didn't wait. The pilot immediately climbed hard to two hundred feet and pointed towards the targets.

The observer got on the radio. At the same time, he started to frantically make switches in the cockpit. A gentle thud was felt through the airframe as the first missile was released and suddenly the outside was lit up as the rocket motor in the first Sea Skua ignited as it fell clear of the aircraft.

'Bruiser Loose, Bruiser Loose,' the observer called, meaning they had fired missiles. It would tell the other Lynx to do the same if they hadn't already and also let the ship know that they had detected something that represented a threat. In a matter of seconds, four Skua were in flight, from two different directions. Two were targeted at the lead ship, the other two at the second vessel. The other weapons were kept in reserve as previously agreed.

However, the observer was dismayed to see the lead ship had continued to fire missiles of her own. He counted four in all and radioed the information back. Then the horizon lit up.

On the first missile boat, as soon as the last weapon was away, the Captain ordered the wheel hard over. He wasn't keen to stay in the area any longer than he had to. He had known that the British would be aware of his presence. However, he had absolutely no idea how closely he had been observed and what threat there actually was to him and his ship.

The first missile travelling at over Mach 0.8 slammed into his bridge. The 70 pound warhead wasn't that big but at that speed, the kinetic energy of three hundred pounds worth of missile would probably have been enough without a warhead at all. As it was, the bridge was blown to bits and everyone inside with it. A few seconds later, the second weapon impacted the side of the ship near the stern and blew it off. With such a large hole in her, the ship immediately started to settle. With no one to give the command, the remaining crew started to abandon her.

The second ship wasn't so lucky. Her missile tubes were still fully loaded and the first Skua scored a direct hit on one of them. The subsequent explosion set off the warheads and rocket motors in all four tubes in what ordnance experts call the 'Popcorn Effect'. The whole ship disappeared in a massive blast and disintegrated. No one survived.

In Formidable's Ops room there was a muted cheer when the Lynx reported that the attacking ships had been hit. However, there was no time to contemplate the action because they knew there were four modern sea skimming missiles inbound.

'Is Hampshire in position? Jon asked urgently.

'Yes Sir,' Ops answered. 'Her Captain just sent you a message. He said, covering your ass usual.'

'Tell him I'll buy him a pint afterwards. Now is there anything else we can do?'

'All countermeasure have been ordered. Chaff has been fired by all ships Sir.'

This meant that the incoming missiles would be presented with dozens of targets to choose from rather than just three when they turned on their seeker radars.

'And all our close in systems are ready. Swansea is hoping to help as well. We can only wait.'

Suddenly, there was a call over the intercom. 'Missile targeting radar detected. Bearing one two five.'

Jon called to the bridge. 'Come hard left, head Three Zero Five.' This would present their stern to the incoming weapons and narrow their silhouette.

'Hampshire is turning towards Sir. We have the tracks of the missiles now on datalink from Hampshire.'

Jon looked at his radar plot and could clearly see four tracks heading inbound. They seemed to be well spread out. The information was coming from Hampshire's 967 radar which was optimised to pick

Formidable

out fast moving, low level targets. He picked up the main broadcast. 'This is the Captain we are under missile attack. Brace Brace.'

Throughout the ship, everyone who could, threw themselves down and covered their heads.

The four missiles were flying at four metres above the sea. During their inertial flight they had separated slightly so that when their radars came on they saw a slightly different picture. However, they all selected a target and locked on.

In HMS Hampshire, Brian Pearce waited patiently. The incoming missiles were quite clear on his plot. He had already given command authorisation for his Sea Wolf anti-missile system to engage as soon as they were in range. There was nothing else he could do. If nothing else, his ship was a physical barrier between the threat and the Formidable but he really would rather not use his ship in such a way. As the first missile came within range there was a dull thud from the ship and the first vertically launched Sea Wolf left its silo. As soon as it was clear, it altered course and fired its main booster. Accelerating to over Mach 2 in under a second the booster cut out and it coasted the rest of the way. It was still travelling over Mach 2 when under the guidance of its 910 fire control radar, it impacted the first missile and blew it to bits.

In quick succession, the next two missiles were blasted out of the sky. The fourth one was a different matter. During its transit flight, it had wandered further away than the others and when it did acquire a target it had had to perform quite a large change of course. This meant it would come in on a track that didn't intersect the Hampshire's Sea Wolf engagement zone. It also meant that most of the chaff blooms that it could have chosen from were less spread out.

Brian's Ops room team had seen the problem in advance and warned the other ships but Brian had to look on helplessly as the missile streaked safely past him.

In Formidable, they were also aware of the problem. Even if the missile didn't have lock on them exactly, it was clearly coming their way. Jon ordered another turn to continue to present their stern and minimise their size as a target. Then the distant sound of their CIWS guns firing was heard. Jon couldn't but remember how badly they had performed a few years ago in the Gulf when an American ship had used them. They had hit the incoming missiles but only shredded them and the ship had been clobbered by tons of very fast moving shrapnel.

Formidable wasn't even that lucky. The intact missile struck the stern on the starboard side and detonated. The shock throughout the ship threw several people off their feet.

Simon Gross was in his cabin at the rear of the ship. He had been given anti-flash gloves and a hood as well as a lifejacket but had decided he didn't need them. He was far too busy writing the denouncement of his treatment by the Captain of this bloody ship. He had also ignored the order to brace when it came over the intercom. After all, what did it have to do with him? In the end, neither anti-flash nor lying on the floor would have made the slightest difference. The warhead of the weapon actually pierced the bulkhead of his cabin before it detonated. In a micro second he was turned into red mist and a micro second later it all burnt to carbon dust in a massive blast of flame.

Chapter 39

Jon looked around the Ops room. It all felt weirdly normal. He stifled the urge to call for a damage report. That was the sort of thing you saw in the movies. His people were on it and knew they had to report as soon as they had any information. Instead, he called out to the room. 'Everyone alright? Anyone hurt in here?'

There was a cry from one corner. 'Chief Ops here Sir, one of my girls was thrown from her chair. I think she knocked herself out on the deck as she fell. If it's alright I'll get her down to Sick Bay?'

'Go ahead,' Jon said just as the intercom came to life. 'Captain this is HQ1. We have an initial assessment.'

'Go ahead MEO,' Jon replied.

'Impact was at the stern just below the quarterdeck Sir. It seems the missile came in at an angle into the officer's cabin flat at the rear and then exploded. However, most of the blast seems to have gone straight back out. There's a bloody great hole our side but is fifteen feet above the water line.

'Casualties Dave, how many?'

'That's the really good news Sir. We don't think anyone has been killed by the missile. The place should be empty at Actions Stations, although there are a few people in the ship with minor injuries.'

'Good God,' Jon said. 'Who said Formidable was an unlucky ship? So we have full power available and the steering wasn't damaged?'

'Sir, apart from losing a few cabins and a couple of store rooms below them we're fine.'

An alarm bell rang. 'Hang on MEO, where did we put that bloody journalist? Wasn't he confined to his cabin down aft?'

'Oh shit, you're right Sir. Let me look into it.'

Jon put down the microphone. Despite his distaste for the man, Jon wouldn't wish that on anyone. He hoped he had been on the other side of the ship. However, he still couldn't believe how lucky the ship had been.

His thoughts were interrupted by the Ops officer 'Just had a call from the Harriers they are about to sort out the airfield Sir. And I take it we are alright to conduct flying operations again? Wings had been asking as we have cabs getting low on gas and he really doesn't want to divert them to the only airfield within range. Especially as we are about to bomb the crap out of it.'

Jon grinned. 'No, Formidable is good to go.'

Miles inland, four Harrier GR7s escorted by two FA2s were lining up on the main runway at the airport. Each attack aircraft was carrying three, one thousand pound bombs. A few minutes ago they had been told to execute the plan they had devised. Shutting down an airfield runway was a tricky business. In the Falklands War, a Vulcan bomber had dropped twenty one, one thousand pounders to virtually no effect. That had been because they had to do so from height and the only way to give any chance of a hit was to drop them obliquely across the runway. In the Second World War, despite heavy bombing by the Luftwaffe, most airfield runways were in use again only hours after they had been hit. Bulldozers and top soil could easily fill in a crater. The aim tonight was different. They didn't need to deny the use of the runway for more than a few hours.

As the two fighters remained at altitude and kept watch, the four GR7s dived down one after the other along the axis of the runway. The place was pitch dark, someone had sensibly turned off all the airfield lights. It wasn't going to help. Not only that, it meant they were not flying at the moment and anyone interrupting from elsewhere would have the fighters to deal with. The place was defenceless.

Bob Everrett led the attack in a steep dive. He could clearly see the runway through his NVGs. This was going to be fun. This was why he had always wanted to be a pilot. Pulling five G, he grunted with effort as he pulled out of his dive only twenty feet above the runway. The military compound was on his left. They had all studied the layout from satellite images. The idea was to lay down his bombs opposite the only tarmac entrance to the military hardstanding. He hit the bomb release and felt the jolt as they fell clear. He then pulled another five G, climbing hard at full power. As the nose came up he rolled the Harrier over onto its back to look at his handiwork. He could clearly see a blast of dust and debris still climbing into the air in exactly the right place.

'Number two go,' he called and then turned left to keep clear. They had a separation procedure agreed. Colliding with one of your own aircraft was just not going to happen.

Formidable

On the ground the noise was appalling. There was the thunder of multiple fast jet engines overhead and every few minutes that increased tenfold as another jet dived down and dropped its load of explosives on the runway. Four times it happened and then the noise disappeared as the aircraft left. As silence descended once again, the only noise left was the sound of earth and stones dropping back into the massive craters surrounding the military hard standing access. There would be no flying from the field for some time to come.

As the six aircraft climbed back to height they checked in with the ship. The four GR7s, now empty or ordnance were ordered back to Mother. However, the two fighters were told to link up with the two aircraft that had been providing top cover for the Special Forces raid. There were still six other aircraft somewhere that needed to be found.

Despite all that had been going on, it was less than half an hour since the first shot had been fired.

The two aircraft providing top cover over the Commando Sea Kings were starting to get low on fuel. They had heard on the radio that the two FA2's that had supported the raid on the airfield would be with them soon. Pete Moore was glad. His bum was starting to get sore and he was really regretting not going to the heads before he launched. It was standard practice for him and had been for years but just for once, in all the excitement of a real operation, it had completely slipped his mind. However, he was also very conscious that there were other enemy aircraft out there and he had been watching his radar carefully. They had been too far away to track them when the launch had been reported to him, not that he could have done anything about it at the time. What he couldn't understand was that if they were coming his way then they should have been here some time ago. He knew two fighters had been shot down at sea. He had heard the excited call of Fox 4 even from this distance. So, where were the buggers now? Then he had a thought. The Nigerian border wasn't that far to the north and they had been given strict instructions to stay out of their airspace. Would the Ukundu aircraft do the same?

He pulled the aircraft into a tight turn to the north. His Blue Vixen radar was a typical fighter sector radar and could only look ahead. 'Got you, you sneaky buggers,' he muttered to himself before calling the contact over the radio. They had discussed this contingency on board. Now that the airfield was out of action these guys didn't have

Formidable

that many options. It was just that they didn't know it yet. He would be delighted to inform them.

He switched his radio over to the emergency frequency. 'Unidentified fast jets approaching over the Nigerian border, this is British Sea Harrier callsign Whiskey Echo calling on Guard. Be advised, your home airfield is no longer available to you. The runway has been bombed. There are no other diversions in your country, you have no choice but to turn around and head for the airfield at Gombe.' Pete had a pretty good idea of the range and endurance of the enemy machines and he wasn't bluffing.

He watched the radar contacts carefully. They were closing fast and would soon be in range of his AMRAAM but showed no sign of changing heading. He tried again. 'Unidentified aircraft, this is British Harrier Whiskey Echo on Guard. Be advised if you do not turn, your actions will be considered hostile and I will fire on you. You should be aware that the two aircraft sent to attack British Warship Formidable have been shot down. Turn away. If you do not do so in two minutes I will be forced to fire on you.'

There was no reaction from the aircraft. Pete waited until he had a good firing solution and when the time was up fired one AMRAAM. 'Fox 4, this is British Harrier, I say again Fox 4. I'm sure you guys know what that means.'

Suddenly, the contacts on the radar scope scattered. It wasn't going to help. Pete counted down under his breath. A few seconds after his estimate, one of the targets disappeared. He watched intently as the other five all turned and headed north east. With a sigh of relief, he turned his aircraft west towards the two jets who were coming to relieve him. He called to his GR7 wingman who was even lower on fuel than he was to join him and then he could go home and get relief of another sort.

Chapter 40

In the Ops room there was satisfaction all round. Despite the one missile hit on the ship, all had gone well so far. However, Jon was less ebullient than his staff and decided they needed to settle back to work. This wasn't over yet.

'Listen up everyone. We've seen off their attempt to take us out but may I remind everyone that this operation is to rescue people ashore. We haven't done that yet and we have aircraft and Royal Marines out there who need our support if it's to be successful. As soon as the GR7s are back on board I want them bombed up and back in the air to support the ground attack if needed. The final two fighters are to escort them. We may still have a threat from the air. Let's plan for the worst.'

His words hit home and everyone looked down and started concentrating on their jobs again.

'Ops, I'm going up to FLYCO for the next few minutes.' So saying, Jon put down his headset and headed out of the door.

FLYCO was dark, Jon had completely forgotten that it was night time. In the darkened Ops room with its electronic displays, it was easy to forget what time of day it actually was. Wings was sitting in his chair which was similar to Jon's on the bridge and Little F was hunched over his control console further forward. Neither man saw Jon until he announced his presence.

'Well done chaps,' Jon said.

Wings jumped slightly. 'Oh hello Sir, the Ops room said you were coming but you snuck up on us.'

'Sorry about that. How's it all going?'

'You mean apart from that bloody great missile hitting us. One of the best brown trouser moments of my career. From up here it was quite spectacular.'

'What, you didn't hit the deck like everyone else?' Jon asked in surprise.

'Figured that it would be my only chance to see something like that in my career Sir and if it was that close then lying down would be no bloody help.'

'Good point. When are the light blue due back?'

Little F answered for him. 'Just in the circuit now Sir. We've got the weapons ready to load and the last two Sea Harriers are manned up and ready to go. I just hope our Crab chums don't try to pull their crew duty hours stunt on us. It's way past their bed time after all.'

Jon grimaced at the thought. He'd come up against that particular RAF foible before. In some ways it made sense in ensuring that aircrew didn't get too fatigued to fly. The problem was that often they stuck to it too much. It had caused great bad feeling in Northern Ireland especially when naval aircrew were willing to keep flying until the job was done.

'Don't worry Sir. I had a quiet word with their CO,' Wings said. 'He understands.'

Jon decided he didn't want to know more and changed the subject.

Just then Petty Officer Jenkins came in with a tray in his hand. 'Found you at last Sir. I've got a mug of coffee and some sandwiches if you would like them.'

Jon suddenly realised how parched he was and grabbed the coffee mug. 'Thanks Jenkins you must be clairvoyant. Just put the sarnies down there please.'

Jenkins put down the tray and then as quickly as he had arrived, quietly disappeared. Jon offered the sandwiches around and they all watched as one after the other the three GR7s came in to hover alongside, then move across the deck and thump down. Within seconds of moving clear, they were surrounded by members of the deck crew pushing weapon trolleys.

Within bare minutes, the aircraft had been refuelled and rearmed. 'Bloody Hell,' Wings said. 'That must have been the fastest turn around on record.'

'What? Even faster than when we went to Actions Stations for real the other day? Jon asked with a smile.

'Oh yes but don't tell the Commander that.' Both men laughed.

A few seconds later the first aircraft called ready for take off and they all watched as one after the other, they roared down the flight deck and back into the night.

Almost three hundred miles inland the two Sea Kings flared into a hover and landed. Within seconds, troops were out and scouring the area looking for any sign of opposition. There was none. As soon as he was certain, Captain Shaw indicated to the pilots to shut down the aircraft. They couldn't afford the noise they made even running on the ground and they couldn't afford to stay airborne either. They didn't have the fuel.

As soon as the rotors and engines had wound to a halt, one of the pilots jumped out and approached the Captain. 'We're good here. Couldn't see any indications of movement near us but we will keep a careful watch. The big danger for us is if that bunch of troops manage to catch up with us. So, I suggest that if we see any sign of them, we flash up and fly over you and land the far side of the camp. The camp will have been alerted by then anyway and it'll give you an escape route away from their line of approach.'

The Captain nodded. 'Good thinking, hopefully they are too far away and we should have some pretty serious air cover soon as well. We'll keep in contact by radio and if we can call you in earlier we will.'

The two men shook hands and the marines disappeared into the night. The aircrew took up look up positions and waited.

Half an hour later and Max was completely shot. Luckily, they had arrived. The terrain had started out reasonably flat but as he well remembered, the mining camp was built on open ground up against a steep sided hill. The actual mine entrance was in a narrow gulley that cut into the side of the hill. He looked at his watch. It was half past one.

Captain Shaw dropped to the ground next to him. To Max's annoyance he wasn't even breathing hard. 'See what a few years away from us does to you Sergeant?'

Max was still too blown to give a pithy reply. He merely nodded agreement.

'So, now we can see the whites of their eyes do you have any ideas?' The Captain asked.

They were still over a mile from the camp and there were definitely no eyes in view but Max knew what he meant. He knelt up and studied the whole scene through his NVGs still breathing hard but recovering fast. 'Right Sir, over to the left that long roofed building was a sorting shed. Further on behind it was the accommodation for the workers and the building off to the right is the administration office. My guess is that anyone holding hostages would put them there. The whole place is falling to bits but that was the most intact building when we were here earlier in the year.'

Formidable

A bright light flared up behind the sorting shed and what sounded like American rap music could be heard along with faint voices. Max pulled his goggles clear and the light almost dissipated to nothing. As they waited and watched the music stopped.

'Kicking over the fire and going to bed would be my guess,' Max said as he continued to study the area. 'I still think my idea of approaching from behind the sorting shed is best. It will block the view of nearly everyone inside and give us the best overall cover. I would be surprised if they've bothered with sentries if the way they're behaving is the same as last time I encountered them but I think we should expect at least one lookout. If it was me, I would put him on top of the sorting shed roof. You should be able to survey the whole approach from there.'

'Agreed,' Captain Shaw said and called his team over. 'This is the plan chaps. A covert approach with the aim of getting to the back wall of that long building on the left. After that we'll re-assess but our best guess is that the hostages are in that small building on the right. Smith, I want you to hang back when we are within about five hundred yards and go off to the right so you can see the roof of the shed but also up into the rest of the compound. Then get that bloody great big rifle set up and be ready to cover us. If we see a target, we want taken out, I will designate it with a laser spotter. Otherwise, get ready to support us when we go in. Dexter, you're on point, watch out for sentries. We won't use the mortar but bring it with us. We'll leave it before we go in. We can always come back for it if we need it. Otherwise standard covert ops. Everyone happy?'

There were nods all round. This was something they had practiced many times and for some of them it was something they had done for real several times.

Agnes was just drifting off to a troubled sleep when the door flew open again. The music had finally stopped although despite what one of the girls had told them it was quite some time after they had been returned. They had all been praying for a little rest and at last it seemed it might happen. Now it was obvious they weren't going to get it.

Jamar came in with two other men and shouted at them to get up. Still half asleep they were pulled to their feet and forced out of the door at gunpoint. Once outside, they were led up past a big shed and into a narrow defile. The men had torches, otherwise it would have been a nightmare walking over the rough terrain. There appeared to be the remains of train tracks on the ground and several of them stumbled over the remains of rotting sleepers. At the end of the little gulley was a large cavern. Clearly, at some time there had been barrier of some sort in the way but it had long rotted away. However, there were several large boulders some over waist height that must have fallen from the rocky hill above making it impossible to walk straight into the cave. Once there, they were told to sit by a wall of rock about ten feet inside. Jamar then left, instructing them all to be silent. The two guards stayed and these two actually looked reasonably alert.

Agnes's heart was thumping. Something serious was going on and the girl's earlier comment that she had heard something about the army was preying on her mind. Whose army? And what would they do? One thing was clear, they had been moved to a more secure location and that could only mean that something would be happening tonight and probably quite soon. As she lay back against the cold rock, she could feel the sharp outline of the pistol in her waistband. For the first time, she actually got some comfort from the thought that it was there.

They didn't have to wait long before they knew something serious was happening. First, there was a strange roaring sound. It seemed to go overhead. Agnes quickly realised it was the sound of helicopters and more than one. Then there was the staccato sound of an automatic rifle firing and then it suddenly stopped. For a few seconds, that seemed much longer nothing happened and then all hell broke loose. Massive explosions and gunfire from seemingly everywhere.

The two guards looked surprised and then scared. They turned to the captives and for a second, Agnes thought they were going to be shot. Then the two men started shouting at each other. There was a massive explosion from somewhere and that was enough for them. The two men bolted into the night taking their torches with them. The cave was plunged into darkness lit only by the flashes of the gunfire from outside.

Francois was the first to get to his feet and Agnes joined him as they looked out at the narrow entrance.

'We must get out,' Francois said worriedly. 'This may be our only chance.'

'Don't be so bloody silly man' Agnes replied. 'We don't know who is shooting at who and the only way out is to run into all that gunfire. No, the safest place is here.'

'What if it's the Ukundu army coming for us?'

'Alright, you go and investigate. We'll all wait for you to come back' she gave him a challenging look.

Francois hesitated and then slumped back. 'You're right as usual. However, why don't we see if there is anywhere better we can hide? Before the guards ran off with all the light it looked like this is an old mine and this cave goes back a long way.'

She didn't have time to agree or not as a light suddenly shone in their faces. It was Jamar. There was blood on his face and he looked in a bad way. However, not that bad that he couldn't point his AK47 at them.

Chapter 41

The crew of the two Sea Kings had been keeping careful lookout using their NVGs and it wasn't longs before one of them saw lights in the distance. It was hard to judge exactly how far away they were but they were clearly approaching fast. There was nothing they could do except get out of the way. Without hesitation they jumped into their machines and started up. As agreed, they got airborne as soon as they could and flew over the mining camp. At the same time, the lead aircraft made contact with the Harriers who were now above them.

'Three Bravo this is Victor November, one of them called. 'Bad guys approaching, estimate they're about five miles. Due south. Any chance you could make them think again?'

'This is Three Bravo,' Bob Everett replied. 'Leave them to us, over.'

The Sea King pilot grinned. He was glad he wasn't in that convoy.

The marines had made the shelter of the rear wall of the sorting shed without being seen. There had indeed been someone on the roof but he was either asleep or looking elsewhere. They had the advantage of being able to see as if it was daylight, albeit in monochrome green. All the man on the roof could see was blackness as the moon had now set. Once in position, the Captain detailed two of his men to do a recce around the end of the shed. They all waited patiently for several minutes and then they returned without alerting anyone.

'The shed is full of what looks like stores and a couple of trucks. They've obviously been using it for a party as well, judging by the empty bottles everywhere but there's no one in it,' one of the soldiers reported. 'That building over the other side, the one that might have had the hostages in is empty. There's one window with bars on it but I was able to see inside. The building further on which Sergeant Llewellyn said was the old accommodation block has about thirty blokes in it on old camp beds all snoring their heads off but no sign of hostages anywhere.'

'Max, where could they be?' the Captain asked.

'The only other place could be up at the mine itself. We'll have to get past all this lot to get there.'

Formidable

They were interrupted by the growling sound of two helicopters approaching fast. 'Shit, that means we might have company. The Ukundu army must have been travelling faster than we thought.' The Captain said looking up. 'Right everyone, spread out. I want as many sixty mils into that sleeping hut as we can. Now.' As he spoke the sentry on the top of the roof must have woken up as he opened fire at the helicopters which were now flying overhead. He didn't get much time as a single shot from the sniper rifle took him out. They could clearly hear his body clattering down the corrugated roof as he fell. The marines ran around both sides of the sorting shed and as soon as they were clear they knelt down, took the green plastic tubes off their backs and pointed them at the long low building. No one waited for the order to fire, the enemy had fired first so the rules of engagement were now clear. A few men were already spilling out of the building which erupted in flame and smoke as fifteen anti-tank rockets blasted it to bits.

The marines then grabbed their rifles and started to pour fire in the survivors. Despite the mayhem they had caused, several brave men managed to return fire but it couldn't last. They couldn't see who was firing at them. They were effectively out in the open, with no cover and silhouetted by the flames of the burning building behind them. Within minutes of the engagement starting, there was no one left standing.

'Cease Fire,' the Captain called, although it wasn't really necessary. There was no one left to fire at. 'Search all the buildings now for survivors and try and find out where the hostages are.'

It soon became apparent that there were no survivors and there was no sign of the hostages. Captain Shaw called over to Max. 'Where's this mine entrance Sergeant?'

Max indicated up between the buildings. 'About five hundred yards up there Sir. But it gets very narrow and the sides are quite steep.'

The Captain was about to say something more when the familiar roar of a jet engine was heard behind them. It became louder and louder and then there was the sound of three massive explosions, one after the other.

'Seems we have our six o'clock secure.' He said to Max and then called to his men to regroup. They carefully made their way forward as more explosions were heard behind them.

Jamar was raving. He was screaming at them all to move together and threatening them with his rifle. It seemed to Agnes that he had completely lost his mind. She could see a wound on the side of his head, presumably from a bullet.

'You will now all die,' he screamed at them. 'You think you can escape this, you won't.' and he levelled the AK47 at the huddled group.

Before he could do anything more there were three enormous explosions. They were so violent that things started to rattle down from the rock ceiling above them. Jamar spun around with his mouth agape. Clearly, he was unable to process this new development. Then there were more explosions. Jamar continued to stare outwards seemingly oblivious to the people behind him.

Agnes knew she only had one chance. Despite everything she believed in, despite all her vows to the contrary, she knew that if she didn't act now they would all die.

Jamar was still turned away and pointing his torch out of the entrance. Which was probably a mistake if anyone was approaching. Agnes reached into her waist band and pulled out the pistol. Grabbing the slide on the top, she pulled it back and cocked the weapon. Then she released the safety catch. She got to her feet holding the pistol with both hands as she had been taught all those years ago and took several steps closer to Jamar.

Although amazed to see that a nun was now holding a pistol in her hand, Francois was quick to react. 'Shoot him, Shoot him now,' he said urgently.

All she had to do was pull the trigger she was only a few feet behind him. She couldn't miss. But she couldn't do it. She knew it would almost certainly mean her death and that of the rest of them but, dear God, she just couldn't do it.

Jamar must have sensed something going on behind him because he turned around and saw her. She still had time to shoot and still she couldn't do it.

He smiled at her and started to pull up the rifle in his right hand. She knew, because of her ridiculous hesitation, that she had condemned them all to death.

His head exploded. Bone fragments, blood and other matter splattered her face and she had to stand back to avoid being hit by his falling body. Completely stunned, unable to take in what had happened she just stood there incapable of rational thought.

Suddenly, a familiar voice brought her out of her paralysis as a pair of arms went round her and a hand delicately removed the pistol from her grip. 'There you are, you stupid bloody nun. You said you couldn't use it and you were right. I also said I'd come and get you.'

Chapter 42

Formidable and her escorts were almost home. In the best naval tradition she was having an 'up channel night', a final celebration before going alongside in Devonport the following day. The wardroom had decided to have a formal dinner and had invited Jon as well as all the released hostages. Even the two young girls who had been violated had accepted the invitation. The attention they were getting from the ship's officers seemed to be as good a therapy as any. They had also invited Max on the basis that he wasn't really a Sergeant anymore and everyone wanted to hear his side of the story.

After the dinner, Jon and the Commander were back in the bar surveying the goings on and wondering whether they should put a stop to it, as many of the aircrew were going to have to fly off tomorrow before they got alongside.

'Midnight Sir, I'll pull the plug then.' Paul Taylor said.

Jon nodded agreement. Although he was remembering similar evenings in the past when he had partied much later into the night and then managed to fly ashore the next day. *'Best not admit to that,'* he thought.

Wings came up to join them. 'It seems the light blue have integrated rather well,' he observed as the RAF squadron mess rugby team scored a try with a bottle of champagne at the far end of the bar.

'Yes, I'm bloody proud of the whole ship,' Jon said.

Just then Max and Sister Agnes joined them. Jon was surprised to see the size of the glass of whiskey in her hand.

She caught his glance. 'The one vice we're allowed Captain.'

'Bunch of stupid bloody rules her lot insist on,' Max commented sourly.

She gave him a hard glance but didn't rise to the bait. Instead she turned back to Jon. 'So Captain, what has been happening over the last few days? I presume there has been a major international incident over all this. Mind you, the BBC World Service seem to be treating it very lightly.'

'You're right Agnes,' Jon replied. 'No one wants to admit to what actually happened. The Chinese can't really say anything as they denied being involved from the start. As for the Ukundu government, they don't want to look stupid. The big thing in their favour, which I

Formidable

know has been pointed out to them diplomatically, is that they still have the Lithium. France and the UK have offered expertise to set up a clean extraction plant for them and they've accepted. It might have put Chinese noses out of joint but there's not a lot they can do about it.'

'And what about the bastards who killed my friends?' Max asked tightly. 'I suppose they just get away with it?'

'Sorry Max. We know that that Zhang Li character is no longer in the country. I suspect he will be dealt with quite harshly in Beijing. But what else can we do?'

'No, you're right. I understand that.' Max acknowledged with a resigned sigh. 'I wonder if I can get some work with the company that's setting up that extraction plant. They'll need a geologist.'

'What? Go back to that God forsaken place?' Agnes asked in a surprised voice.

'Well, you told me you're going to go back and you'll need someone to look after you.'

'They're my people, they need me and I don't need your bloody help, you pompous man.'

Jon looked at his two commanders and they discreetly left them to it.

The next day, enough reasonably sober aircrew were available to fly the aircraft off. Wings and Jon were in FLYCO to watch them go.

'You know it always amazes me,' said Wings. 'Ever since we embarked the Air Group, there have always been at least three unserviceable aircraft sometimes a lot more than that. Yet now they're all working well enough to fly home.'

Jon laughed. 'Come on Wings, you know damned well nothing stands in the way of getting home. Anyway it's our turn now. We should be alongside by lunchtime.'

That evening the ship was eerily silent. As they had entered Plymouth Sound that morning, a small armada of boats had come out to greet them. The news had only reported the successful rescue of hostages. There had been no mention of other matters and probably wouldn't be for many years to come. The damage to Formidable's stern was covered in a large tarpaulin but even so it was quite obvious she had literally been in the wars. The explanation given to the press was that there had been another fire on board. Jon wasn't happy about that but hadn't been able to come up with anything better.

A massive crowd had been waiting on the jetty to greet all three ships. Family and friends cheered as the ships finally put their gangways down and the crews were able to reunite. Those in the know were under strict orders not to say anything but apart from the aircrew and SBS Marines there were remarkably few who actually knew the full story.

Now it was all over. Only a few duty personnel were left on board. Even the Captain had gone ashore with his girlfriend. On the aft gangway, Leading Seaman Bell and Able Seaman Jones were standing duty as Quartermaster and Bosun's mate. Neither had family ashore so had volunteered to stay as duty watch.

'Well that was bloody fun,' Jones said.

'What was Taff?'

'All that flying and missiles and all that. You know rescuing those blokes.'

'You call that fun. I was fucking scared to death half the time. Thank God we've got a good skipper.'

Jones stared moodily out over the darkened dockyard. 'Yeah, he's alright but it was the ship that did the best. Bloody lucky ship this.'

Author's notes

During World War Two, one our most successful Aircraft Carriers was HMS Formidable. On board were 888 Squadron flying single engine fighters – Martlets, later known as Wildcats. I am personally interested in the ship and squadron as one of the Pilots was Lieutenant Dennis Jeram RN, my father. It was fun therefore to resurrect the ship and the squadron for this novel. Mind you, although she is fictional, one has to wonder at some decisions made by the MOD. HMS Ocean on which Formidable is based, only cost £154 million which was peanuts even at the time she was built and she is now classed as the Royal Navy's flagship. The new Queen Elizabeth carriers should finish up at about £3BILLION each. I actually worked on the QE carrier programme as a consultant after I left the navy and although they are wonderful ships one has to wonder about cost versus effectiveness. I'll say no more.

Lucky or unlucky ships are, in my opinion, a myth although they often do seem to get a reputation. In my view, its lucky or unlucky ship's companies that make the difference. I've seen a ship totally transformed purely when the Captain changed. People, not welded steel plate make the difference.

'Three Badge ABs' are pretty rare these days but I can recall several from my day. They would always have an opinion, having served in many ships and seen many officers. Their opinions were often colourful but could also be quite insightful, after all, they had in all probability, really been there, seen it and got the T shirt.

Diesel engines do sometimes refuse to stop. I know of two occasions. One where a friend of mine was bringing his minesweeper into HMS Vernon and one engine kept going. The crash into the dockyard wall was apparently quite spectacular. The second one was a 'Cat' class frigate who was going into the north part of Portsmouth dockyard and the same thing happened. She had time to drop an anchor which she spun around for a while and in the process picked up the main electric power cable to the naval base at Whale Island. The lights stayed off for quite a while I believe. In both cases, the cause was high crank case pressure forcing lubricating oil into the cylinder bores which acted as fuel. Basically the engine was running on its own oil.

Hydrogen fires have happened and are a nightmare to deal with. In 1980 I was serving in HMS Bulwark and we were in Philadelphia. One morning, they were flashing up the boilers for us to leave and in one of them a boiler tube burst. This took out several more and superheated steam was blasted into the boiler. Before the burners could be turned off the temperature rose so high that the metal started to burn. The boiler room was evacuated. However, if it had been left at that the ship would almost certainly have sunk as the mass of metal melted through the hull. A brave decision was taken to re-enter through the boiler room air lock. There was a high vacuum in the boiler room by then and the blast of cold air that came in when the inner door was opened was enough to cool the reaction and blow it up the funnel (which subsequently caught fire but that was an easier problem to solve). The heat was so intense that the hangar floor was being boundary cooled and the water was turning to steam. All eight of our Sea Kings were on deck within half an hour and all could have flown ashore or onto the neighbouring American carrier's deck. I remember going down to the boiler room several days later and where there should have been a massive great wall of steel, was a massive great gap with just the steam drum hanging by its pipes above it. It had, in fact, burnt through the inner of her two hulls which made the subsequent trip back across the Atlantic amusing to say the least. It's also the reason she wasn't available two years later to travel south to the Falklands which is a shame as she would have been invaluable.

Pass the Pigs is a great game and the story about the aircrew winding up the rest of the wardroom is true. The only modification being that it was in HMS Hermes in 1979. The Commander got so fed up with shouts of 'double leaning jowler' or 'making bacon' that he told us to bloody well shut up. The next day we did indeed make up cards with the words on them and waved them frantically at the appropriate moments. He gave up after that. Aircrew one, Commander nil.

Could you get so many people on one side of a carriers flight deck to make it list dangerously? HMS Ark Royal found itself in just that situation in New York some years ago. A friend of mine was the liaison officer for the visit but managed to duck the flak when it was discovered that the consulate had just received a colour photo copier and got carried away somewhat!

Peter Yorrick was 'real'. I pinched him from 814 Sea King squadron for this story. He was exactly as I describe. He started life as the squadron Grimmy Trophy and took on a life of his own after that. My only disappointment was that when I visited HMS Invincible some years later, with 814 embarked I asked after him only to be told that no one knew what I was talking about. I hope his demise was as spectacular as his short but very productive life.

The navy can be quite cruel with 'wind ups': getting green oil for the starboard nav lights, looking for the 'golden rivet' in the ships keel, going on a Malta Dog Shoot (the 'Dog' is naval slang for getting diarrhoea), getting an electricity bill for your bunk light, the list is long and often very funny. However, being a Splash Target Coxswain seems to be a recurring one that causes great amusement as the hapless victim is shunted around the ship to various departments for endless extra clearances. We kept one lad going for over two weeks in HMS Bulwark some years back.

Aircraft lifts have been known to operate all on their own. It happened on one of our Invincible Class with a Sea King half on it. Getting the lift back up without damaging the aircraft proved impossible but they did manage to repair it. For this book I just wanted to have the fun of pushing an aircraft over the side.

Unauthorised use of the ship's main broadcast is another RN foible. In HMS Hermes we had someone saying 'Cocopops' at random intervals, he was never found, nor I believe, was the 'Phantom Crapper' in the old Ark Royal.

Lithium is known today as 'white gold' and even back when this story was written it was the up and coming mineral to have. Apparently, they have discovered deposits in Cornwall but attacking Truro didn't seem quite as an exciting prospect.

The RAF. Hmm - several of my followers have commented that I have been rather hard on my light blue cousins in previous books. Alright, I did make the bad guy in several of them an RAF Air Marshall! However, in this book I've actually been rather nice to them compared to what really happened when they were asked to take their Harriers to sea in the 90s.

Firstly, I would like to go back in history. On 1 April 1918 the RAF was formed out of the Royal Naval Air Service and the Royal Flying

Corps. For the next twenty years there was continual in-fighting between the three services over the issue. The situation for the navy was very difficult. For example, when aircraft were embarked at sea they were required to work under Admiralty regulations but when ashore they came under the Air Ministry. This meant they had to comply with two sets of often conflicting regulations. In 1937 the Minister for Co-ordination of Defence, Lord Inskip was asked to report on the matter. I have the whole report in my possession and if anyone wants to read it contact me via Face Book or email and I'll send it over. He explains the situation in great detail and it makes fascinating historical reading. However, in my view the key paragraph reads:

'If it was possible to draw a line between the ship and its personnel and the aircraft and its personnel and to treat the latter as part of an external entity finding accommodation in the ship but not being in any way concerned with the life of the ship, I should take the view that the aircraft in question should be administered by the Air Ministry. But the air unit in a carrier or in a capital ship is a great deal more than a passenger in a convenient vehicle. It forms part of the organisation of the ship and as such is a factor in naval operations. The naval officers primarily concerned with the working of the ship are not only in some degree responsible for work of the aircraft but they have to accept a large measure of responsibility for the safety of the crews of the aircraft. I find it impossible to resist the inference that when so much that concerns the air units depends upon the naval element in the ship and in the fleet, the Admiralty should be responsible for the organisation of the Fleet Air Arm.'

In other words, when aircraft operate from ships – they are part of the ship.

The result of this report was that the Fleet Air Arm of the RAF was transferred back to the navy on 24 May 1939. Cynics might also say that it was not before time as maritime aviation was a low priority for the RAF in the interwar years. The result was that the only indigenous fighter available to the FAA at the outbreak of the war, had guns that could only fire backwards! The Blackburn Roc. This was one of the reasons my father was flying Martlets. The original batch of aircraft produced by America for export was an order of thirty aircraft for the French, which by the time they were ready for delivery, no longer had a customer. The FAA managed to snaffle them.

In the late 90s, I was on the staff of Flag Officer Naval Aviation and was part of the team staffing the integration of all Harrier forces into one and sorting out the issues of operating RAF aircraft from our ships. It wasn't an easy ride. I actually circulated the Inskip report around at the HQ at the time and got a bollocking for being subversive! An example of the problem was exactly the same that Inskip had commented on in his report – regulations. I was at RAF High Wycombe one day discussing the issue. The navy had all their aircraft maintenance regulations in one book called NAMMS – the Naval Aircraft Maintenance Manual. It was the holy bible to all Naval Maintainers. The A4 size book was about four inches thick. The RAF direct equivalent was Air Publication 3456 – volumes A to F, each one as thick as NAMMS, in addition there were Command Orders – another thick volume and then station orders. When placed side by side, the stack was ten times higher than the RN book. I left the RN soon after this but still wonder if anyone got it sorted out. Whatever happened, I strongly suspect that the slimmer RN rules were not the ones adopted.

I also had a nose to nose debate with the CO of a Harrier squadron about who authorised his sorties from a ship. In the RAF the 'authorising officer' is the final arbiter. I pointed out to him that there is another level of authorisation in a ship which must come from the command. He wouldn't have it and we parted agreeing not to agree. However, I think he might just have had other thoughts after he had been at sea and couldn't leave the deck until a certain light turned green. This debate is apparently still going on now and it will be interesting to see how it is resolved in the new carriers.

I mention 'crew duty hours' in the novel. This has been another bone of contention. Basically, once aircrew in the RAF have flown a certain number of hours they are required to rest for a minimum period. I think this is a fine idea. The only problem is that it's a peacetime rule that has no place once real military operations start. The RN have always just got on with it and allowed the individual aircrew to use their judgement. I am not aware of any time when it has caused a problem. That said, I did once wake up in a Sea King in the hover to find out that the other pilot had also nodded off and it was pretty quiet in the back as well!

Certainly the early light blue deployments were interesting. RAF personnel were definitely not used to being away from home for protracted times and living in the conditions that matelots have been used to for ever. From the feedback I received they did a pretty good job of integrating with the ship, it's just that on occasions it was clear that the 'rules' needed to be sorted out. For example, the incident in this book is partly based on events in Sierra Leone at about the same time. HMS Illustrious was there with a mix of FA2 and GR7. RAF rules say you should not fly unless you have a diversion to go to in case you can't get back home. This is regularly impossible in maritime operations. If the RN implemented it they would hardly ever fly at sea. You won't find it mentioned in any publication but when Illustrious arrived, the GR7's were not allowed to fly because there were no suitable diversions. But that was alright, the Sea Harriers did the job anyway.

So with this book, I didn't want to highlight these issues as it would only detract from the story. I have made many friends in the Air Force and they are great at what they do. As a matter of course naval aviation requires some different disciplines and approaches to situations. The best way to sum it up is to quote the first verse from the first song in the Fleet Air Arm Song Book:

They say in the Air Force and landing's OK
If the pilot gets out and can still walk away
But in the Fleet Air Arm the prospects are grim
If the landing's piss poor and the bastard can't swim

CONSPIRACY

The terrorist attack in New York on 9/11 starts a chain reaction that alters the balance of power in the Middle East.

Jon Hunt, having left command of the Formidable and newly promoted to Commodore is thrust into the middle of events just as the allies invade Iraq looking for Weapons of Mass Destruction. But do they even exist? Why is the British Government so convinced that they do? He is given the task of finding them despite his personal misgivings over the war. What he discovers is a conspiracy going right to the top.

Will he intervene to stop an even greater tragedy taking place?

Printed in Great Britain
by Amazon